LIKE MIND

CORBYN TRAVERS

CHAPTER 1

I REALLY NEEDED TO EAT.

Even so, I hesitated as I stood outside the glass doors, my legs trembling slightly under the weight of my backpack, suddenly reluctant to enter. It was always scary, doing what I was about to do, because nobody likes to be the object of negative attention. And my appearance would certainly draw that. Sure, there were enough people on the streets who looked like me—unkempt hair, dirty clothes, could use a bath—that no one paid all that much attention to me when I was in the pedestrian flow. But entering an establishment puts you in the spotlight. You become a lone diva on the stage. Regardless, I knew I had to do this, so I sucked it up and pushed through the doors.

I'd spent all but the dregs of my money on yesterday's lunch at Burger King, and the dude who finally picked me up in Mount Shasta that evening didn't so much as ask me how I was doing, let alone offer to buy me a meal. Our sporadic attempts at conversation died out long before the six-hour trip ended. But that was okay. I didn't want to talk to him, either. He had a vibe. Even our opening exchange had been terse.

"Where ya headed?" he asked, leaning across the seats as I bent to the passenger window.

I shrugged. "North."

"I'm going to Portland."

"That'll work."

He dropped me off in the parking lot under the Morrison Bridge, on the western shore of the Willamette River. He raced back onto the street almost before I got the car door closed.

It was past eleven at night, and the area was virtually deserted. There was no hope of scrounging up money or food at this hour, so I just gave in and waited for morning. It wasn't the first time I'd gone to sleep hungry.

I scrunched into my sleeping bag, squeezing my bunched-up jacket into my stomach to stifle its complaints. Exhausted from the strain of the day, I slept like the dead until a piercing scream jerked me out of the troubled depths of the nightmare I thought it was part of.

I bolted upright—or at least, I tried to. The restrictive sleeping bag got in my way. And that immediately reminded me of where I was. I glanced around, to find that the unearthly sound was actually quite earthly, simply the metal-on-metal screeching of brakes as the Metropolitan Area Express trundled past, slowing for the station on Yamhill Street a block south.

I watched until the last car passed by me. Then I dragged myself out of the sleeping bag, shivering a bit. The temperature was well below what I was used to, and the overcast sky, coupled with a heavy wind coming off the river, made it feel even colder. I quickly dug out my jacket and threw it on.

Checking out my surroundings in the cloud-shrouded sunrise, I noticed that cars were lining up at the huge lot's fee booth.

I knew I needed to get going, but suddenly, something took hold of me, and I stiffened, unable to move. I became filled with a strange, disorienting sensation that drew my attention to the river. I stood for maybe thirty seconds, intently listening, my eyes straining to see beyond the concrete bridge pillars as the traffic noise faded to an unattended thrum in the back of my mind. But I only succeeded in glimpsing patches of the deceptively narrow-looking strip of water through the gaps between these obstacles. And I honestly didn't even know what I was searching for.

Suddenly, a car pulled past me, startling me back into the world. I quickly rolled up my bag and hurried down the access walkway that ran through a gap in the chain link fence to the narrow back street, pausing at the curb to judge the lay of the land. Across the double MAX tracks, a sixteen-story office building loomed in my way, almost daring me to defy it.

Since the wind was coming from my left, I headed for the right-hand side, to use the wall as a shield. Reaching the corner of Alder Street and Second Avenue just as the light was changing, I made a snap decision and continued west on Alder. Vehicle traffic was heavy, the sidewalks were busy, and the gusts pummeled me as they were funneled between the blocks of multistoried buildings.

When the street is your world, you never know what you're going to find. What I found was a tiny coffee shop called Java Man. And it would change my life forever.

Three cops, seated in brown vinyl easy chairs around a knee-high square table near the door, cast their attention my way as I entered the warm space. Their conversation didn't stop, but it lagged for the briefest of moments. And my forward motion slowed for that same tick. Though I forced myself not to look at them, I could feel their disapproving gaze on me.

Trying to make myself inconspicuous by pulling my arms close to my sides and ducking my head, I skirted past the group as quickly as I could, doing my best to pretend they weren't there.

Even though these precautions narrowed my own visual field, I couldn't help but notice the young dark-haired woman in the far-right corner. Her red pullover sweater, with its colorful psychedelic swirls, was impossible to miss. And I could feel her eyes following me.

I reached the counter and picked up a bag of chips at random. I dug out my last two one-dollar bills, limp as boiled cabbage, and placed them on the counter. The Southeast Asian woman behind it appraised me closely. This made me stiffen, and I mentally prepared myself to be given a tongue-lashing and get kicked out. It wouldn't be the first time that happened to me. But she surprised me.

"That's your breakfast?" she asked in a mother-hen tone of voice.

All I could bring myself to do was nod.

Leaning toward me across the counter, she asked more gently, her voice lowered so only I could hear, "How old are you?"

"Seventeen."

"How long since you last ate?"

I shrugged.

Straightening, she pushed my money back toward me. She twisted around and said something in what I later learned was Cambodian to an older woman who was standing behind her. Then she turned back to me. "You go ahead and sit down," she said. "We'll bring you some food."

"But I can pay for this," I said stubbornly, motioning to the bag of chips. Pride is a demanding master.

"You go sit down."

I have rarely encountered such kindness. Gratefully, I nodded and slid my dollars off the counter. She pushed the chips toward me too. I offered her an embarrassed smile and mumbled, "Thank you." She smiled back broadly and winked, then looked to the customer who had come up behind me.

The young woman in the sixties sweater was still watching me, so this time I gazed back openly, and my heart skipped a beat. Black shag with blue highlights clinging to her cheeks in tight curls that reached to the base of her neck. Hazel eyes. Slightly pointed ears, which made a silly thought flash through my mind that she might be part fae. I guessed her to be college age. She was seated at one of a line of green-topped octagonal tables in front of a mirrored wall with glass shelves on which stood Buddhist statuary. And even as I took her in, she beckoned to me with a tick of her head and an inviting smile. So I walked across the room to her table.

"Well played," she said.

I was genuinely puzzled. "What do you mean?"

She gestured with her chin toward the counter. "The number you did on her."

"I didn't do anything." I inwardly chastised myself for my slightly belligerent tone. I really didn't mean to come across like that, but I was worn out and half-starved and not in total control of my emotions. I made a better effort. "She was nice to me, is all."

"She doesn't do that for just anyone. You must be special."

I snorted. "Not hardly."

"Well, let's find out." She gestured with her hand to indicate the green-padded metal chair across from her. "Sit."

I happily accepted her invitation, relieved that I hadn't blown it with my initial attitude. I dropped my backpack on the floor and draped my jacket over the back of the chair. "So do you always stare at people when they come in?"

"Isn't that the point of being here?" She slowly glanced around the small room, her gaze briefly resting on random customers. "I watch people. They have stories, and I like to figure out what they are."

"You're curious about others, eh?"

"Something like that."

I grinned. "So what's mine?"

"Your story?"

"Yeah."

She pushed her iPad aside and crossed her arms on the table, resting her weight on them. She scrutinized me with an intense expression on her face.

I swore I could feel an actual pressure emanating from that gaze, feel it *inside* my head, searching out my deepest secrets. I tried to be cool, but it was impossible to prevent myself from squirming a little.

At last, to my relief, she finally broke off her gaze and leaned back in her chair.

"You're looking for something," she said, a puzzled frown on her face. But before I could open my mouth to respond, her face lit up. "Wait—no! That's not it. Something is looking for *you*."

"Looking for me?" I asked, dumbfounded. "What are you talking about?"

She shrugged. "Dunno. Your destiny, I guess."

I shook my head dismissively. "I don't believe in destiny."

"Everybody has a destiny."

"I don't think so. I make my own future."

Before she could reply, the older woman from the kitchen area showed up carrying a tray bearing a Styrofoam cup of coffee and a sausage, egg, and cheese croissant. I watched hungrily as she set this before me, then thanked her. She just smiled and gave me several short nods. I began digging in before she even moved off.

"You were hungry," my new companion said blandly, as if she were noting the time.

"Yeah," I said, my mouth full. I placed my hand over it.

"How long have you been on the street?"

I swallowed. "I just got here."

"Oh. On the road long?"

"A while." I counted backward in my head. "Five weeks or so, I guess. I took off in early February."

"That's a long time. Where you headed?"

"I'm not really headed anywhere."

"Rambling man, eh?" She laughed. "I've never hitched before. Was it hard to get rides?"

"Mm, sometimes. Depended on where I was. I tried to find drivers who were headed up I-5 if I could. That way, I could cover a lot of ground quickly."

She offered me a slightly mocking smile. "Were you in a hurry to get nowhere?"

This was a more accurate insight than I was comfortable with. I didn't have a ready answer.

"Sort of," I stumbled out. "Maybe. I mean, I had no idea where I was going, so I just kind of followed my instincts. When I felt, um, *antsy*, I guess you could call it, I took off."

"Okay, so you're antsy. But I don't think that's what you really mean."

To be honest, it would have been embarrassing for me to answer her question the way it actually needed to be answered. I'd scare her off for sure. So I simply skirted the issue. "It's hard to put into words and would probably sound strange to you, anyway."

"Strange is no stranger to me," she said.

I didn't doubt this one bit. But I still wanted to avoid the subject.

"Anyway," I said, "if it looked like scraping up bread wasn't gonna happen, I took off. That's what I did most of the time. But I hit the mother lode in Stockton. I was able to score day jobs working in the fields there. So I hung around for a while."

"Why didn't you just stay in Stockton, then?"

I shrugged. "Because it wasn't where I was supposed to be."

"Is this where you're supposed to be?"

"Well, Portland kind of *became* where I was going. I realized it this morning."

"Just this morning?" Her eyes glinted, and I could tell she was holding back another laugh. "How did that happen?"

I certainly wasn't going to tell her about the odd sensation I'd felt at the river. But I could sidestep that issue and still be honest.

"Well, I guess what I mean is, I didn't set out to come here. But when I got here, I knew it was right. Like it was in the air, or something."

At this, her eyes widened, and she leaned forward eagerly, stabbing with a finger for emphasis. "Now, *that's* what I'm talkin' about! You feel it, don't you?"

I was nodding briskly before I even realized it. No one had ever understood my intuitions before, and the thought flashed through my mind that maybe I had something going here. Whatever, my words burst out of me before I could stop them. "Yeah. I feel it."

"Now, that I get. It's about time you came clean with me." She leaned back once more, crossing her arms and giving me that gaze of hers, that looking-right-through-me gaze, that *you-can't-hide-from-me* gaze. The one that made me not *want* to hide from her, even as I was squirming inside. "So what's waiting for you at your destination?"

I hesitated. I didn't know how much I wanted to reveal to her about my motivations. I wasn't particularly comfortable with them myself. Because, truth be told, I had no reason for staying here. No believable reason, at any rate. But I couldn't look into her eyes and not give some kind of response, however stupid it might sound.

At last, I said, "I don't know yet."

So, yeah, I went for stupid.

But she only became more intrigued. She leaned forward yet again, this time with her elbows on the table and her chin lightly resting against her loosely clasped hands.

"Now, that is interesting," she said. "You came all this way, looking for something without even knowing what it was."

"Pretty much, yeah."

"But you weren't just wandering aimlessly," she persisted. "You knew to come this direction."

Again that impulse to squirm, which, this time, I was able to squelch. "Well, I wouldn't call it *knowing*. When I started out, I really didn't have much choice. And I guess I just stayed on that course."

"As long as it felt right." She was prompting me, filling in the gaps I was deliberately leaving unfilled.

"Well, I suppose. I just had no urgings to veer off it."

"So you did have a beacon, after all." Once again, she leaned back in the chair, a triumphant look on her face.

At this point, all my protests dissolved, and I couldn't respond. I made a deliberate show of opening the bag of chips, trying to appear nonchalant. But it was hard for me to concentrate on anything but her face, with her staring at me like that, her eyes alight, that little half smile at once judging and accepting me. She saw right through me as she once more searched me out, as she had when I asked her about my story, and I just knew she was reading my innermost thoughts. I wondered if I'd ever be able to keep anything from her. And suddenly, I realized I didn't want to. I met her gaze and held it.

She said, "You'd fit in well with my friends."

I smiled. "Are you asking me to be your friend?"

She laughed. "Well, maybe I am."

"So what's your name, anyway?" I asked, jumping at this opening.

"Sari," she said. "What's yours?"

"Arthur."

"Well, Arthur, I thought you were going to take a finger off, the way you were going at that sandwich."

"Been a while since I last ate."

"I know what that's like. But sometimes we have to go without in order to be brought to the right place to get what we need."

"A restaurant?" I asked, deadpan.

Sari laughed. I loved the sound of it and wanted to keep making her laugh.

"Sometimes," she said. "But I wasn't talking about material things. You and I were supposed to meet."

"So you think this is some kind of mysterious plan?"

"I'm the future you made."

That stopped me in my tracks. I had no response to offer. Thankfully, she changed the subject.

"So where you from? Besides Stockton."

"San Diego."

"That's a long slog, cowboy."

"I walked enough of it to know." I laughed. "And how about you?"

"I grew up in Hillsboro, about half an hour from here. Quiet place. Farm country."

"And what brought *you* to Portland?"

"I needed a new vibe."

I nodded. "I can get that."

Suddenly, she became animated and leaned forward yet again. She looked directly into my eyes as her voice lowered conspiratorially, her hand gestures emphasizing her points. "What I like about Portland is that it isn't the *status quo*, y'know? It's a confabulation of everything from conservative to bonkers. Nobody has trouble fitting in because *nobody* fits in. There's nothing to fit *into*. It's its own organic entity, swallowing people up, transforming them, and recreating them. You never know what you're going to become here." She dropped back against her chair again and finished with a happy sigh, "It's impossible to be bored in this town."

I have to say, I loved this display of animation, of excitement, in her. Mesmerized, not quite knowing how to respond, I merely took up where she left off. "Were you bored before?"

"Deathly." She sipped her coffee, which prompted me to pick mine up as well. "How about you? Were you *deathly* bored? Is that why you ran away?"

"I didn't run away," I said, shaking my head. "I was kicked out."

"Oh my gods. I'm so sorry."

I waggled my hand in a *fuhgeddaboudit* gesture. "Don't be. It was crap where I was, anyway."

The conversation died on this note, so I finished my breakfast. Then Sari suddenly became animated again.

"You know what?" she said. "You've got to meet Carl. He'll figure out what your destiny is."

"What is this, *The Wizard of Oz*?"

She laughed. "Well, this is one wizard behind a curtain you'll want to listen to! If there's anyone in this city who can transform your life and put you on the right path, it's him. Come on. It's just across town. I have a car."

She was pretty and seemed to like me. And when you came right down to it, I had nothing else to do.

CHAPTER 2

S ARI STOWED HER iPAD IN its carrying case while
I quickly cleared the table, dumping the trash on our
way out. At the door, I paused to raise a hand in acknowledgment to the woman at the counter, who responded with
a nod and a smile.

The entrance let out onto the corner of Fourth and
Washington. Pointing to our right, Sari said, "I'm parked
just up the way there."

"Cool."

As we ambled along the two blocks back to the river,
she talked about where she was taking me.

"It's Carl's house, but he doesn't act like it is. He
doesn't believe in authority; he lets us do our own thing.
There are seven of us living there, besides him. We're kind
of a commune."

"I didn't know those still existed."

"I don't know how many there are, but we have one."
She laughed. "We all share in the upkeep of the place. It's
really big, so we have to work together. It's kind of fun,
actually. During the week, we have family dinners, and
on Sundays, we all go out for brunch. Everyone who can
make it does. And we always have each other's backs. It

feels good to know you have someplace where everybody accepts you for who you are instead of what your story is."

This hit me hard, harder than I wanted to show. My father had never had my back—except as one of his targets. I swallowed in a suddenly dry throat.

"Yeah," I said, my voice catching. "I could use that, for sure."

To my relief, Sari gave no sign that she had noticed my moment of weakness.

We reached the small, open-air parking lot at Second Avenue and crossed the asphalt to her car. A patchy blue 2003 Dodge Neon, it had seen better days.

Sari unlocked the doors, and we placed our packs in the back seat. It was not an impressive vehicle, but considering it was fourteen years old, it wasn't in too bad a shape. Besides the paint, the interior was a little worse for wear, the upholstery faded and the driver's seat sporting a small tear. But she told me it served her purposes nicely.

"Doesn't look like much," she said as we settled in, "but it always starts."

And it did, with a single turn of the key. She shot me a "told ya" look.

"Fire," I said.

Exiting the lot, we turned right onto Second and drove southward a number of blocks, then turned away from the river and continued on for even more blocks until we reached the 405 Freeway, which marked the western edge of the downtown district. From there, we wound our way along wooded hills through quiet, secluded residential neighborhoods, some more affluent than others.

Sari pulled the car to the curb in front of a sprawling three-story Victorian mansion surrounded by a ten-foot-high wrought iron fence. The front yard of the place stretched along the street for—well, forever, I think. The property could have been its own subdivision. I grew up in an upper-class neighborhood, but I'd never encountered anything like this before. There was no sidewalk and no neighboring houses on this side of the street, because there was no room for any.

The landscaping was simple but meticulously maintained. A well-manicured lawn was studded with trees—black hawthorn, maple, white dogwood—and artistically designed planters filled with various flowers; one held a fountain. A long cobblestone sidewalk led to a portico accessed by three broad wooden steps. A gable rose up behind it, and there was also one on each wing of the house. The right wing was greatly extended, making the structure look a little off-balance.

It gave me an odd feeling, as if I'd seen it somewhere before. *Déjà vu*, I thought. Aloud, I said, "Unreal. Looks like something out of a ghost flick."

"Well," Sari replied, laughing, "nothing goes bump in the night here. But other things happen."

I left asking what those might be for another time.

As we got out of the car, she said, "You can just leave your stuff here. I'll give you a ride to wherever you like when you're done with Carl. Although," she added with a sly grin, "I don't think you'll need one."

"I hope I'm not keeping you from anything," I said.

"Oh no, not at all. I work anytime I like. I run my own business."

"Sweet."

She looped the strap of her laptop carrying case over her shoulder, and we walked up to the arched double gate. She pulled what appeared to be an ancient skeleton key from her purse, unlocked the gate, and swung one side open. We traipsed up the cobblestones, bits of crabgrass pushing up here and there between them, to the wooden veranda and climbed the three steps up.

She unlocked the front door with a normal key, and we entered. The old wooden floor beneath the worn, dirt-stained beige carpet creaked softly as we stepped into a simple entryway the size of a bedroom.

I followed her lead and removed my shoes, placing them in a cubby alongside the door, and I hung my jacket on an available hook above it.

She said in a hushed voice, "I'll be right back."

I simply nodded. I watched her climb the spiral staircase in the far-left corner until she rounded the second curve and disappeared. Then I stuck my hands in my pockets and tried to stifle my nervousness.

But there was no helpful distraction to be found in this square space. The eighteen-hole cubbies and the line of coat hooks were accompanied only by a round, single-pedestaled oaken table, which was set in the right half of the room. This held a large and lovingly cared-for Ficus. That was it.

An archway in the wall directly in front of me opened onto a white-carpeted hallway as wide as the foyer. This extended so far into the house that the laws of perspective started to come into play. Curious, I crossed the room to get a better look.

There were three arched entrances along the wall to my right and two—more widely spaced—on the left. The first set were near enough to sneak a peek into, so, taking a quick look up the stairs to make sure no one was coming yet, I took the liberty of doing just that.

On the right was a large dining room. A rectangular, carved mahogany table stood in the center, in front of a wall tapestry depicting a medieval scene. Around it stood ten chairs with curved arms and legs, and backs carved with lions' heads. An imposing, intricately engraved hutch stood against the back wall to the right of the table. All the furniture was old and worn but deeply polished. I half expected a knight to accost me for intruding.

Directly across the hall from this was what I took to be a study. A six-shelf bookcase stood against the outside wall. An executive desk was on the right, with a high-backed swivel chair behind it. Four other chairs were scattered throughout the space; they looked like the type you might find in a public library. Two round display tables had been set among the chairs, each holding a bronze statue. The closest one, just inside the entrance, depicted a stick man walking up a long flight of stairs. It was oriented so that he was moving away from the door. The other consisted of a ring of fire surrounding what I assumed was a deity, as it had four arms. It looked like it was performing some kind of yoga move or something. I frowned, not getting it.

Overall, the house was cavernous but didn't seem as ominous as it did on the outside. I stepped back into the foyer just as Sari returned.

"He'll be right down," she said, a note of excitement in her voice.

"Okay."

"I'm going up to my room. I'll come back down when you two are finished."

"Cool. Thanks."

"Good luck." She flashed a smile and retreated back up the stairs.

It didn't take long for Carl to appear, although, in my nervous state, time was hard to measure. He wasn't what I expected. It may sound crazy to say this, but he didn't seem to occupy much space—and yet he might have been taking up *all* space. He was taller than me, of average build, maybe a hint of an impending paunch. But his presence was heavier, if that makes any sense. The air seemed to warp around him, like something from *The Matrix*, except far more subtly.

Optical illusion, I told myself. *I'm still hungry and tired.*

He had flowing, shoulder-length graying hair whose natural color was pretty much washed out. A scraggly brown-and-gray beard. Wire-rimmed glasses with round lenses. He wore loose-fitting beige clothing, a tunic over baggy trousers; the material looked like hemp. A handful of bead and string necklaces, some with symbolic medallions, hung in increasingly long loops to his solar plexus. He was barefoot. There was no question he was beyond his midlife crisis years, yet he gave off a younger vibe. His eyes were so dark blue they were almost black, as if his pupils were dilated. He held my gaze, and I felt a touch of vertigo.

"So," he said gently. "You're Sari's friend."

"Well, we just met. But yes, sir. I'm Arthur."

"Hello, Arthur." He smiled. "And please, honorifics are not permitted here. I'm Carl."

He leaned forward toward me. Recognizing his physical cues, I bumped fists with him. I chuckled despite myself; I'd never done that with a grown-up before.

"Please join me in the parlor."

He seemed more to drift than to walk, ambling softly on the thick carpet. I remained a step behind him so I could snatch glances into the other doorways as we passed them.

The rooms varied in size, but all of them were far larger than any I'd ever seen in a house before. The one next to the study, on our left, was a library that seemed more like a wing, as it extended well into the property. Its outside wall was slightly concave and almost totally made up of window, the expansive arced glass divided into many panes. Its purple drapes were open, and I caught a brief glimpse across a section of the lawn to the western fence, which was half a football field away. A white gravel driveway ran close to the house. Inside, mahogany book-shelves lined the other walls, while a number of reading chairs, along with a few tables of diverse sizes and shapes, were scattered around the space. It looked inviting.

Down from that one, on my right, was a huge kitchen with all the most modern fixtures, including an oval island with the requisite hanging pots and pans. I wondered if it had been recently renovated.

Next, once more on my left, was an open vestibule containing ornate wooden tables on which stood statues and plants. Its floor was parquet, its walls painted rose. This space extended beyond the end of the hallway, and in its far wall were two carved doors that I assumed opened into separate rooms. Both of these were closed.

Across from this, the final archway opened into a sitting room. It contained six easy chairs and a desk on which stood a twenty-four-inch computer screen, with a rolling studio chair on a translucent plastic floor pad before it. The floor was laid with a brown carpet; the walls were painted avocado. Centered on the outside one was a small fireplace surrounded by a swarm of unframed photos of various sizes, both in color and in black and white, posted at random angles. I assumed these had been taken by the residents.

At last we reached the parlor. While I was impressed with the other rooms, I was downright blown away by the opulence of this one. I took a slow spin around to take it all in. The walls were painted eggshell white; the carpet was forest green. The art on the walls was eclectic, all of it original works. Five glass display cases stood in strategic spots, containing expensive statuary, some of it appearing to be rather old. The furniture was a seemingly random blend of ornate and everyday fashion. Chairs of various styles were scattered about, seemingly randomly, except for the two wingbacks at the coffee table set before a char-coal-gray sofa halfway along the left-hand wall. Maroon drapes enfolded a sliding glass door in the far wall, which let out onto a large furnished patio and a sprawling back-yard. An area rug of the same color was laid out before it. A massive fireplace stretched from the right-hand corner to a third of the way along the wall. Its blocks of white unworked stone, threaded with gold, flashed in the warm light of a flickering wood fire. An alder bay window, framed with cream-colored drapes and a coral design area rug, took up another third of the wall, centered in the space between the fireplace and the south corner. It looked out eastward onto a thick stand of evergreen trees beyond a wide patch of grass.

As my twirl completed, I found myself stopped in my tracks, captivated by a stunning painting centered in front of a plush white couch that faced it. It depicted a green woman bedecked in sparse but fine clothing and draped in jewelry, sitting on something like a cross between a seashell and a candy dish floating in water. She was surrounded by halos and flowers. The vivid colors drew my eye in, and the free-flowing lines lent a sense of movement to the piece.

"Do you like that?" Carl asked from behind me.

I reflexively glanced back at him. "Yeah. I really do."

"It's called a *thangka*. It's a traditional Tibetan artwork, painted on fabric. This one is of the goddess Tara, who was the first female bodhisattva. Some consider her to have been the first feminist as well, as she rebelled against the teaching that only men could reach nirvana. So she vowed to always reincarnate as a woman until all men had attained Enlightenment. There are several versions of her, each denoted by a distinct color. Green is for compassion."

"That's pretty cool."

"She's the patron saint of our household."

I nodded again, approvingly.

My interest seemed to please Carl. He gestured toward the couch as he turned and moved to its far end.

"Please have a seat."

I automatically glanced down at my clothes, which I had worn for well over a week. My jeans in particular were quite dirty, making me hesitant to sit on that pristine piece of furniture, but Carl casually dismissed my fears.

"Don't worry about it," he said nonchalantly, his back still toward me.

How did he know what I was thinking? I wondered, startled. Still, I automatically nodded before gingerly taking a place on the edge of the couch cushion on the right, leaving the center one open between us. I leaned forward with my hands clasped beyond my knees. I wanted to touch as little of the upholstery as possible.

"So," Carl began. "Sari tells me you're from California."

"Yes. San Diego."

"What brings you up this way?"

I was still reluctant to reveal my motivations to strangers. But somehow Carl didn't feel like a stranger. I had this weird sense I'd known him my whole life. There was something about him that drew me out, made me comfortable with the idea of exposing my entire being to him. I fought against this urge but, nonetheless, ended up saying something I absolutely had not intended.

"Actually," I said, horrified to hear the words coming out of my mouth, "I came here because of a dream."

I cringed inwardly, trying not to let it show in my expression even as heat rose in my cheeks.

But Carl did not react. "I'd like to hear about your dream," he said calmly.

"Okay. I had it on New Year's Eve. My birthday is the first, so that made the dream seem even more significant to me."

"And how old are you?"

I berated myself for opening this door. The more times I admitted my age to people, the more precarious my situation felt to me. It had been embarrassing in the coffee shop; here, I was afraid it might jeopardize something that, although I had no idea what it might be, I suddenly felt I wanted very much. After a couple of seconds of contending with myself, I swallowed my reluctance and told him.

His demeanor did not change. He only nodded as he took the information in. I waited a bit for him to make a comment, but when he did not, I decided to continue on with my dream.

"Okay. So. I was in a desert at night, standing on an asphalt road that ran perfectly straight through it. The sky was full of stars, more than I'd ever seen in my life, and a full moon hung low above the horizon in front of me. It cast an eerie light on the ground, just enough to be able to make out the terrain. The desert was completely empty, except for the road. No plants, animals, buildings, or anything. Nothing but sand stretching out in all directions. It made me feel lonely.

"Just before I became overwhelmed with sadness, the moon disappeared and the sky lit up, illuminating everything clearly. But I couldn't find the sun. Halfway to the horizon, I saw that the road rose up, not like a hill, but suddenly and straight up at a perfect right angle, climbing, like, forever, until it was lost in a large cumulus cloud that hung only above that part of the road. The rest of the sky was clear.

"And then I saw that angels were walking up and down this vertical part, traveling between heaven and earth.

"And that's when I woke up. I was filled with a sense of urgency, like something was prodding me to act. I didn't know what any of this meant, but I did know one thing."

I fell silent as I cast my gaze down to my folded hands. I felt embarrassed to say what I knew I had to say next, suddenly afraid Carl would think I was stupid or something.

He waited for me to go on, but when I remained silent for more than a few seconds, he prompted me.

"And that was?"

I forced myself to meet his gaze, summoning all my strength. "That I had to find that road."

Carl's face lit up, and his eyebrows shot up. This was the most emotional reaction I'd received from him yet. "You're on a quest." He sounded pleased.

This startled me. I certainly had never thought of my journey in those terms. To me, a quest meant having an objective in mind, and I had none. I had only known that where I was, was not where I wanted to be.

I shrugged.

"I guess so."

"And that quest has led you here."

I unclasped my hands and spread them a bit, then re-clasped them. "Seems like it."

Silence rested between us for two beats before Carl spoke again.

"You are a man who takes his dreams seriously."

His use of the word startled me. I'd never been called a man before. Other things, maybe.

"Yeah," I said, drawing my wandering thoughts back. "I guess you could say that. My dreams sometimes affect my life."

"I know something of that."

"Do you think dreams have meanings?" I blurted impulsively. I felt heat in my face again.

"Not all of them. But we tend to recognize the ones that do."

This struck home. But I had nothing more I wanted to say about my dream and its effects on me, so I remained silent.

"Now that you're here," Carl asked, "how do you plan on fulfilling this dream?"

I felt a spark of hope. "You think I can fulfill it here?"

He didn't answer. The spark faded.

I shook my head. "I haven't really thought about that yet. I guess I was just waiting to see what might happen."

He smiled. "And Sari happened."

I smiled back. "Yeah."

"What's home like?"

The unexpected question, the abrupt change of subject, caught me off guard. I had to think hard before answering, working out in my mind how much I wanted to tell him and what I might be able to get away with not saying.

"My father hated me," I said at last, struggling to keep my voice level as it warred between anger, sorrow, and self-recrimination. "My mother abandoned us immediately after I was born. I've never even seen her. My father said she never wanted me. And that she resented him for not letting her get an abortion." I turned my head in shame, not wanting to look Carl in the face, and ended up gazing at my right knee. Finally, I said in a hushed voice, as if to myself, "Maybe he should have."

We sat in silence. I could feel his gaze on me as the seconds dragged on. Although I still couldn't bring myself to look at him, I knew there was compassion in his eyes. Somehow, strangely, it was as if I could feel that too. An emanation of its energy seemed to wash over me.

"No," Carl said finally, in a gentle but authoritative voice. "It was different than you think."

I frowned, and now I did look him in the eyes. "What do you mean?"

"I mean that things are not always the way we remember them."

An odd feeling, one of hope mixed with foreboding, arose in me. He hadn't uttered these words consolingly, like a counselor might, but rather as someone who knew the intimate depths of my being.

His gaze held mine. His eyes were like deep wells, falling away from me. It was what they might be falling into that disturbed me.

I looked down at my folded hands again.

"Anyway," I went on. I desperately wanted to move away from this subject, didn't want to talk about myself at all anymore, but knew that I had no choice in the matter. So I turned to more pleasant aspects of my life. "He hired a woman to watch over me while he was at work. She was also a professional tutor, so she did some of that too. I still went to school, but she supplemented my normal studies. She taught me all sorts of cool stuff." Now I looked at him and smirked. "And she let me get away with a lot of things my father never knew about."

Carl smiled broadly, eager curiosity shining in his eyes. "Care to indulge me?"

I chuckled. "She let me watch all the DVDs I wanted to from his collection. No way he would have approved of that."

"She sounds like just what you needed. And you seem fond of her."

I considered this. "Yeah," I said quietly. "I guess I am." I waited for him to speak again, but when I saw he wasn't going to, I went on. "Anyway, so I was able to skip a semester. But a few weeks after I received my diploma, my father kicked me out of the house. That was on New Year's Day."

"Your birthday."

"Yeah. I saw it coming, though, so I'd already arranged to stay with a friend."

"That must have been hard for you."

I shrugged. "It was, and it wasn't. I try not to get upset about things. They just are what they are."

"That's a very wise way of going through life."

I didn't know how to respond to this, so I fell silent.

Carl appeared to be weighing me, considering me, deciding what to do with me. His eyes bore into mine again, and this time, I couldn't keep myself from squirming. I didn't want to hold his gaze, but he was holding mine, and I felt trapped by it.

Finally, I broke away and stared at my hands again.

At last, he spoke, abruptly returning to the subject of my dream.

"The psychologist Carl Jung was famous for his study of dreaming. He kept a journal of his own dreams, along with his thoughts about them, and he even painted pictures that were inspired by them. He called it his 'red book,' and he kept its contents secret until he died. But eventually, his family gave their permission for the entire thing to be published, including the artwork. He said something in it about dreams providing a paved path for us in the direction we're supposed to go. We in this house are dreamers. We let dreams pave our way."

Of course, the word *pave* struck me. How could I be faulted for associating it with the road in my own dream? Surely it couldn't just be a coincidence?

And then he startled me again, saying something that made me wonder if he was reading my mind.

"Jung developed a concept he called *synchronicity*," he continued, "which he defined as a 'meaningful coincidence.' When things or events fall together and seem to be significant. It's a key part of his philosophy of mind and human existence. If we allow ourselves to be open to this kind of thing, to pay attention and think about it, it can guide us in our lives and put us on the right path."

"Do you think I'm on the right path?"

He smiled broadly again, and his eyes took on that odd glow once more.

"We could find out, if you like."

CHAPTER 3

ARL LEFT ME IN THE parlor and headed back upstairs, then Sari appeared in the doorway.

"So," she chirped, "Carl told me he invited you to dinner!"

"Yeah. I was kind of surprised, actually. I think we hit it off."

"*I'm* not in the least bit surprised. You are so in!"

"You really think you know me, don't you?" I laughed.

I wasn't sure what to make of the look she gave me. There was something hidden in it. Something subtle, something poignant.

"Oh, you have no idea," she said. Then she smiled brightly again. "C'mon. I'll introduce you to the city before I settle down to work."

"That sounds cool. But…"

"But what?"

I looked down at my clothes. "I'm kinda dirty."

"Already on it. You can use my shower. I even replaced the sliver of soap with a new bar."

I laughed. "That's nice of you, but are you—"

She showed me her palm. "Don't try fighting me. I always get what I want."

I had no reason to doubt her. I smiled. "All right, I give up. And thanks."

We walked down the long, perception-tricking hallway back to the foyer. There she handed me her keys so I could retrieve my backpack. I slipped my shoes on for the task, leaving them untied, and when I returned, I placed them back in the cubby.

Then I followed her up the stairs, lugging my backpack with me. The dimly lit second-floor hallway gave me my second hit of vertigo for the morning, as it stretched away before me like a tunnel.

"It's all bedrooms on the right and bathrooms on the left," Sari said. "It's kind of a weird setup, because they're not the same size. I don't know what this wing originally was, but it's been changed a lot over the past century. I think they just tacked on stuff as they felt like it."

Her bathroom—the third one in the line—was another modern renovation. Judging from its slightly awkward layout, I figured that adding indoor plumbing had probably been tricky.

I turned on the bath water and took off all my clothes, but I still had to wait a bit for it to become good and hot. The shower felt indescribably luxurious, washing away all the grime that had accumulated over the days since my last chance to clean up. That had been merely an above-the-waist sponge bath in a gas station restroom. This morning, I pampered myself and washed my hair twice.

After I dried off, enjoying the slightly feminine scent lingering on my skin and hair from Sari's bath products, I leaned on my hands at the sink and gazed into the mirror. What I saw peering back at me was not perfect but didn't look as bad as I felt. Black hair swept back in a loose and long cut that had grown below my shoulders since I'd left home in January; watery blue eyes; straight nose. I was never particularly well muscled, but my abs were flat. My latest bruises had finally healed, while the small scars on my arms and chest were still visible if one looked closely enough. They were more noticeable when I was suntanned.

Overall, I wasn't as haggard looking as I'd imagined. I could deal.

I had one set of good clothes I had kept in reserve for when I reached my destination. I figured that this was probably it, one way or the other, so I put on my olive-green chinos and black Thrasher T-shirt. The sun was now playing hide-and-seek with the clouds, which I figured would make the air warmer, so I decided to leave the jacket behind and wear my dark blue Wanakome Cascade hoodie instead. It was much more comfortable. The clothes were a touch wrinkled, but those would work themselves out. At least nothing smelled of the street—including me, now. I felt myself beginning to relax, both emotionally and physically.

Sari must have heard me come out of the room, because she immediately joined me in the hallway.

"Wow, look at you!" she said teasingly. But I noticed admiration in her eyes.

"Thanks," I said, grinning to hide my embarrassment. "Let's go."

Once settled in her car, we wound our way through the hills back to the downtown district. The streets seemed a little confusing to me, at times twisting around on themselves. As if reading my mind, she mentioned this.

"I hope you have Google Maps, because I'm going to leave you on your own for the afternoon, and you would for sure have trouble finding the house without it. Let me give you the address and my phone number."

I pulled out my phone and entered her information.

"There are a couple places I'd like to show you this morning," she continued. "They're kind of like landmarks, notable things about the city's history. So you can get a taste of its flavor."

"Sweet. I'm up for it."

We were lucky; we found available parking in the underground lot of the Jackson Tower directly across Yamhill Street from the main entryway to Pioneer Courthouse Square. The official center of town, the square was a bustling place, made up of salmon-colored bricks filling the entire block.

We stood at the top of a wide bank of curved steps leading down into the gathering space. Centered on the western flank next to us was a white horseshoe-shaped wall that opened into the main concourse. This served as the entranceway to an underground exhibition center, its inset ticket window reached by a wide sidewalk lined on either side with decorative shrubs. Next to that stood a Starbucks built of glass and wood. Three camping trailers were parked on our level, just to our right.

"Food carts," Sari said, as I stared at them with a puzzled expression. "We're famous for them."

It didn't take me long to soak it all in. We veered around the food carts and walked beneath the trees to the corner.

After the MAX pulled out of the stop, we crossed Sixth Avenue and stood before the courthouse itself. I was a little disappointed to find it less than impressive. Smaller than I expected, dwarfed by its surroundings. With its gray stones, blocky wings, and central bell tower, it appeared to me like a cross between the Capitol Building and a penitentiary.

"It's the second-oldest federal building west of the Mississippi," Sari recited, sounding like a tour guide.

"What's the oldest?"

She gave me a blank stare, as though she had never thought of the question before. Then she giggled, putting her hand to her mouth.

"I don't know," she said.

I chuckled.

"There's an even older building I'd like to show you," she said. "It was a business, the first one built here. It's only, like, ten minutes away, but I want to stop off at the river first."

I felt that strange longing again, which caused my words to catch in my throat. "Awesome," I said after swallowing. "Let's do it."

We strolled eastward along Yamhill Street, chatting in that light, getting-to-know-you way people engage in when feeling each other out. Sari was an artist, a painter in the abstract style.

"I want to be the next Jackson Pollock!" she exclaimed, laughing.

I had never heard of him, so she tried to describe his work to me. It sounded intriguing, if a little difficult to picture in my mind. Selling her art online was the nature of the business she had mentioned to me.

"I would love to see some of your work," I said.

"It could happen," she said, the words tossed off casually.

The street teed at Naito Parkway, a broad north–south artery that served as the easternmost border for the district.

We crossed at the light, pausing to laugh at Mill Ends Park, which consisted of a single six-foot-tall tree occupying a two-foot-diameter space within a concrete ring located in the precise middle of the crosswalk.

"It's the smallest official park in the world," Sari said, a hint of pride in her voice.

We paused a little too long there, as the crossing signal was counting down before we moved on. Determined to make it, we jogged across the northbound lanes to Tom McCall Waterfront Park, where we paused to catch our breath and stop laughing.

We then continued across the grass to the tree-lined sidewalk that ran along the river. There we stood, resting our arms on the top rail of the barrier fence—a set of two aquamarine, tubular metal pipes—and looked out across the green water coursing twenty feet below the vertical ledge.

"This," Sari said, sounding a little dreamy, "is why Portland exists."

I shared something of her feelings. Standing before this powerful flow of water, the calling—or whatever it was—returned even more strongly in me now. The river felt to me like a living thing, grabbing hold of my heart and wrenching it, filling me with a longing I had never experienced before.

What's happening to me? I wondered.

Sari turned to me with an odd expression on her face, and with a small shock, I realized I had muttered those words under my breath.

"Are you all right?" she asked.

I hesitated, then decided to go for it. I felt safe with her. "I don't know, to be honest. I feel kinda weird here. I don't know how to explain it."

She nodded with a small knowing smile. " 'Keep Portland Weird' is our motto. We're proud of it."

I smiled ruefully. "So I can look forward to more of it, then."

"Oh yeah."

We stood in silence for some time, gazing out over the powerful water. Then she glanced at her watch. "Why don't we go on now?"

"Okay."

We sauntered northward along the sidewalk, crossing under the six-lane-wide Morrison Bridge.

I pointed out the opening in the fence on the far side.

"That's where I slept last night," I said.

"My gods. I'm so sorry."

I just shrugged.

Coming out from under the concrete canopy, we walked for another five minutes until we reached the Oregon Maritime Museum. This was a converted steam paddleboat that was the last one to serve the city. The vessel's pristine white wood was trimmed in robin's-egg blue. I noticed it didn't rock at all at its mooring.

"It was only decommissioned, like, thirty-five years ago," Sari said. "I've never been inside. Not really my thing."

From here, we cut across the lawn and recrossed Naito Parkway to the corner at Oak Street and stood in front of the Hallock-McMillan Building. I can't say I was particularly impressed with it; it was pretty nondescript. It basically looked as if a huge brick had been placed on top of another one, half as tall, after the left corner of the bottom one had been chipped off. This formed a triangular open space, which was buttressed by a round pillar and housed a glass door and several windows. The Naito side had sets of casement windows on both floors; some of the upper panes were broken, their jagged holes seeping blackness from the building's interior. The bottom floor held another inset door, which was protected by a modern, barred security gate. The entire structure was painted a dull, faded rose white.

"It's the oldest building in the city," Sari said. "It was built before Oregon was even a state."

"Kinda looks like it."

Sari laughed. "The pioneers were conquering a wilderness; they weren't worried about fancy."

I felt heat in my face. "Yeah, that makes sense." *Idiot*, I chided myself.

I tried to imagine this bustling cityscape with no buildings or streets in it, just endless trees extending from the riverbank to the hilltops. The difference kind of boggled my mind.

"It was almost the only thing left standing in this area after a fire fifteen years after it was built," Sari was saying. "Half of downtown was burned down."

"Dude."

"I think it survived because it's actually made of brick. They started restoring it six years ago and plan on making it just like it used to be."

"Doesn't look like they've done anything."

"Well, you know how these things go. All the red tape and stuff. I read that, right now, they're remaking the decorative castings that used to be on it—doing it by hand from sand moldings, the way it was done back then—and that they expect to start work on the building itself in two years."

I nodded as I swept my gaze around it again. "What was it used for, anyway?"

"I dunno," Sari said, "but I do know it was commissioned by an ironworks company in California." She glanced at her watch. "It's ten to eleven. You hungry?"

"I can always eat."

Sari laughed. "I don't doubt that. Feel like pizza?"

We wound our way around the three blocks to Checkerboard Pizza, where Sari bought us two slices each. I chipped in my two sad dollars, overriding her protest.

"So," she said as we ate, "do you feel the vibe?"

"Yeah, I think I do. It's totally different here than in San Diego. That city's too touristy for me. But this place is pretty cool."

"Awesome," she said, her voice muffled with pizza. She swallowed the bite, then said, "I've only got one other place I want to show you. It was redesigned by a company called McMenamins. They're a thing here. They do a fab job of turning old buildings into completely new venues. They call it 'resurrecting.' " She laughed. "The one we're going to is Crystal Ballroom. It's an old dance hall where some sixties groups like Grateful Dead used to perform. But the city closed it down because the squares hated rock 'n' roll"—she made a crazy face, rolling her eyes and letting her tongue loll out "—and just let it go to squatters. Can you believe that?"

"Totally cringe."

"I know, right? Anyway, McMenamins bought it twenty years ago. We can't go in, but no one can stop us from looking in the windows."

She laughed, and I caught her laughter, joining in. "I love it."

"But then," she said, sounding disappointed, "I'm afraid I'll have to leave you on your own. I have a painting I have to work on for a customer."

I hid my own disappointment. "Oh, yeah, that's no problem. Don't worry about me. I feel like I've taken up enough of your time already."

"You fit into my time. Don't even think otherwise."

I liked hearing this. "Cool. I don't know what I would've done if I hadn't met you. I'd be totally lost here."

She gazed into my eyes with an intense expression on her face, causing my heart to pound.

"I don't believe you could ever be lost."

CHAPTER 4

I ARRIVED BACK AT THE HOUSE a few minutes early. I had texted Sari when I was close, so she was waiting for me at the gate. I was happy to see her again, while she seemed genuinely excited.

I had left my backpack in the foyer. Noting it as I removed my shoes and hoodie, it felt foreign to me, like something out of a past life, something I had discarded. Something of myself that I had shed.

Many more of these weird feelings, I thought, *and I'm going to start questioning my sanity.*

As I turned from the shoe cubbies, Sari pointed at my socks.

"You might be more comfortable barefoot," she said. "It's what we do here."

"Oh. Sure. I get ya."

I could hear sounds of busyness emanating from the kitchen. Staccato clinking and clanking punctuated a steady drone of voices and laughter.

"They have fun cooking," Sari said, nodding toward the sounds. "They'll begin serving in a few minutes."

"Cool." Whatever it was they were making, it smelled wonderful.

Carl appeared at the end of the hallway, entering from the vestibule next to the parlor. He paused as a woman joined him, and the two of them headed our way. When they reached us, she stood back while he stepped forward to greet me, surprising me by embracing me in a gentle hug.

"Welcome to our home," he said.

"Thank you for having me here."

The woman was stunning. She was as tall as he was, but slender and catlike, with green eyes and long flowing red hair that tossed wisps across her face. At least ten years younger than him, I judged. She wore a black-and-green paisley dress that flowed around her, the hem swirling softly at her ankles, like sea foam. There was a knowing but joyful sheen in her eyes, and behind that, an authority equal to Carl's.

I felt a little breathless and found it difficult to take my eyes off her. The same way I felt around Sari.

Fortunately, Carl didn't seem to notice my reaction. Or maybe he was aware of the way she affected people and was cool with it.

She hadn't touched Carl on their passage along the hallway, but it was obvious they were an item. The way she would glance at him, with a radiant look on her face, was a dead giveaway. But more than that, I sensed a kind of vibration between them that seemed to intensify whenever they moved closer together. It was like the way it feels when you place your finger on the track of a toy electric train set. I admit I was a little freaked by this energy, which filled the foyer.

"So you're Arthur," she said. Her voice was sweet but serious, with a soft Kentucky accent.

"Yes," I said, with a little nervous hitch in my own voice.

"I'm Melanie." She held out her hand to me, palm down. No one had ever greeted me in this fashion before, but I quickly realized what she was expecting, so I simply gave her soft fingers a light squeeze, as if we were a Renaissance lord and lady. Reflexively, I bowed slightly, which made me blush when I realized what I was doing. But she smiled and nodded in acknowledgment, the gaze of her cat's eyes never leaving mine.

"Carl tells me you hitchhiked all the way from California."

"Yeah."

"I didn't know people still did that." She laughed, a light, breathless sound that made me believe she was a very gentle person. "It seems such a sixties thing."

With her attire, hairstyle, and vibe, I could easily imagine her as a product of that long-ago era, but she was far too young to have been part of it, or even to have been born during it. For some reason, I found that disappointing.

I didn't know how to answer her, so I just smiled.

A man popped his head through the dining-room entrance. "We're ready," he announced, then popped back in.

Carl motioned to me. "Shall we?"

I let the grown-ups lead the way, Sari keeping pace with me. The dining table was elegantly set with a white embroidered tablecloth and fine china. Melanie directed me to a chair, facing the tapestry, next to her place at the foot of the table, while Carl moved to the head, near the arched entrance to the kitchen. The others took seats randomly—except for Sari, who made a point of sitting next to me, casting an impish smile my way.

I could get used to that smile.

Dinner consisted of thick vegetable stew, two fresh salads—one green, one tomato—and hot hard-crusted bread with lots of butter. Melanie doled out servings of stew from a large black cauldron, and the hefty bowls were passed around.

Then the man who had called us to dinner, who was sitting to Carl's left, sent a bottle of red wine down his side of the table. When my turn came, Melanie hesitated, looking questioningly at Carl.

After a moment, he said, with a wave of his hand, "Oh, what the hell. We've taken in a stray. We might as well contribute to his delinquency too."

She splashed a little wine into my glass, with a wink at me.

Once the wine had made its rounds, I waited for Melanie to pick up her spoon before I dug in. She noticed this and offered me a nod signifying both approval and recognition of my upbringing.

The incredible flavors of the warm, homemade stew, after so many hungry days and meager meals, made me close my eyes and want to cry. I felt as if I were discovering real food for the first time.

At this point, Carl said, "Now that we're no longer in danger of starving, introductions are in order. We're short a couple members tonight, but that's okay. Everyone who hasn't yet, please welcome our guest Arthur."

I acknowledged the ensuing chorus with a shy smile that I directed around the table.

"On my left, here," Carl said, placing a hand on the shoulder of the man who had called us to dinner, "is John." He appeared to be in his midforties, athletic, with neatly trimmed black hair. He might have been a corporate executive. "He's my right-hand man. He keeps me in my place."

John stabbed a finger at him. "Stay," he said. "*Stay.*" He cocked an eyebrow at me, making me chuckle.

"On my other side"—Carl indicated a woman who reminded me a bit of Blake Lively, sitting next to Sari—"is Janis. Janis has been with us the longest. What is it now, ten years?"

"Ten and a half," Janis said.

"A world record for putting up with me," Carl said, chuckling.

"It's true," Janis said. "I'm in *Guinness*."

"You'll notice they have weird senses of humor. They are true Portlanders."

Finally, he indicated the young woman sitting across from me. She was the only one not having wine. Her short, wiry body, multicolored punk spike haircut, pearl nose ring, and intense expression brought one word to my mind: *rebel*. She challenged me with steely gray eyes. There was something behind those eyes, something I couldn't quite discern, that made me a little uncomfortable.

"And finally, this is Emily. She's our resident college student."

"Oh, sweet," I said, trying to sound more casual than I felt. "What are you studying?"

"Feminist theory."

Woah. The challenge in her voice took me aback: "Argue with me," it seemed to say. I decided right then and there that I would always treat her with caution and respect.

Swallowing, I said again, "Sweet."

She continued to stare intently at me, sizing me up.

Trying to push down a growing uneasiness, I broke our gaze and cast a glance around the table. "Well, it's nice of you folks to invite me here. Thank you very much."

"We're so happy to have you," Melanie said.

"It's been a long time since I felt welcome anywhere." I cringed inwardly. To my ears, it sounded like I was looking for sympathy, an impression I certainly didn't want to give everyone.

Janis seemed to pick up on my vibe.

"You can be yourself here," she said quietly. "It's okay."

I looked at her inquisitively, as once again I felt like something was happening behind the scenes that I wasn't aware of.

"Arthur," Carl announced to the group, "is a resilient young man."

"He is," said Sari, looking into my eyes.

I listened awhile as the others began talking about their day, and I was glad that I was no longer the focus of attention. It was nice to be with people who were so engaged with each other. I certainly hadn't experienced this at home.

Sprinkled into the conversation were references to various esoteric things, which kind of blew me away. Not so much the things themselves, which I didn't understand, but the fact that they talked about them so matter-of-factly.

When a lull occurred, John addressed me.

"So, Arthur. What brings you to Portland?"

I glanced at Carl, wondering how much he had told the others about me. His expression, however, was unreadable.

"I had no actual destination," I said. "I was just moving north. It was the most obvious thing to do, since I lived near the Mexican border. To the east was mostly desert, so I didn't really have much choice."

John nodded. "Yeah, I guess not."

"I don't know why I kept going. There were lots of places I could have stayed if I'd wanted to. Decent places to work. But, with one exception, I didn't seriously consider doing that. I felt like I needed to keep moving."

"It sounds like something was guiding you," Janis said. "Something inside you. Or maybe even outside you."

This was the second time someone had suggested that to me today. I wondered if all the residents believed in such things. But I didn't like having to address the subject again. I felt as if I was being forced to defend my views or something.

"I didn't really think of it that way," I said carefully. "In fact, I didn't really think about it at all." I glanced at Sari, and she calmly held my gaze. "At least, not until I got here."

"Arthur has a destiny," Sari said, "that he hasn't quite accepted yet."

Melanie rescued me by saying, "This is a good place for people like you." She swept her gaze around the table. "For people like us."

There was a murmur of general agreement. I wasn't sure what she meant, how she thought I fit in here. But I didn't get a chance to ask her.

"So," John said, determinedly returning to his subject. "What did you consider to be a 'decent place to work'?"

"Anywhere that would hire a kid and not tell anyone about it." This made them all laugh, pleasing me. I shrugged. "I did all sorts of stuff. Washing dishes, warehouse work, sweeping floors. But the one I liked best was working the fields around Stockton. It was really hard, but I made friends with some of the Mexicans, who showed me some of the tricks. It was the only place I seriously considered settling in. But like all the other times, that urge to leave finally came over me."

"Ever cook anything?"

I frowned, wondering why he would ask me that. "My tutor taught me some stuff. I can flip fried eggs without breaking the yolks." I said this with a touch of pride.

John looked duly impressed. "What would you say to flipping some burgers?"

"Sure, I could do that."

"I have a food cart over on Fifth. I could use some part-time help."

His offer was unexpected but perked me up. "Sweet. That'd be rad."

John nodded.

Carl said to him, "Let's not put the cart before the horse."

I wasn't sure at first if the pun was deliberate, but as neither of them smiled, I decided it wasn't.

John shrugged. "I want him to work for me, regardless."

"Fair enough." Carl studied me. "I happen to have a spare bed at the moment. After we discussed the conversation you and I had this morning, John and I think you might be a good addition to our little group here. But there's something we need to know about you first. If you don't mind spending the night with us, I'd like to find out if you truly do fit in."

"You mean, I might be able to stay here?" I had understood what he was saying; I just found it too good to be true. Things were moving so fast, my head was spinning. So my question was impulsive and just blurted out.

To my relief, Carl was patient with me.

"Live here and join us in our dream work, yes. If you pass the test."

Although I felt some hesitation at the prospect of undergoing this "test," which Carl remained silent about, I felt excitement bubbling up within me at the thought of living in a place like this.

"That would be awesome."

Carl cast an inquiring glance around the table. Everyone expressed agreement.

"Sounds like a plan, then," he said.

CHAPTER 5

AFTER DINNER, THOSE MEMBERS WHO had not cooked did cleanup. I was surprised to find they didn't have a dishwasher, but upon reflection, I decided I shouldn't have been. It fit right in with what Sari had told me, that everyone pitched in with the chores. They had no need for such a luxury.

While they attended to this, Carl took me up to the second floor, where he offered me the second-to-last bedroom at the end of the east wing of the house. It was large and furnished with all the essentials: a twin bed, a nightstand with a lamp and a digital clock, a two-drawer dresser, a standing closet, and a small writing table with a wooden, spindle-backed chair. There was plenty of room for spreading out, if I wished, and I was pleased with the gray walls and the navy-blue curtains on the sole window that looked out on the front yard. It was at once simple, practical, and inviting. I immediately decided that I could be happy here.

I dropped my backpack next to the closet, then followed Carl back to the stairwell, where we climbed up to the third floor.

"Have you ever meditated before?" Carl asked me as we climbed the spiral of stairs, the smooth wood, slightly indented from a century of use, at times creaking softly under our bare feet.

I shook my head, even though, since I was following behind him, he couldn't see this. "No."

"Mm. Too bad. It would prepare you for what we're about to do. But don't worry," he added hastily, looking back at me over his shoulder. "It's not absolutely necessary tonight. We'll teach you how to do everything over time. All the activities we do in this house are interrelated. Everything builds on and supports everything else. It doesn't matter where you start."

The stairs ended on this floor. Randomly scattered, low-lumen LED lamps set into the baseboards illuminated the hallway with a soft glow. There was no other lighting that I could see.

Carl paused at a doorless entryway on our right, one-third of the way along the hall. Reaching around inside, he found and flipped a wall switch. A stronger—but still soft—glow spilled out.

I followed him inside and paused after two steps to take the space in. It was a large, windowless rectangular room, its long side stretching along the hallway. I guessed it to be a little more than twice the size of my new bedroom. A residual smell of pot hung in the air. Its walls, whose corners were set with rounded molding, were painted cerulean blue, and the carpeting was charcoal gray. This latter was unusually plush; my feet pleasantly sank into it. The light in this room, which made me think of an autumn sunset, seemed to be holding its breath as it infused the air from a string of three LED pendant lamps suspended along the length of the room on two-foot-long cords. Or maybe it was me holding my breath.

Nine black meditation cushions, also known as *zafus*, had been placed in a rough circle in the right-hand half of the room. This quantity struck me as an indication that they had expected me to accept their offer. Two of these sat more closely together against the far wall; the ring of *zafus* was centered on them. Before those sat a short-legged birch table on which lay a remote control. I figured that was for the Antipodes MP3 player set up on a Korean rosewood ceremonial table immediately to the left of the door. Differently colored and patterned cushions of various shapes and sizes were scattered about, as if they had been tossed around the place during some kind of game.

"Everyone sits wherever they like," Carl told me, "except for Melanie and me. Our places are fixed. Tonight, though, I'd like you to sit next to me, please." He pointed to the *zafu* on the far wall that would place me to his right.

"Sure, no prob."

We took our places as the others began flowing into the room, chatting in hushed voices among themselves. I grimaced as I settled onto the hard-packed *zafu*, which barely gave way beneath me, making me have to scrunch my way onto it to make even a shallow dent.

To my delight, Sari plopped down next to me, a bright smile on her face and a memory foam pillow under her arm. I grinned back at her, hoping my nervousness about the upcoming evening didn't show.

"I'm so excited for you," she said. "You're going to be blown away!"

I made a wry face. "Just what I need," I said sardonically.

She playfully slapped my arm. "You'll love it. I promise."

Just then, a larger-than-life figure appeared in the doorway. He was even more hippie-like than Carl. His thick, wavy brown hair cascaded wildly over his shoulders. He was Carl's height, but weighed considerably more. I judged him to be about twice my age. He was dressed in jeans and a black-and-purple dashiki shirt, with a three-inch-wide wooden peace symbol dangling from a leather cord draped around his neck.

He immediately proved himself to be by far the most boisterous of the bunch, entering the room with a shout of "Let's rock!" and flinging his arms out to his sides as if he were trying to hug everyone. They greeted him with laughter and welcoming words, albeit in a much more subdued manner. The whole scene reminded me of Norm entering the pub on *Cheers*. He quickly noticed me and flashed me a peace sign, as if he was not surprised to see me here.

Carl picked up the remote control and fiddled with the MP3. Soon the room filled with steep crescendos and diminuendos that accentuated the lilting, yet masculine, cadences of Gregorian chants.

The quiet voices, combined with my nervousness and the energy I felt emanating from the other members of the household, made me feel like I was floating on gently rolling waves. I closed my eyes, relishing the sensation, until Carl spoke.

"Well," he said, surveying the room and offering everyone a beatific smile. "Here we are, at it again. Another week gone by. Hard to believe, isn't it? Time just slips past us."

"It just means we're all fully engaged with life," Melanie said.

"Indeed we are." Carl turned to address me. "Normally, we would meditate and then have a freeform discussion. But tonight, we're going to skip all that. You need to be initiated."

He grinned, and I swallowed hard.

"Don't worry," he said. "We're not going to ask you to do anything embarrassing. We're not a frat."

Everyone laughed. To be honest, his use of the word "initiated" *had* sparked in me a fear of being humiliated, but I realized, even before Carl's reassurance, that such a fear was childish and unwarranted. I couldn't even imagine these people behaving in such an unseemly manner.

"Okay," I said. "That's cool."

"Good." Carl appeared to be studying me, but it turned out that he actually was focused inward, marshaling his thoughts. "We talked about Carl Jung this morning. His ideas about psychology are the basis of what we believe here. Whereas his teacher, Sigmund Freud, believed personality to be driven by internal conflict, Jung's theory grounds human psychology in spirituality. In his concept of the mind, there is no conflict. Rather, there's an interplay of what he called 'archetypes,' mental energies that work in us at various stages of our life. They reside in what he termed 'the collective unconscious,' a part of our minds that is inaccessible to us but shared by everyone."

I indicated I had a question, and Carl paused. "What do you mean by 'shared'?" I asked.

"That it's the same for everyone. The archetypes are universal and unchanging, and they mean the same thing for all of us."

"But if it's inaccessible, how do we know what's in it?"

"The archetypes often appear to us in dreams."

"Are the dreams also the same for everyone?"

"No, because they're regulated by the *personal* unconscious. The archetypes infiltrate that individual's mental space and influence our normal dreaming."

"Hmm." I twisted my mouth. "I guess I get it."

"I know it sounds confusing," Carl said with a smile. "But it's easier to grasp if you remember that all the functions of the mind work in conjunction with one another. They're not completely separate entities. The big leap here is the idea of *sharing* 'brain space' through a common pathway that we can't deliberately access. But once you experience it, it's really quite revelatory."

"Will I get to experience it?"

"That's what we're going to find out."

"Oh. Okay. I'll shut up now."

"No, no. Break in anytime you like. I want you to get a reasonably clear idea of what this stuff is all about, before we put you in the fiery furnace." He offered me a sly smile before continuing. "So. Where was I? Oh yeah. Okay. In the 1960s, psychologists became interested in hallucinogenic drugs like LSD. Not only did they engage in clinical trials of them with volunteers, but they took it themselves as well.

"One of these men was Stanislav Grof. The things he experienced on the drug convinced him that current psychological theories were inadequate to explain them. Expanding on Jung's theory of the collective unconscious, he posited the existence of a collective *conscious*. This is a realm of shared spiritual experiences, such as feelings of being one with all things."

"Okay, that I do get." I'd had intimations of this sort on our annual autumn trips to see the leaves changing in the local mountains. I had a real affinity for trees.

"Excellent." Carl sounded quite pleased. "Grof coined the word 'holotropic' for these expanded states of consciousness. He believes we can enter them at will, and he invented a technique for doing so—something he called 'holotropic breathing'—which is part of his overall theory of transpersonal psychology, the science of transcendence.

"Melanie and I got interested in his program shortly after we moved into this house, about"—he looked to Melanie—"what? Fourteen?" When she nodded in confirmation, he continued, "Fourteen years or so ago. After undergoing a number of sessions with him, we both took the certification course and became authorized Facilitators. I then opened my own clinic. Janis was the first of my victims."

He looked across the room to his left and, grinning, nodded to Janis, who offered him a namaste bow in return.

"The technique enables us to call up our most deeply buried memories," Carl went on, "all the way back to when we were born. It's a powerful method of treating subconscious issues, but we discovered that it has some interesting side effects. Things that Grof doesn't talk about and that we now think are experienced only by certain unique individuals. We've gathered as many of those together here as we've been able to find so far. And now, we'd like to find out if you're one of us."

This put me on the spot, and I blushed deeply, as I in no way thought I was special. I thought the opposite to be true. But before I could respond in any way, Melanie leaned forward, around Carl, to address me.

"What we discovered," she said, "is that it lets us read each other's minds."

I suppose Carl left this announcement to her as a way of softening the blow. But it didn't work. I was stunned. I didn't know what to say, because I had no words to express anything at all. All my words had fled from me, making me feel lightheaded and empty. So I responded the only way I could: I laughed.

Carl smiled. "You don't believe us."

I shook my head, embarrassed for my outburst. "I'm sorry, but I don't."

"Of course you don't. Who would? But we'd like you to give us a chance to convince you."

"You want to read my mind?" I recoiled in horror at this prospect.

"No, no." Carl briefly raised both palms to me in a calming gesture. "We wouldn't intrude on you in that way, even if we could. It would be unethical, and both parties have to be willing in order for it to work, anyway. It would put you on the spot to ask that of you tonight, pressuring you to say yes even if you mean no. So instead, I'd like *you* to read *mine*."

"Me to read yours?" Carl may have meant this to be reassuring, but it only made me feel more bewildered.

Sari placed a hand on my arm, and I turned to her, glad to be grounded by her touch.

"It's not intrusive or anything," she assured me. "But it can be a little startling at first."

That wasn't the issue I was having, but her touch eased my real concern. I couldn't help but think that this ability was what she had displayed in the coffee shop. If so, I saw no real harm in it. And after all, I had requested her to do it—if a little naively. Why should I balk now?

"Okay," I said. I turned once again to Carl. "I guess I'm game."

"Excellent!" he said.

Janis clapped triumphantly and called to Melanie, "I told you he'd be an adventurer!"

The others cast approving glances in my direction.

Then Carl went on from where he had been interrupted.

"After me, Harold"—he indicated the retro hippie—"is our most accomplished practitioner." Harold punched his fists into the air over his head, making everyone laugh, and Carl continued, "He's agreed to be the control element of our little experiment."

I acknowledged Harold's accomplishment and willingness with a formal nod in his direction.

"This will take at least an hour," Carl went on. "What we're going to do this evening is the first step in learning the skill. Once you're reasonably proficient at it, you won't need this anymore."

Again I noticed that he spoke as if he expected me to succeed.

"The foam pad underneath the carpet," he continued, "is triple thick, just for this purpose. It should be comfortable enough for you. Go ahead and situate yourself over there in a way that will let you lie still for that long. I suggest lying on your back, with your arms at your sides."

As I got up to move toward the center of the room, Sari handed me the memory foam pillow that she had brought in with her.

"Thanks."

"No worries. Enjoy." She smiled.

I offered her a here-goes-nothing expression, making her laugh. I then noticed that Janis had come to stand beside me, carrying one of the plusher cushions she had picked up on her way into the session.

"I'll be your sitter," she said, smiling. "I watch over you."

"Cool," I said.

I stretched out on the surprisingly comfortable carpet as Carl had suggested I do, palms down.

Janis placed her cushion close to my chest and settled herself on it. She instructed me in a quiet voice to close my eyes and try to relax. After less than a minute, she said to Carl, "I think we're set."

"Good," Carl said. "Arthur, please try to stay awake." He laughed lightly. Then, addressing Harold, Janis, and me, he asked, "Shall we begin?"

I nodded as Harold said, "Right on."

The room fell silent around me as Carl switched off the Gregorian chants. A few seconds later, the air became infused instead with the sound of rhythmic, ritualistic drumming, at a volume just loud enough for me to hear it.

As I let this repetitious pounding flow through me, I soon felt my nervousness dissipate, leaving me feeling surprisingly relaxed amid the drifting of my thoughts.

I didn't know how many minutes I had lain there before I heard Janis's calm, even voice again. Funnily, somehow it seemed to hover somewhere over my closed eyes.

"Okay, Arthur," she said. "I'd like you to start breathing slowly and deeply."

It didn't take me long to realize that Carl's admonition to stay awake had been made only half in jest. I was more fatigued from my long, emotional day than I had realized, and deep breathing tended to make me sleepy.

As my energy seeped into the air, my mind turned to odd thoughts, disturbing me with their weirdness. I wasn't dreaming, but the imagery was similar to it, some of it rather nightmarish. Each time I startled back to normal wakefulness from one of the latter, I became more determined to not let it happen again.

"Struggling against your thoughts is a natural reaction," Janis said quietly. "But it will only make your brain become more insistent. Instead, focus on the drums. They will impart energy to you and clear your mind."

I didn't allow myself to wonder for more than a moment how she knew what I was experiencing. I just did as she suggested, and my fatigue gradually fell away.

After another passage of an unknown amount of time, I no longer had to fight off drowsiness. Janis seemed to sense this too.

"Okay," she said, "breathe a little faster now and a little deeper."

I obeyed but immediately felt her lightly place her hand on my chest.

"Slower," she said. "We don't want to rush this. It can make you hyperventilate."

I slowed my breathing a notch, and she removed her hand.

I got into the rhythms, as Janis gradually drew me into deeper and more rapid breaths. I was surprised at how pleasant it felt to breathe in this way.

I can't say how long I was at this; all awareness of time had slipped through my mental fingers. All I knew in the world was the sound of the drums, the pumping of my lungs, and Janis's occasional voice. But at some point in this self-produced eternity, I heard Carl speaking in a gentle and soothing tone.

"Okay. Harold and Arthur, I'm thinking of an object that I've mentally placed on the coffee table in the parlor. Imagine yourself walking into that room and seeing that object. Arthur, you remember the room, yes?"

I nodded dreamily. The movement threatened me with nausea, so I put a quick stop to it.

"Good. Don't try to guess, and don't force it. Let the awareness of it come into your mind of its own accord. And don't settle for the first thing that shows up. That's almost never the right one. Instead, just let objects come and go. The right one will *feel* right to you. Wait until that happens, and when it does, squeeze Janis's hand."

Janis gently turned my right hand over, so my palm was facing up, and placed hers in it, which I found comforting.

I followed Carl's instructions as best I could. It took a while for me to get to the point where potentially correct images started appearing—things that made sense and weren't just random blips in the cavern of my thoughts.

At last, one presented itself that persisted, even when I tried to dismiss it. On this basis alone, I felt like it might be the right one. Unfortunately, the object that had come to my mind was so ridiculous that I was embarrassed to tell everyone about it. But it did feel right. When I was as satisfied as I was going to get, I gave Janis's hand a quick, light squeeze.

A few seconds later, the drumming stopped, a low-toned bell sounded, and the chants returned.

Janis let go of my hand and placed hers on my chest again.

"Let's start to slow down," she said gently.

We reversed the process in which we had earlier engaged, but more quickly.

When my breathing was back to normal, she said, "You can go back to your *zafu* now."

When Janis and I were settled in our places once more, Carl glanced around the room.

"Thank you, everyone. Janis, you were marvelous, as always. And Harold, thanks for lending us your mind."

Harold raised his right fist and gave it a short, tight jerk in acknowledgment.

Carl smiled at me. "So, Arthur, why don't you tell us what you found."

Put on the spot, I felt embarrassed and reticent. I was sure the group was going to laugh at me. But I saw what I saw. I murmured, "A pitcher of red Kool-Aid."

Everyone laughed, just as I'd feared. Everyone, that is, except Carl and Harold.

"You got in the ballpark," Carl said. He sounded pleased.

"Ballpark, hell!" Harold exclaimed. "Lil bro *groks* it!"

"What?" I was at once surprised and relieved. I wasn't a fool after all. But I also wasn't exactly correct.

"Harold's a bit excitable," Carl said, laughing. "But yeah." He motioned to the retro hippie. "Tell us."

"It's a book."

"Very good. And what is the title of this book?"

"*The Electric Kool-Aid Acid Test.*"

I felt my stomach drop with my jaw. But Carl continued on nonchalantly.

"Dead on. Have you ever read that book, Arthur?"

I frowned and shook my head. "I've never even heard of it before."

Harold said excitedly, "It's from the sixties. A true story all about the Merry Pranksters—a group of LSD-stoned beatniks led by the novelist Ken Kesey—who traveled the country in a psychedelically painted bus; wreaking havoc wherever they went; following no rules, not even their own; living just for the experience of being alive. Comporting themselves like deranged, psyched-out clowns and drawing anyone who was susceptible into their lunacy. It's a classic, man, the start of everything antiestablishment and real, the roots of the counterculture movement."

Blown away by this stream-of-consciousness onslaught, all I could do was gape. Carl rescued me from looking like a complete idiot.

"So do you see what happened?" he asked me. "Your mind had no reference point for the object, but it was definitely tuned in. It made a best guess."

I didn't know what to say, so I said nothing.

"That was incredible," said Janis.

"No kidding," said John. "You're a natural."

Melanie leaned forward again to address me. "No one's ever done that well on their first try."

It goes without saying that I enjoyed hearing these compliments. But it was the look on Sari's face that really meant something to me.

It verged on awe.

CHAPTER 6

SO THAT WAS HOW MY first experience with Likemind went.

The next day was mundane and boring, perhaps even a bit of a letdown, after the night's mindboggling experience.

I was awakened by a light rapping on my bedroom door. Groggily, I opened my eyes, wondering where I was. A moment later, it came to me. I sat up in bed, making sure the covers were pulled up over my boxers, then I called for the visitor to enter.

In the doorway stood a striking woman with a serious demeanor, as serious as Emily's, but different. Not scary like the younger woman; just no-nonsense. I judged her to be the kind of person who never took no for an answer. She had mousy hair, verging on blonde, which she wore in a Jane Fonda style, and mahogany-brown eyes. She was dressed rather conservatively, even more so than the manner John favored. I was kind of surprised to find these two seeming conformists living here, in a place that clearly flaunted social norms.

"Good morning," she said. "I hope you slept well."

"I was literally dead. And this bed certainly beats the hard ground."

The woman's piercing gaze didn't waver. I felt like she was weighing me, judging me. Looking right through me. I seemed to be experiencing that a lot here. "I imagine so," she said. "And then we kept you up half the night."

"Last night blew me away."

"Likemind has a way of doing that." At last she flashed a smile, mitigating some of her prim demeanor. But it was brief. "My name's Priscilla. I'm John's wife. I'm kind of in and out around here. My job keeps me on the road a lot."

"What do you do?"

"I'm a tech consultant to small business owners. I travel the country."

It seemed to me that a lot of the members of this group worked for themselves. I liked that.

"Awesome," I said. "That sounds really cool."

She responded to this with a tilt of her head. "It is."

Grimacing at the clock, which I couldn't read because it was skewed on the table, I said, "What time is it, anyway? I feel so good, it's like I slept for days."

She laughed, and the slight discomfort I had been feeling in her presence dissolved. "It's the day after, around seven thirty. John and I are about to have breakfast, if you'd like to join us."

"Oh, bet. That sounds great."

"Sweet. See you downstairs."

The door closed softly behind her. I sighed in satisfaction and lay back on the bed again, the covers disheveled around my legs. I really did feel good.

Last night's events had worked magic on me. I could still feel a kind of vibration, an electric tingling along my skin that had set in when my breathing had been at its fastest. A powerful energy seemed to pulse everywhere this morning, inside me and around me.

After a minute, I got up. I had no choice but to throw on the same clothes I'd worn the day before, but fortunately, they were still basically clean. With any luck, I'd be able to do my laundry today. Unfortunately, Priscilla had given me no time for a shower right now. I got ready quickly and headed downstairs.

John was sitting at the dining table when I arrived. Priscilla stood behind him, her hands on his shoulders. They were chatting quietly—he, tilting his head to look up at her; she, lowering hers to him. They stopped when they noticed me.

"We've got scrambled eggs and toast," she said, "if that's to your liking."

"Works for me."

"Coffee?"

"Oh-yes-please." This came out almost as one word.

She motioned to a chair across from them. "Go ahead and sit down. I'll bring everything out."

"Thanks."

I pulled out the heavy chair and sat, facing the tapestry as I had the previous evening.

"So," John said, "how was your night?"

I wasn't sure if he was referring to how I slept or to the events of the evening, so I offered an answer that covered both. "Totally out of it."

He laughed. "That's the correct answer."

"No, really. It was good. I feel really good." That was something of an understatement and didn't fully express what was happening inside me, but I didn't know how to put it into words. "I mean, I've never felt like *this* before. I can't even describe it."

"That's the holotropic practice for you. You actually entered a higher spiritual state. It's the kind of thing yogis and shamans do."

"Whatever it is, I want more."

"No one has ever taken to it as quickly as you did."

From the entrance behind me, another voice broke into the conversation. My heart leaped at the sound of it.

"Didn't surprise me in the least," Sari said.

I twisted around to watch her enter the room. She moved like Catwoman, stirring a different feeling inside me.

"When has anything surprised you?" John asked her, laughing.

"The fact that I'm awake and up at this ungodly hour on a Saturday surprises me." She lightly tapped my upper arm with the back of her hand. "How are you doing, kiddo?"

"I feel like I might float away."

"I feel that all the time."

"Why *are* you up now?" Priscilla asked as she entered from the kitchen, carrying a silver tray laden with steaming plates.

Sari wagged a finger at me. "I'm responsible for this dude. I needed to make sure he was okay."

"You're responsible for me?" I asked her.

Sari frowned at John. "You dudes didn't tell him?"

"Didn't think we needed to." He addressed me. "Allow me to officially welcome you as a member of the household. Assuming that's what you'd like, of course."

"Oh absolutely," I said, ticked at myself for gushing, but unable to stop. "I'd like that very much. Thank you!"

Sari laughed and said, "We kinda like it too." Indicating the tray that John was offloading, she asked Priscilla, "Any of that left out there?"

"Of course," Priscilla said. "I had a feeling you might want some."

"So," John said to his wife, "you actually *weren't* surprised to see her."

"Nope."

"I can't get away with anything around here," Sari said, rolling her eyes in disdain.

"It's not like you're hard to read," Priscilla said, flicking her eyes in my direction—and making me blush.

"That's me," Sari said. "An open book." She headed for the kitchen.

I carefully settled the plate John handed me onto the table, then accepted a cup of coffee from Priscilla.

"Anyway," John said to me, "we don't normally do the holotropic thing for reading minds; that's just for beginners. None of us needs it for that anymore. Instead, we use it the way it was originally intended, as a form of psychological therapy. Carl doesn't charge us for a session."

I thought I could probably use some therapy, but was kind of scared of what I might learn about myself. I decided not to mention that last part.

"I'll keep it in mind," I said. "Thanks."

John gave me a look that made me wonder if he *was* reading my mind. But then I remembered Carl had said I had to be willing in order for people to be able to do so. Again, I decided to trust that that was true. Of course, I had no way of knowing for sure; my subconscious might very well be a leaking sieve.

"I have to do some shopping this morning," Priscilla said to me, switching to a more mundane, practical subject. "You can come with me, if you like. Pick up some toiletries and stuff."

"Thanks, but I don't have any bread. I have to wait for my first paycheck." I couldn't prevent an involuntary glance at John.

"I can give you an advance, if you like," he said. "I have some company cash around that I haven't put in the bank yet."

I opened my mouth to speak, but Priscilla cut me off. "I'll just use my debit card, John. It's less complicated."

"Well…"

"I'll do separate transactions." Her tone indicated that there was an unspoken *of course* somewhere in that assertion.

"Okay. You win."

She pecked him on the cheek. "Of course I do."

I grinned as John gave me a doleful look.

"Would it be possible," I asked, "for me to do some laundry when we get back? This is my only good set of clothes, and I wore them yesterday."

"No problem," Priscilla said. "We have machines in the basement. I'll show you when we get back."

"Sweet."

"Maybe we could get him some new ones?" John suggested. "Just a few things. If his other stuff was ruined from—"

"We could do that," Priscilla interjected, talking over him.

"—the trip." John reacted as if he was used to this pattern with his wife. Which is to say, he didn't react at all.

"That would be awesome," I said. "I don't really need a lot."

"We'll take care of it," Priscilla said with finality.

"You folks are too dope."

John laughed. "I don't think anyone's ever accused me of that before."

I decided not to respond to this.

In the lull, Sari addressed me on her way back to the table, full plate and coffee in hand.

"When you get back, I have something planned for you. It'll only take an hour, so you'll have plenty of time to do all your other stuff."

"What's up?"

"The second part of your initiation."

Priscilla said, grinning, "She's going to sell the city to you."

I frowned, not understanding. I thought she'd done that yesterday. But before I could say anything, Sari addressed me.

"Priscilla's lived in Portland her whole life, and she still hasn't gotten hip to what it's all about."

"So I'm a stick-in-the-mud, eh?" Priscilla rejoined. "Well, somebody has to keep you kids in the real world. Disco is dead, y'know."

"Don't listen to her," Sari said to me, rolling her eyes again. "It's hardly *disco*."

Priscilla laughed. "Wait'll you see the setup."

This sparked me to ask about something I had been curious about since my arrival. "Why is this house so weird looking, anyway? There doesn't seem to be any logic to it."

"It wasn't always like this," John said. "The land the house is on was first bought as a small tract by Carl's family back in the 1800s, when Goose Hollow was first getting established. It was just big enough for a small Victorian house. But when Portland was incorporated a decade later, Carl's great-great-great-grandfather was savvy enough to realize that the city was going to boom. So he bought up the four acres around the original plot, and the house slowly expanded into it over the next century. That's why it doesn't fit any architectural style anymore; it's mostly just a bunch of tacked-on rooms."

Priscilla interjected, "That's what gives it its character."

"It has that, for sure," I said approvingly.

"It has spirit," John said.

This made me think of the jest Sari had made when I first arrived. "Any bumps in the night?"

I grinned at Sari when she laughed, but John gave me a cryptic smile. "Energy," he said. "Energy moves here."

I nodded absently as I pondered this. There did seem to be something in the air, a sensation of *presence* I couldn't put a name to. "It's not scary, though."

"No," John said. "It's not scary."

We finished eating, and I offered to do the cleaning up, because I hadn't helped the previous night.

"I can figure out where stuff goes," I said.

When I was done with my task, I took a shower, again using borrowed items, but this time, in my very own bathroom. There were enough of them in the house to accommodate the nine of us living there, plus one for good measure: eight on the second floor, each directly across the hall from the bedroom it was assigned to; and one each for the two master bedrooms on the first floor, which lay side by side behind the doors in the vestibule. These accommodated the two married couples.

Afterward, Priscilla and I spent a leisurely morning shopping for everyday items at Fred Meyer, a northwest-based hypermarket superstore located across the river in the Hawthorne District. I came home with everything I needed to get started in my new life. She had also—despite my protests—bought me a pair of jeans to replace the pair I'd torn at some point on the road, plus a set of pajamas. I was grateful for her trust and generosity.

I changed into the jeans and tossed my chinos into the laundry basket we'd also bought. I then offloaded the backpack into it and headed for the basement. After I finished doing my laundry, I met up with Sari.

She took me up to the television room on the third floor of the western gable. Its presence surprised me, making her laugh.

"We're seekers," she said, "not monks."

The space was completely at odds with the rest of the house. Against the south wall, an old, clunky forty-inch Sony Trinitron sat on an oak shelving unit; an equally old and clunky Panasonic DVD player was set up on the first shelf below it. A rose-patterned white couch and a brown La-Z-Boy recliner took up the opposite wall. Three beanbag chairs were scattered around the room, each accompanied by a fifteen-inch-diameter pedestal table, one holding a lava lamp, and the others, candles. The window behind the television was cloaked with heavy brown drapes, and on each side of it stood a six-foot-tall spiral wrought iron DVD stand. Colorful bead curtains cascaded down the western windows, casting halos of red, green, and blue into the room. The walls were painted purple, and an oval beige rug covered the space between the couch and the TV. Variously sized and colored cushions were randomly scattered across the floor. Everything seemed worn, and while the room was clean, it intimated a little dust. I felt like I'd been transported back in time.

"Carl gave me free rein to decorate," Sari chirped happily. "I'm a hipster, so I did my own thing."

And what a thing it is, I thought. Aloud, I said, "That's pretty cool of him."

"He digs my nineties style."

"I could get into it." I frowned as I studied the ancient equipment. "What do you do if it breaks?"

Sari laughed. "How do you think I got it in the first place? There's a repair and resale shop in Vancouver, just over the state line, that specializes in old electronics. About half an hour away."

"Cool."

Sari closed the door, then motioned toward the couch. We settled in, and I wondered what it was she wanted to show me. As it turned out, it both surprised and intrigued me.

"This," Sari said, operating the remote, "will be your *cultural* initiation into Portland."

We leaned back on the couch, close together, and watched the first episode of the old cable TV series *Portlandia*. It was odd and quirky and funny and cool. But it was the opening that grabbed my attention and stayed with me, changing the way I viewed the city. A large crowd of people—done up in outlandish costumes and makeup—danced, sang, and rode odd bicycles along a broad concourse, with glimpses of the river, a bridge, and skyscrapers behind them. In this extremely bizarre way, they were celebrating the eclectic freedom that was to be found in Portland.

When the episode was over, she turned the devices off using their separate remotes and twisted around to face me, an expectant look on her face.

"Wow," I said. I was pleased to see her light up at my reaction. "Is that really what this place is like?"

"At its heart," she said. " 'Dream of the '90s,' baby." This was the title of the song performed in the show. "You can do or be anything you want here. There are no boundaries. Time has no meaning."

I marveled at this prospect, while not knowing quite what to make of it. Feeling as if I were floating on the exhilaration Sari exuded, I said the first thing that popped into my head.

"Let's become something."

CHAPTER 7

A s Sari had intimated to me on Friday, Portland's food carts were iconic, crunched together side by side in a number of parking lots around the city.

John's, set on a stretch of Fifth Avenue between Stark and Oak Streets, drew the polo-shirt-and-khaki office crowd from the riverside business towers. Others had their own particular clientele, depending on their location.

John's business was called Flash Burger. A wooden sign on the front of his cart sported a hand-painted picture of a double-decker burger with a superimposed yellow lightning bolt jutting diagonally across it. The name was hand carved above this. It was a pretty decent amateur's work, I thought.

"Made that myself," he told me proudly as he un-locked his shop.

"I like it."

Inside, it was cramped, with just enough room to slide past each other as we moved back and forth between the large griddle and the customer window. A small space heater stood against the back wall, but John only used it in the winter and, even then, just until the griddle heated up.

It was overcast and breezy when we arrived to do lunch prep at nine o'clock, and the temperature didn't even reach fifty degrees until my shift ended at one o'clock that afternoon. By then it was raining. I was used to a much warmer and sunnier clime in San Diego, but I was stalwart and didn't complain. I'm just saying, it was mid-March; it should have been spring by then.

I had accompanied John in his vintage 1969 Chevrolet Camaro RS Z28—a sweet ride. He parked in his regular spot—for which he maintained a monthly pass—in the underground lot of the building I had skirted on my way to Java Man. From there, we walked to his trailer, roughly retracing the route I had taken three days before on my quasi-random trek. After I was fully trained, he said, I'd be responsible for getting myself to and from work, because his hours were different from those he needed me for.

My days quickly became routine. The lunch crowd would begin gathering in earnest about a quarter to eleven, and by the stroke of that hour, it was hard to weave one's way along the sidewalk. Over time, I came to think of my work period as "the Lunch Crush," because it reminded me of the video game. Keeping up with orders required some concentration and adeptness, but nothing I couldn't handle. In fact, once I got the rhythm of it down, I kind of enjoyed the work.

After the daily lunch cleanup, John no longer needed me, so I would head back to the house. Sari had told me that Portland is considered a walkable city, but the streets were bumper-to-bumper with vehicle traffic, nonetheless. Aside from the cars, my senses were frequently assaulted by buses and MAX trains as well. Downtown was a bustling place, and I felt the energy of it infecting me with a kind of buzz that flowed along my nerves.

Often I would ramble off the direct route home, changing streets and directions on a whim, trusting Google Maps to rescue me if I should become hopelessly lost. But it was actually hard to do that. When I came across establishments, I peered into the open doorways of those I wasn't allowed to enter, and I stepped inside those I was.

I got lost one afternoon for over half an hour in The Fossil Cartel, wandering among its variously shaped wooden display stands and glass cases overflowing with such treasures as ammonites, hand-sized chalcedony rocks, and custom jewelry. Some of the stones were reputed to have magic qualities. I found myself reluctant to leave the place.

However, I was always glad to get back to Carl's house, where I felt welcome—even if no one else was home. There was an aura about the place, something I couldn't define but that seemed to call to me from every corner. I decided early on that I was going to like my new life very much.

CHAPTER 8

I KILL MY MOTHER AND BURY her in a field. But that night at dinner, her ghost sits beside me at a long banquet table. I struggle with my feelings.

"And now it lies," she says, her voice hollow and devoid of emotion, "where the blood has stopped."

"Where the life has stopped," I say miserably, holding back tears.

My father thinks I don't care about her death. He glares at me from across the table, a cold and callous expression on his face. But I am capable of feeling, I insist to myself, as I avoid his gaze. Still, I have no appetite, and I pick listlessly at my plate.

——◆——

I jerked out of sleep with the words *it's your fault* reverberating in my head. I lay there on my back, with my eyes closed for a few seconds, until my heart stopped pounding. I'd had variations of that dream every so often over the years, but this night's was the most disturbing yet.

A light spattering of rain tapped tentatively at the window, calming me. The darkness of my bedroom became a cloak I now wrapped around me, hoping it might shelter me from the harsh recriminations of my nightmare's whispers.

I turned my head to check the digital clock on my nightstand: 3:43 a.m. This was the morning after the vernal equinox, a yearly turning that was supposed to bring the hope of renewed life to the earth. I wanted to embrace that, to take it to heart, but—as this macabre dream indicated— I was still far from escaping my past. Maybe it was just too soon; maybe I was just expecting too much.

I drifted back to sleep just as the rain was tapering off.

Two hours later, my alarm chirped. I immediately got out of bed, anxious to shake off the gloom of the night.

After I showered and dressed, I met up with John, Melanie, Janis, and Emily in the kitchen, where they were preparing breakfast. Because I had bragged about my prowess at frying eggs, John always gave me that task whenever he and I ate together in the morning. It had become kind of a standing joke between us, although everyone agreed I was the best one for the job. He held out the spatula to me, and I happily took on my privileged duty.

"Coming up on your two-week anniversary already," Melanie said to me, after we had settled around the huge dining table.

"Yeah," I said. "It went by quickly. Time's fun when you're having flies."

My silly joke, meant more to prod my own feelings fully out of the night's bleakness, produced some chuckles, although Janis made a face, while Emily merely raised an eyebrow at me. I was pleased enough with these reactions.

"You fit in nicely here," Janis said.

"Thanks. It's the first time I've ever felt at home anywhere. Although," I added, glancing around at the room, "there's something else about this place, something I haven't figured out yet."

"The house has that effect on people," John said. "It's at once comforting and unsettling."

"It has a very long history," Melanie said. "Not all of it pleasant. Carl and I have worked to mitigate the negative vibes, with some recent help from Emily." The two women exchanged knowing looks but didn't offer any details. "Can't get rid of them all, though."

"You learn to live with the ghosts," Janis offered with a cryptic smile, making me wonder once again what the truth actually was about bumps in the night.

After eating, we all pitched in doing the dishes, although there weren't actually enough tasks for all of us to do.

Then John headed off for Flash Burger. I followed him into the foyer.

"It's supposed to rain pretty hard this morning," he said as he put on his shoes. "Would you like a ride? I don't have anything for you to do at the cart before your shift, but it might save you a soaking later."

"No, thanks. I was thinking that I've focused a lot on exploring downtown but haven't even seen the neighborhood yet. I think I'll take a quick look around before heading for work. If you don't mind."

"Of course not. I think that's a good idea. There are some decent views from the higher spots, although the heavy weather may blot out some of them. But I think you'll like it, either way. It's a nice area to walk around. See you at ten, then."

We headed out the door together, but parted as he veered off to the right to get his car out of the garage on the western side of the house, while I made my way to the front gate. The vehicle gate, which had a remote-controlled lock, opened outwardly, so I skirted it to make sure I didn't get tapped by it accidentally.

The sky was a battle between white, gray, and a bit of blue, but the weak sun and heavy winds didn't do much to mitigate the temperature, which was still too cold as far as I was concerned. But whereas I huddled in both my jacket and hoodie, I had noted that John was in short sleeves. I wondered how long it would take me to get acclimatized so I could stop looking like a schmuck.

Carl's house was on a tree-lined street that rose and dropped and twisted its way among differing neighborhoods. Some were parceled out in the same anal-retentive blocks as the city layout below. Others were more like Carl's property, sprawling between a few houses.

For the most part, the streets this morning were devoid of traffic. I exchanged idle glances with the few drivers who did pass by me, more due to surprise at seeing each other than anything else.

I walked at a moderate clip, mindful of the thickening clouds and the limits of my time.

I found myself at the Vista Bridge, a landmark on the northern border of the neighborhood, where I stopped to gaze out eastward over the city.

From this vantage point, I could just discern, rising out of the distant misty hills beyond the towers of downtown, the silhouette of Mount Hood, a dormant volcano seventy miles away. Although the top third was cloaked in cloud, I had seen photos of its peak on the internet. Contemplating its eleven thousand feet of pyramid-shaped rock, almost all of which was still buried under ice and snow at this beginning of spring, I was struck by a passing curiosity about what it might be like to watch it erupt. But my mind immediately jumped from that thought to a memory I really wished I'd not called up.

Southern California is earthquake country. When I was five years old, the entire region had been rocked by three high-magnitude temblors, one after the other over the course of four days in June of 2005, moving northward in succession from San Diego to Yucaipa.

I had been playing in my bedroom on that Sunday morning when the first one hit. There was a powerful jolt that knocked me onto my butt, followed by a massive rocking that seemed to last forever, the floor beneath me rising and falling as if I were being tossed on ocean waves, preventing me from standing up again. I screamed, then began sobbing in abject fear. It felt like forever before everything finally settled down again. A few seconds after it did, my father strode down the hallway—not to check on me or to comfort me, but to berate me.

"What the hell are you bawling about?" he demanded. He slapped me across the face, hard enough to sting. "Don't be a baby."

Shock stifled my tears. My father had berated me on occasion, but he had never struck me before. I couldn't believe he had done so then. But after a moment of stunned silence, the blow galvanized me to react in a way *I* never had before, which was almost as shocking to me: I yelled back.

"I'm not a baby! I hate you! I want Mommy!"

"Well, she doesn't want *you*."

And for a second time, I was stunned into silence. *She doesn't want me?* This was incredulous beyond my imagination, and my words dried up. Up until that moment, my father had always responded to my questions about where my mother was with dismissive statements like "She's gone on a trip" and "She's busy right now." This was the first time he had openly blamed me for her absence. I just sat there with my mouth agape, my eyes burning, as confusion and fear fought for dominance within me.

"You have no one to blame but yourself," he went on. "Now get out here and eat your breakfast." As he turned to leave, he said over his shoulder, "And turn off the damned waterworks."

Now, as I stood on the bridge, looking out at the distant volcano, these memories and emotions roiling inside me, I realized that, while the earthquake had not destroyed my house, it certainly had destroyed my home.

A light drizzle blew into my face, jarring me out of my unpleasant thoughts. I allowed myself to believe that this was the only source of the dampness on my cheeks.

Once again moving quickly, I finished crossing the bridge and made my way eastward across town to Flash Burger, half an hour away, hoping I would be able to build some new, better memories in this city and to put away the old ones for good.

CHAPTER 9

BY THE FRIDAY THAT MARKED both three weeks of my living in the commune and the end of the month, I had scoped the house out pretty thoroughly, both inside and out. While the backyard was easily my favorite part of the residence, I had decided that the parlor was my favorite room. The mixed styles and casual layout of the furniture, the changing quality of the room's natural light (due to the bay window's eastern exposure and angled panes), and its collection of artworks made it feel like a secret hideaway, a respite from the noise of the outside world.

So that was where I headed around four o'clock, hoping to spend half of the sixty minutes left before dinner contemplating there, before the rest of the house members not on cooking detail would begin arriving home.

I started where I usually did, gazing at the green Tara *thangka* just inside the door. The artwork's symbolism, that of compassion, certainly was fitting for this household. They had shown that to me in abundance. I felt I owed them a great debt. More than that, I felt I owed a debt to the universe itself—and wondered how I could possibly pay *that* back. I resolved to do my best to find a way.

After a few minutes of contemplation, I moved to the bay window. The side lawn extended for about twenty yards to a stand of mixed pine, fir, and alder trees—which, in turn, stretched for another half a football field to the perimeter fence—and ran southward along that for thirty-five yards to the front wall of the house. I was told this was a remnant of the original forest that Portland had been hewed out of (earning it the nickname "Stumptown"). Carl's family had kept it in a quasi-natural state, and he continued that tradition, having the arborist do only enough pruning of the blackberry tangles to prevent them from growing over the narrow footpaths that wound through the woods. I had strolled along some of these and had found myself filled with a strange but strong reluctance to walk out again. Something in there beckoned to me even now, a tugging in my chest.

"You look like you've gotten lost somewhere."

Startled, I quickly twisted around to see who my visitor was, even as I recognized her soft voice, with its perpetual good humor and optimism.

"Oh, hey, Melanie." I took a final glance at the trees, feeling my cheeks heat up at the coming confession I was not able to keep myself from making. "Maybe I did."

"They call to you, don't they?"

Somehow, I didn't think she meant the plants. I turned to face her fully. "Do you feel it too?"

"Of course."

"What do you think it is?"

She smiled but didn't answer my question. Instead, she glanced around the interior space of the parlor. "You know, we built this room to facilitate dreaming."

Right from our first meeting, Melanie had struck me as a woman whose words did not reflect what she wanted me to hear. But instead of finding this puzzling, I had become enamored of it, discovering that I enjoyed parsing out her true meanings.

There were several tacks I could have taken this evening in response to her comment, and I took a moment to decide which one to follow. Then I asked, "Do you think I'm just imagining things?"

"I think we're always just imagining things."

I couldn't prevent a small smile from touching my lips; I had chosen correctly. "Is imagination real, then?" I blushed again, as the words sounded childish in my ears, but Melanie took me seriously.

"Everything is real." She offered me her light, pixyish laughter, a sound I couldn't help but be entranced by. "You can take whatever path you like."

At this, I felt compelled to turn once again to the window, where I studied the not-so-small patch of woods, imagining myself wandering among the untamed-yet-tamed growth. I thought of the meandering paths winding around like serpents among the trees, shrubs, and black-berry tangles, and my mind chose one for me to follow. The shadows closed in around me as I moved deeper into the woods, which I now thought spread out around me forever. I was filled with intrigue and nervousness, and I sensed magic in the cool air that breathed lightly on my cheeks. The shadows thickened, pressing in on me, causing me to stand still, my senses heightened and expectant. My heart raced, but it was calmed almost immediately by soft auras that began coating the leaves and pine needles, reassuring me with their living glow. Rapture now filled my heart, and my feet drifted a few inches off the ground, my body buoyed by the breath in my lungs. I didn't want to leave this place yet, at the same time, was terrified that I never could.

But just as this tangled web of emotions threatened to overcome me, I heard Melanie's gentle voice again. It seemed to emanate from my own mind.

"Come home."

Immediately, I was fully in the parlor, looking out the bay window on the thickening evening, heavy with dark clouds now covering what little sunshine there had been. I turned to face her, my mind blown.

"What did you do to me?" I asked, at once amazed and fearful.

"You might as well ask," Melanie said with a gentle smile, "what *you* did to *me*. Because neither of us did anything to the other. But both of us experienced the Dream of the Room."

"The Dream of—"

"The Room," Melanie finished for me. "Yes. The room is always dreaming, but you can't just join in with it. It has to let you in. I opened the door for you, and you went further than I did my first time. The room must like you."

I studied her face. "You're serious, aren't you?"

"Serious as a heart attack."

"This is kinda freaky."

"It takes some getting used to."

I just shook my head. *This is a dangerous place*, I thought. I wondered why it didn't scare me.

"Anyway," Melanie said, changing the subject, "I came here to tell you that dinner's almost ready. Come and eat."

On Friday nights, the household would engage in something Carl called Bohm Dialogue, a technique created by David Bohm, a quantum physicist who, like Jung and Grof, had devised a spiritual theory of mind. He had applied his theory to serve as the basis for a therapeutic practice designed to bond people together into a kind of groupthink. It was a discussion method in which there was no moderator, no set theme, and no requirement to make a contribution. Topics could be on any subject (personal or general), were allowed to arise pseudorandomly, and would "flow" until either they were exhausted or the raised issue was resolved.

I kind of liked this practice; it had an easy feel to it. Being somewhat shy, I had not yet introduced a topic, although I had made some small comments on other people's. But tonight I had something personal I wanted to talk about—if I could push myself past my natural reticence about being in the spotlight.

As it turned out, Carl had a remedy for that.

"Have you ever smoked pot before?" he asked me.

"Yeah," I said. "My best friend's parents were stoners."

"I like them already," Harold announced, to general laughter.

"We consider it a sacred substance," Carl said, ignoring Harold, "that can help to alleviate inhibitions. We use it as a ritual for cleansing our psyches on the Friday closest to the first of each month."

I nodded. "Cool."

The drug, as usual, let me open up—although it made me a little groggy, also as usual.

"I had a weird dream last night," I said.

Of course, I instantly became the focal point of the room. My immediate reaction to this was to wish I could crawl back into my tortoise shell and disappear, but I pushed through my inhibitions.

"Well," I said, "I dreamed I was in a wooden rowboat floating through a jungle. I think the trees nearest me were mangrove trees—they had thick twisted roots that were lowered into the water, like the trunks were on stilts or something."

"Yeah," Priscilla said. "That's a mangrove."

I nodded. "Cool." Then I chuckled. "I got this silly feeling that they were actually gripping the water, like huge wooden fists or something. And there was lots of other vegetation too, vines and shrubs and all sorts of stuff.

"So I was in this boat, in the middle of a swamp. But even as I was looking around me, the swamp suddenly became a river, and I saw a young woman with long, curly golden hair, sitting in the stern, guiding the boat with a paddle. She hadn't been there at first. I was instantly struck by a sense of immense power emanating from her. Her expression was dead serious, but her blue eyes kind of danced with laughter. Does that make sense?"

I looked around the room and received reassuring nods and affirmations.

"Anyway, I wanted to hide from her, but I couldn't even look away, let alone move. Just as I was about to freak, she said to me, 'Arthur. Wake up.' Immediately, I jerked awake, just a few seconds before my alarm went off."

The room was still for about fifteen seconds.

Emily broke the silence, saying in her typical droll way, "Well, at least you were obedient." This made everyone laugh, but she continued speaking, ignoring them and going on as if we were the only two in the room. "I think it's interesting that this woman was guiding you in a boat. Taking you along a river."

"Dude," Harold interjected, laughing, "he's not dying."

I frowned and looked back and forth between the two, puzzled.

"Charon," Emily explained. "Taking you across the River Styx."

My one class in Greek mythology reared its head. *Oh,* I thought. *Of course.*

Aloud, I said, "Yeah, I guess I could see that. Except Charon's a bro."

"Dreams aren't always perfectly aligned," Melanie said. "The imagery can vary, depending on what the meaning of the dream is."

"Spiritual death, perhaps," Janis offered. "Moving from one life lesson to another."

"But I don't even know what the first lesson was."

"Sure you do," Sari said, laughing. "You learned how to strike out on your own, to make your own way and do your own thing."

"And to leave everything behind in the process," John interjected. "Pretty damn adult, if you ask me."

"So," Janis said, glancing around at us, "moving into adulthood, then?"

"Well, yeah," I said, shrugging. "I mean, it'll be official in nine months."

"Again," Janis corrected me, "I'm talking spiritually. Just because the body grows up doesn't mean the inner man does. But you're already well along in the process. Further than most boys at your age, I'd say."

Carl made a noise as if he disagreed, and everyone turned their attention to him.

"This is an okay way of looking at the dream, I suppose," he said, "but it's kind of mundane, don't you think? It might just be a disguise." He addressed his next words directly to me. "I think you've encountered the anima—the deep feminine aspect of a man that most men don't even realize they have."

I frowned. "Feminine aspect?"

"See?" Carl laughed, prompting some of the others to join in. "Every man's unconscious contains female energy, and every woman's contains male energy. Jung referred to these as the anima and the animus. They play a vital role in every person's development and may show up in dreams at specific stages of our lives. You're at one of these stages now—spiritually, mentally, emotionally, and, yes, physically too. What intrigues me here, though, is what your anima says to you. 'Wake up.' It doesn't really fit what I would expect at this point in your journey. You should be leaving the first stage, where you rely on your mother as a model of how to interact with women, and entering the stage where you're looking for your own ideal wife. And I'm not saying that's not already taking place; in fact, I'm certain it is." I noticed his eyes flicker to Sari for an instant.

"But the dream doesn't reflect that. To tell the truth, I think you've somehow skipped a couple stages."

Melanie, I was learning, was a quick study. She knew Carl intimately, and she understood his mind and how his thinking process worked—quite literally, actually, given her extensive holotropic practice. She now interjected, "You think he's encountered Sophia, don't you?"

Carl nodded thoughtfully, gazing at her. "Yes," he said. "I think he has."

"That would be remarkable," John said. "And I'm not sure it can even happen."

"Well, it's not rocket science, of course," Carl said. "There's no divine law demanding that Jung's order of things must be followed to the letter in every case. To everything, there's a season."

"You folks sound like you think these beings actually exist," I said.

They all just gazed serenely at me.

Becoming increasingly uncomfortable as I looked around at them, I decided it might be best to drop that particular line of thought. I took and released a deep breath.

"So—what is Sophia, then?" I asked.

"Sophia," Carl said, his dark eyes like black holes sucking me in, but his expression and voice reflecting an unusual level of enthusiasm, "is the goddess of spiritual enlightenment."

CHAPTER 10

I SLEPT FITFULLY THAT NIGHT. THE group didn't break up until well after midnight, and it took me about twenty minutes or so to fall asleep once I was finally in bed. My mind was just moving through some odd spaces, and while I didn't have another dream like the one we'd discussed, I did have some rather surrealistic ones. I don't remember their content anymore, but I do know they made me feel uneasy.

I woke up from each one of them basically every hour, which meant my sleep was insufficient, which in turn meant I was still rather groggy when I finally decided to get up at 6:25 a.m. I felt antsy—needing to move, to engage myself physically with the world, in order to shake off the bad feelings the night had left in me—and I knew exactly where I wanted to go. But I needed to wait for daylight to arrive.

Once again, rain spattered against the windowpane. *Spring is a wet season here*, I thought. I wasn't used to that, just like I wasn't used to the cold. But to my relief, by the time I finished showering and getting dressed, the rain had stopped for the day. So maybe the universe was on my side, after all.

Although I had slept later than usual, the others were still not downstairs. I figured that my first morning here, with so many gathered in the dining room, had been an unusual thing for them, prompted by my unexpected arrival. I was something of a novelty back then. This idea made me chuckle. *You're old news already*, I thought.

I made some buttered toast and jam to eat on the way, put on my shoes and jacket, and quietly slipped out the front door, headed for the river, to the spot where Sari and I had first stood together, contemplating my being here.

It took me thirty minutes to get out of the hills and into the city, and another twenty-five to reach the river.

Arriving at my destination, I once again rested my arms on the top piping of the two-railed fence and gazed out across the deceptively slow water. The wind had picked up during my walk and had shifted so it was now blowing diagonally into my face, giving it a greater expanse of water to cross and thus cooling the air temperature even more. The overcast sky prevented the sun, which had risen just before I set out but was now lost in the clouds, from doing much to rectify this.

The Willamette's northward course was rare among Oregon's rivers. But the thing I liked about it was that it split Portland right down the middle, with distinct types of neighborhoods on each shore. Separated by more than a third of a mile, these neighborhoods had been developed differently, creating a contrast in energy, layout, and architecture, almost as if they were disparate cities. The low skyline of the suburban sprawl, in the distance before me, lay in stark contrast to the tightly packed swarm of high-rises looming behind my back. For some reason, I found this dichotomy pleasurable.

The river was deep enough to accommodate almost any size of ship, although the bridges were built low and had to be raised for larger vessels. Most of the commercial traffic on the river was accomplished by barge. The water was empty this morning, which suited me just fine.

I was struggling to come to grips with the previous night's revelations, and I had hoped the relative solitude of the shoreline—surrounding me with empty water, empty grass, and nearly empty streets—would provide a haven for doing this. But it was not to be.

I was soon startled out of my reverie by the hectic arrival of someone else. I had encountered only a handful of people on my walk here, and most of them were gathered in Pioneer Square, so this dude's bumping up against the railings a few steps to my right both surprised and annoyed me. I mean, he had the whole river to choose from, and this particular spot was the one he had to take? He was deliberately invading my space, and I couldn't help but resent him for that. However, I dared not show this, as a kind of negative vibe—an internal disarray to match his external one—emanated from him. He probably wasn't dangerous, but he was clearly not right. So I pretended to survey the river, while surreptitiously keeping an eye on him.

He dropped his overstuffed, dirt-streaked backpack onto the sidewalk with a loud thud and leaned heavily against the top railing, his arms straining out over the water, his fingers splayed as if he were grasping for the far shore.

My own body was tense, automatically gearing up for fight-or-flight (it would be flight), but I persisted in my effort to appear nonchalant.

He turned his rather wild stare on me. "Got a cig, man?" he asked in a voice as coarse as if he had just spent an hour screaming.

Now, as it happened, I did have a cigarette. One of the crop pickers I had worked with in Stockton had given me a pack, saying they were good for trade. I still carried it with me, out of habit—or maybe nostalgia.

I pulled the somewhat crushed but still serviceable hard pack out of my back pocket and let him take one. He lit it with a red Cricket lighter and took a long drag.

"Thanks, dude," he said. "You're a lifesaver. Much longer, I was gonna get all fidgety an' shit."

"I get ya," I said. "I've gone without stuff before."

He gave me a once-over, then snorted.

"Don't look like no streetie to me."

This was probably, to him, the worst put-down possible. He didn't bother to try to hide his contempt.

"No," I said as noncommittally as I could, returning my gaze to the distant shoreline. "Not anymore."

He also turned back to the river and took another drag. "I could never quit the street," he said.

At least he didn't accuse me of not having been homeless. But my next words surprised me, sneaking out of my mouth before I even realized what I was saying. I had no idea where they came from.

"I'm not sure I have."

They were the right words. He nodded in a slow-bobbing arc. "Hell yeah, bro. The street never leaves you. It's where truth is."

"Truth is a strange thing."

"I hear ya. Street'll do that to ya, man. It blows your *mind*!"

He began to become agitated, sending a shock of alarm through me. Reflexively, I tensed for flight again.

"Makes you question yourself. But you can't let it break ya, dude. Gotta stay in the flow." He took an even longer drag off the cigarette, not bothering to blow the smoke out before continuing his rant. The gray clouds seeping out of his mouth didn't even form before being whipped away by the wind. "You gotta hear the music of the street, feel the beat of the traffic. That heartbeat of the city, y'know? Learn how it all *moves*. Then you're okay. 'Cause if you try to walk against the stream, you come into a world of hurt. But if you stay in the flow, it all flows with you and around you, and you make it. You *make* it, man. You make it all happen."

His words poured out in a rush. Then he abruptly fell quiet and turned back to face the river again, but he didn't look out on the panorama before us. Rather, he crossed his arms on the railing and stared at the cigarette burning down between his thumb and index finger.

I didn't look away; instead, I kept my attention on him. This time it wasn't with trepidation, but curiosity. I wondered what he had experienced in his life to end up like this. A sudden compulsion to ask him made me start to open my mouth, but I instantly checked myself. Still,

I hated to admit it, but his words made some sense to me. And I think this bothered me most of all.

After his final drag, he flicked the butt into the river. Then he spun to face the street, resting his elbows on the rail and throwing his gaze all around him. Finally, his eyes rested on me again.

"I'm hungry," he said. "You hungry, man?"

"Not really, no."

"Oh." A two-second pause. "You got any bread on you?"

And there it was. I had already formulated how I would respond to this question.

"Yeah, a little."

I had no issue with giving him something. After all, he had given *me* something: a lesson in what the street could do to you when you weren't as lucky as I had been. I figured that to be worth a few bucks. I wasn't carrying all that much, so even if he demanded all of it, he wouldn't break me.

I reached into my pocket and pulled out the first bill I touched. It happened to be a ten.

"Here."

"Oh, you are the *man*!" he said excitedly, trembling once more as he stretched the bill between his hands and stared at it as if he'd never seen one before. "You are too much, dude. Listen. You chill out, okay? It'll be okay. You'll make it. You'll make it. Just stay in the flow!"

And with that, he shouldered his backpack and scurried off across the park, his attention focused dead ahead.

I watched until he began to cross the street. Once I was sure he wasn't coming back, I breathed easier and mentally shook the encounter off.

But giving him the money made me remember that I owed someone a debt. I pulled out the rest of my cash, which totaled nineteen dollars. Without hesitation, but feeling a touch of guilt for my former negligence, I shelved my interrupted musings to continue them at another time, and I set off for Java Man.

CHAPTER 11

" **A**T NEXT FRIDAY'S GROUP," CARL said once we had settled ourselves on the *zafus*, "I plan on serving mushrooms. Anyone who wishes to partake is welcome to do so."

"Ah," Janis said, grinning. "Magic time."

I was sitting on the far side of the circle from Carl, one *zafu* in from the door. He caught my eye and said, "I think I can safely assume you have never taken hallucinogens before?"

"No, never."

"Shrooms are bitchin', lil bro," Harold said. "Psy-ch-*oh*-del-*ic*."

Carl chuckled. "Harold is a fan."

"Hell yeah," Harold agreed enthusiastically.

We all laughed.

"Anyway." Carl raised a hand in a call for quiet. Addressing me, he said, "Everything we do in this house is voluntary. I'll let you choose if you want to join in with us. So let me give you some background, to help you make that decision.

"In 1960, a Harvard professor named Timothy Leary discovered the mushroom in an obscure Mexican village.

Thinking it might be useful in his psychiatric practice, he brought it back to the States and had its active ingredient turned into pill form. He found it had a powerful effect, changing the way people think and feel about themselves and about each other."

"That sounds pretty rad," I said.

"It is. Anyway, what the mushroom does is break down the internal barriers each of us has built up between us and other people. For a few hours, we experience what it's like to be one with everyone."

"Like the transpersonal stuff."

"Exactly! You really do grok things."

I can't tell you how good this made me feel. I may even have blushed a little.

"There are constraints on how we do this," Carl went on. "It's not a free-for-all. Leary established what are now the accepted parameters for safely taking hallucinogens, which he called *set* and *setting*. By *set*, he meant our internal condition—mentally and emotionally. We remain relaxed and calm, our minds unclouded with anxiety, and we clear ourselves of as many negative energies as we can before taking the drug.

"*Setting* is the environment in which we take them. We always use this place"—he gestured to indicate the room—"as our meditation and communal center, and it's well suited for the purpose. Places have spirit, and that spirit speaks to our own. The energy in here remains calm at all times."

I nodded, understanding completely. The space had struck me that way the moment I first set foot in it. The peace it exuded exceeded even that of the rest of the house, which itself was already calmer than anywhere else I'd ever been.

"I'm cool with it," I said.

"Our young man," Janis said, a hint of admiration in her voice, "is becoming quite the psychonaut."

"You dudes should listen to me more often," Sari said.

"Maybe we'll raise your rank," John said, eliciting a sprinkle of laughter.

"I deserve to be an officer."

Carl pointed at her, grinning. "Maybe for your fourth anniversary."

"Woo-hoo!"

As I observed this exchange, my heart was warmed by how readily my new friends had embraced me and how the camaraderie they shared with one another had been so quickly extended to include me. And I knew with certainty that I had come to the right place.

CHAPTER 12

T HE WEEK WENT BY BOTH faster and more slowly than I would have liked. Even though each hour seemed to drag on and on, Friday evening was upon me before I knew it.

We skipped dinner, eating only a light snack of various fruits with graham crackers, which would allow the drug to absorb more quickly while also countering nausea.

"Not a good idea to drink it on an empty or a full stomach," John had told me. "And it would be best if you didn't take a full cup. Get a feel for it first. You can always have more if you like."

I settled onto my *zafu* with nervous but excited anticipation.

The circle had been scattered, everyone taking their *zafus* to a place in the large room where they felt most comfortable, some of them picking up cushions along the way.

I chose the northeast corner, for physical stability. It was my first time in that half of the room—I'd had no reason to enter it before—and the perspective of seeing Carl's table from thirty-five feet away made me feel as if I had banished myself to the wilderness.

If I'm already feeling weird, I thought, *what am I in for tonight?*

I was totally pleased when Sari plopped down beside me on my left, flashing me a bright smile.

"I'm so excited for you!" she gushed. "The first time is always the best."

"I'm actually looking forward to it. Although, I have to admit I'm a little nervous."

"That's normal. This is unknown territory for you. *Terra incognita,* as smart people say. But we're all here to support you."

"I know, and that means a lot to me."

"You'll see. You're gonna love it!"

She gave my hand a squeeze, and my heart raced for a different reason.

On the low table before Carl sat a large pot filled with mushroom tea, atop a single-burner hotplate. On either side of it stood a stack of ornate teacups painted with entangled climbing vines. Janis told me these were reserved for the mushroom rituals, another small bit of ceremony to set these times apart in a conscious way.

Eventually, the room quieted down as we sat for a while in personal preparation. Some meditated, while some systematically caught others' gazes, silently communing at a distance. Others just stared at the carpet. I was one of those.

Using some standard of readiness that I was unaware of, Carl announced, "Shall we begin?"

One by one, clockwise around the room and starting with Melanie, each member filled their cup and returned to their spot. Emily had told me earlier that this direction was chosen because it drew in ethereal energy that would raise our emotions to a higher level of positivity, which in turn would both enhance the mushroom's effect and prevent a bad trip.

When it was my turn, I took only a three-quarter cupful. Carl met my eyes and nodded in approval.

"That's going to taste like shit," he said softly, a small smile on his lips.

When everyone had a serving, Carl turned on the MP3 player, which began going through a set of music arranged specifically for these psychedelic sessions. It opened with Jefferson Airplane's "White Rabbit," which made me snort.

Then Carl systematically cast his gaze around the room, alighting on each face for no more than a second.

At last, he raised his cup in a toast and said, "See you in the dream."

He hadn't been kidding about the taste. Even with the honey he had added to the brew, my cautionary sip almost made me gag. Recovering and not wanting to look like a wuss, I took a deep breath, closed my eyes, and downed the entire thing in three gulps. Then I settled myself as comfortably as I could and waited for the effects to kick in.

There were no clocks in the meditation room, phones were not permitted, and I didn't have a watch, so I have no idea of when events took place that night. (Once the drug kicked in, I also lost my ability to track their sequence. Things just happened, spontaneously and randomly. Some of them may have been simultaneous.)

Looking back on it, I would guess it was probably around half an hour or so after drinking the brew when

I started feeling lethargic. My body moved reluctantly, to the extent that even raising my arm took an unusual amount of effort. I also experienced a touch of nausea, and I hoped it wasn't a harbinger of something nasty to come.

I swept my gaze around the room, checking out the others' behavior, but I couldn't tell if they were going through anything similar.

Carl caught my eye and smiled sympathetically.

"Getting a little fuzzy?" he called to me.

"Sorta."

"Just relax into it. Don't fight what's happening; just let your body deal with it. It might help if you breathe slowly and deeply. But don't worry, you'll be okay."

I nodded, but I wasn't so sure at the moment. Still, I did as I was instructed, and after a while, the nausea dissipated, to my relief.

And then the fun began.

The pot on the table, which I hadn't until that moment realized I was staring at, started to morph. At first it reminded me of the kind of light bending that occurs with objects under water. Then it began stretching completely out of shape. At this point, I became fixated on it, bemusedly wondering why the tea didn't spill out of it and onto the carpet. Even though I had been warned beforehand and was expecting weird stuff to happen, I still fully accepted this behavior as real. I thought it amusing that I was more concerned about the tea remaining stable than I was about the pot warping.

At some point, I got bored with the pot. I then turned my attention back to everyone else, curious about how the others were faring.

Janis and Harold were seated in the northwest corner, directly in my line of sight, talking animatedly together, leaning in closely to each other, touching frequently. Their body language sealed my suspicions that there was something going on between them that I hadn't been officially told about. It took me a bit to realize I was staring at them; my mental activity—in fact, my entire world—felt like it had slowed down. I immediately pulled my gaze away, feeling heat in my cheeks for spying on them—even though no one had any idea I'd been doing so, and wouldn't have cared, anyway.

Meanwhile, Carl had crossed to my portion of the room to talk with John about evolution. Snatches of their conversation carried over to me, although I couldn't really follow it. Still, it was obvious they were disagreeing about aspects of the theory, and it occurred to me that perhaps this was part of an ongoing discussion they had been having.

I noticed that neither Melanie nor Priscilla wanted anything to do with their partners' conversation but had gravitated together in the center of the room, where they stood in conversation. I honestly didn't blame them. I was already bored with the two leaders' pedantic topic, so I tuned them out.

Seems like a waste of a good high, I thought—a bit smugly, perhaps.

On the other hand, I decided to follow the two couples' lead and stand up. It was harder to do than I thought it would be, and the effort needed to gain my balance took me by surprise. I was now glad I'd chosen to sit in the corner, and I put it to good use, a hand pressed against each wall.

Once on my feet, I cautiously, hesitantly, unbraced myself. *I'm all right, I'm all right, I'm all right*, I silently repeated in my head, although maybe some of the words did slip out, because I now noticed Sari looking up at me, laughing.

I grinned at her ruefully and shrugged my shoulders.

She extended her hand upward to me in an unspoken request to help her up, and I happily obliged. She rose from the floor like an unfurling flower and seemingly as light as one.

"You're so graceful," I said, "while I'm so cringe."

"I'll be the judge of that," she chided. "C'mon."

She began tugging me into the center of our half of the room, and I happily went along.

Just as we reached it, the MP3 started playing Boston's "Hitch a Ride." Besides the obvious personal connection I found in the song, in this mushroom moment, it spoke to me of a release from the everyday world, assuring me there was a place where I could turn my back on society's expectations and pursue the things I truly valued and wanted. Thing is, I had never considered what those might be before, but now I believed I was looking at the very personification of them.

Letting the music move us, we began to dance.

Almost immediately, the drug distortion kicked in again. Maybe it was the sinuous motion of her body that caused this in me; I don't know. But this time, the images were even more difficult to follow than the antics of the teapot, as they were rapid and erratic. Sari's body became kaleidoscopic, having transformed into countless thin, translucent veneers that at first multiplied out to either side of her like a pack of cards spread by a magician, then began to crisscross back and forth across each other. It was totally disorientating, and once more, I felt unsteady. I somehow managed to keep my footing and, taking a cue from the things I'd been taught here, I concentrated on controlling my breathing. This turned out to be the right thing to do. With significant effort, I was able to slow the movement down enough that Sari's real face stood out directly in front of me, surrounded by ghost images. The relief I felt was enormous.

So I do *have some control over this*, I thought. But I had no control over my feelings for her, which were more solid than even the walls of the room right now. *She's cast a spell over me*. And even as this wonderful thought entered my head, the MP3 switched to Santana's "Black Magic Woman."

That machine is reading my mind, I thought. *Or am* I *reading* its *mind?*

I decided it made no difference, because both things were the same.

Harold and Janis joined us on what had now become a dance floor, followed quickly by Priscilla. To my great surprise, at the next song, stoic Emily took a spot as well.

The mushroom has a deep effect, I thought. *Breaking down barriers. No wonder they do this!*

The energy flowing around me was phenomenal. Light waves and temperature waves and air waves and body waves. Space was a prism of movement and inter-mingling of primal forces. At moments, I thought I was even perceiving the very ground of existence itself, atoms buzzing around each other.

I took Sari's hand again and gently lifted it above our heads. She took the cue and twirled, laughing joyously, her eyes aflame. But as soon as she began her spin, something happened that was weirder than anything else so far. It was so weird I don't think I can describe it properly. Basically, I saw the room from her vantage point, spinning around me. I even saw myself as she faced me again. What was even more incomprehensible, I retained my own viewpoint as well, so that I was also watching her movements. It was as if I were standing in both spots, hers and mine, facing different directions at once.

The initial shock caused me to reflexively squeeze her hand more tightly, as I felt myself stumbling. Seeing her surprised grimace, I immediately let go of her and apologized. As I did, my vision went back to normal.

We danced separately, my mind boggled, Sari grinning.

"All that crop picking seems to have paid off," she called over the music, then laughed again.

I didn't respond to her teasing, because I was so blown away by what had just taken place. Instead, I blurted out, "Holy crap. Did that happen to you too?"

"Did what happen?" she asked, looking puzzled.

"Did you see things through my eyes?"

She smiled coyly. "I see things *in* your eyes."

A thrill shot through me. But I was too hyperfocused on the perception thing to relish it. "So you didn't notice anything out of the ordinary?"

"What? Well, yeah. The drug makes *everything* extraordinary." She laughed once more. I could never get enough of that laugh. "Don't worry. You're just high."

I nodded. "Yeah, I guess so." I tried to smile, but I'm fairly sure it came out shaky.

Sari and I danced for five more songs before we dropped out, returning to our *zafus*, where we sat watching the others. Harold had switched partners, taking up Emily, and Janis had moved over to Priscilla. Melanie had also joined in, moving from couple to couple and dancing with them. As I watched my new friends experiencing their personal trips, the feeling grew within me that I was an integral part of what was taking place here—here in this room, here in this house, here in this city.

The gyrating bodies of the dancers appeared to me like shadows of multicolored light, flickering campfire flames casting their own shadows—and those shadows casting their own in an all-encompassing network of interwoven motion, a tapestry of pure movement. The air of the room vibrated and shimmied, like tiny pebbles dropping into a still pond, broadcasting ripples, like a raindrop striking the center of a cobweb, making it tremble like a drumhead. I was mesmerized by it all and became one with it all. I was filled with a bottomless love and a sheer joy, extending to everything, and I received it, in return, from everything, in a wondrous and overwhelming exhilaration of just being alive.

Every time Sari and I brushed together, every time she touched an exposed part of my body, the entire scene multiplied and washed over me in a roaring river of *happening*.

It was the most glorious thing I had ever experienced, and I wished it would never end.

CHAPTER 13

WHEN I WOKE UP THE next morning, even though I'd slept for less than five hours, I knew I was done for the night.

A deep calm had settled over me during the drug trip, despite the visual antics and the excessive joy, and I still rested in its reassuring embrace. I went outside to contemplate my experience in my favorite spot on the property: the back patio.

The sprawling backyard, which constituted the northern section of the acreage, was for me the perfect refuge from everything. Even the great insulated spaces of the house—which always gave me an odd sense that it was holding its breath, as if in anticipation of something wonderful about to happen—couldn't match the contentment I felt in this gorgeously landscaped spread. The center of the land consisted of an impeccably manicured lawn. A solid line of trees ran along the inside of the back fence, more than a football field from where I sat. These were mostly Douglas firs interspersed with a few maples and dogwoods. A spreading white oak, seventy feet tall and over fifty feet in diameter at the center point of its crown, stood off on its own, almost but not quite in the northeast corner, diagonally from where I was sitting. Priscilla had told me it was older than the house, even older than Portland itself.

"It survived the cutting down of the forest," she said. "The folk tale is, those clearing the land were afraid to take it down. They said it was haunted and refused to approach it while carrying an axe. There were rumors that the axe handles of those who did try broke in half on the first swing." She laughed, and after a moment, I joined in. But it wasn't how I actually felt.

Faerie tale or not, I understood implicitly why those men might want to leave this tree alone. There *was* something about it, something I couldn't put my finger on. But whatever it was, I found my eye wandering to the tree frequently whenever I was out there.

Forty feet south of the oak and twenty feet in from the eastern fence, a twelve-foot-high oblong mound of terraced earth rose, stretching along the property line for fifty feet, ending just before the semiwild stand of trees I had mystically "entered" two weeks ago. A well-maintained landscape of flowering shrubs competed for space on each of three levels. All of them were wild, native to the area: the gangly globe gilia, with pale blue puffballs for flowers; bleeding heart, whose drooping wine-colored flowers attracted butterflies; lupine, with white-and-purple flowers attached directly to tall, slender stems; and salal, a large shrub with dark green leaves and little white, heart-shaped flowers. The birds liked this one, and it spread out along the ledge just below the summit for them, where they could visit it undisturbed.

Interspersed among the plants stood a number of various-sized blocks of unworked stone, mostly basalt but also some granite, the largest being maybe thirty cubic feet in volume and the smallest, three. A six-foot-tall pentagonal basalt column, rusty brown with splashes of gray and blue, capped the center crest of the manmade hill. I was struck with the impression that a kind of aura surrounded it, an energy visible to me in the backlight of the rising sun.

Across the yard from this terrace, toward the western edge of the lawn, a meticulously manicured boxwood hedge had been laid out in the form of a maze. The shrubbery, six feet high and eighteen inches wide, formed walls enclosing a dirt path that meandered within the bounds of a thirty-foot-diameter circle. Priscilla had told me that this was a labyrinth and that the house members used it as a contemplation spot, a place for walking meditation. She was enthusiastic about it, but I was too ashamed to tell her that my intense claustrophobia made it forbidden ground for me. I shuddered at the very thought of setting foot in it.

Not visible to me from my vantage point because the house was in the way, on the western side of the property stood a modern four-car garage, with a turning circle connected to the gravel driveway.

Ten deck chairs were haphazardly scattered across the flagstone patio in various configurations to each other, along with a number of round, white wire-mesh outdoor tables.

I pulled one of the chairs close to the lawn edge and settled myself in it, hugging myself to hold my body heat in. The temperature had actually dropped a little after sunrise, leaving me slightly shivering in the unexpectedly winter-like air. I'd never experienced such a cold spring before; the weather here was going to take some getting used to. On the bright side, the house's solid presence behind me blocked the early morning breeze.

I estimated that my psilocybin trip had basically ended a bit after one o'clock that morning, although I hung around for maybe another half hour as I drifted down off the high, languidly watching everyone, reluctant to be the first one to leave. But when Janis headed for the door, I dragged myself to my feet and followed her lead, pausing to contemplate Sari talking with Carl across the room from me. I wondered what they were saying to each other.

Priscilla and John then interrupted my brief reverie as they passed across my visual field, and I followed behind them as we silently trundled off to bed, leaving the others to continue along their inner journey. The remaining members had each taken another half cup of the tea and probably wouldn't get to bed much before dawn.

For my part, I woke up every hour during the night, taking about five minutes to fall back to sleep as my head spun with the remnants of vivid, drug-inspired dreams.

Now, from my perch on the patio, I let my attention wander as it would, beginning with the play of clouds in the sky. Directly above me, the cloud cover was torn in places, ragged pale blue windows opening onto eternity and allowing me to peek into the secret depths of the universe. I marveled at the beauty of this, the contrast in feelings it produced in me. Then I felt myself falling upward toward one of those infinite holes. It sucked me in, promising me wonders I could not imagine. My chest ached with the breath I was holding, and my heart raced in anticipation of perfect freedom. Vaporous wisps gathered around me as I plunged into a blue lake set in heaven.

Suddenly, I collapsed back into myself, my body jerking as if I actually had fallen from the sky and landed back in the chair. I remained dazzled for a number of seconds before realizing I was simply still in the mushroom's glow, a pleasant aftereffect I had been told to expect.

I returned my gaze to the yard and contemplated the trees on the back perimeter, again allowing my mind to wander. This time, it didn't wander far. My thoughts kept returning to my psychedelic adventure of last night—particularly the multiple-vision thing. Sari was the only person I had touched during my trip, and she obviously had not experienced what I had. No one else *appeared* to have done so either. Although I knew this was very scant evidence, it was all I had to go on at the moment, so I had to tentatively conclude that it had only happened to me.

And if that were the case, the next question obviously followed: why?

I wondered if I should ask John about it. Although Carl was more experienced in these matters, as head of the commune and de facto spiritual leader, he kind of intimidated me. I hadn't had particularly good experiences with authority figures in my life. On the other hand, due to our working together every day in his cramped food cart, John and I had started to hit it off. I knew I would be more comfortable approaching him.

In the end, however, I decided to just let it go. It was probably nothing more than a fluke. Like Sari had said, I'd just been high.

I didn't realize that, as I had been going over these things in my mind, I had been gazing at the oak tree.

Although it was no longer barren, from my viewpoint on the patio—basically behind the parlor—it was much too far away for me to be able to see the new leaf buds. Thus its skeleton was fully exposed. The trunk split in two, perhaps fifteen feet above the ground; from that point, the branches spread out in a great tangled ball. I sensed movement among them—although, of course, this was merely an illusion. It somehow gave me the impression of being at once three-dimensional and two, an incongruity that played with my head. And I thought I heard a voice emanating from it, a soft, sibilant voice. I felt myself wrapped in an illusion of floating through the air, as the tree called me to itself.

Suddenly, I once again awakened to what I was doing in the real world, and found myself inexplicably standing in front of the tree. I had no memory of having walked across the two hundred feet of grass to get here.

The mushroom is crazy, I thought. But to my surprise, after the initial shock, I wasn't troubled by this unconscious behavior. It wasn't frightening—merely a curiosity.

I remained at arm's length from the nearly three-foot-diameter bifurcated trunk, studying its furrowed, blocky gray bark. The long vertical rectangles, positioned quasi-randomly yet rhythmically along the surface, appeared to be cascading downward, like the computer code in *The Matrix*.

For a second time this morning, I knew, intellectually, that I was experiencing an illusion, but it seemed so real that I couldn't stop myself from reaching out and pressing my palm against one of the smooth, flat sections. It felt like a dried-hard sponge. A faint vibration ran along my arm. Laughing in childish pleasure at this, I stepped up and embraced the trunk in an act of love for the living being, pressing my ear to another facet of the bark.

Emanating from deep within the tree's interior, I distinctly heard a heartbeat.

CHAPTER 14

A WEEK LATER, WE ENCOUNTERED A weather anomaly: the temperature took a sudden leap to seventy degrees for just that one Friday. Not surprisingly, since people were reluctant to lock themselves indoors that afternoon, the streets were bustling with refugees from the office towers when I left Flash Burger at one o'clock. Like everyone else, I was quite glad to see the sun again as I ambled along on my way home.

As I wandered down the canyon of office buildings that was Park Avenue, something astounding happened to me. It was even more unsettling than the being-in-two-places-at-once syndrome I'd experienced with Sari on the mushroom, because I had at least recognized what the cause of that event was. But this episode was downright disturbing and left me questioning my sanity.

One moment, I was nonchalantly threading my way through the bustle, and the next, I was stopped dead in my tracks, as the world around me vanished. I lost all awareness of my surroundings—the people, the buildings, the vehicle traffic. I saw and heard none of it. Even more strangely, I couldn't feel my body. I felt as if I had left it—

but not gone anywhere. I was nowhere, in the middle of nothing. A mere point of consciousness and nothing else.

I retained clear cognizance of only one thing: the sound of a resonating male voice that spoke to me with absolute authority, a voice that could not be tuned out or disobeyed. It, too, seemed to be everywhere and nowhere at once.

"Arthur, wake up."

And then I was back in the world. The entire episode lasted only about two or three seconds, but that was long enough to wreak a little havoc on the sidewalk. Pedestrians coming up from behind me were stumbling to avoid running into me, while those approaching me from ahead cast puzzled and disapproving glances at me. I felt my cheeks heat up.

Then I suddenly realized that I was walking again. This was not voluntary on my part; my legs just started moving again without my doing anything, almost as if I had never stopped. My body was no longer subject to my volition; I had no choice about where I was going, or even if I wanted to go there. It had been my original intention to follow Morrison down to Burnside, which I wanted to use as my access point to Goose Hollow. This would have put me in the hills for a longer time before reaching the house. But it was as if something had taken over my will, making its intention my intention, and instead, I crossed Morrison, continuing on to Yamhill.

I wanted to freak out, but even my emotional state seemed to be under a spell. I felt calm, although my thoughts were a jumble of confusion. The dichotomy was jarring.

As if it understood my confused state, whatever it was that was controlling me had me cross Yamhill and pause at Teachers Fountain. There I took note of the simple pleasure that arose within me as I watched a few children splash in the shallow water. I stood in the shade of a large tree, noting the thin jet streams that spouted above the horseshoe-shaped pool and fell back in long graceful arcs to make small ripples in the water. I allowed myself to appreciate the simple beauty of the architect's design, and I felt my anxiety dissipate.

"Time to cross over," the Voice said, in a gentler manner than the first time.

I was making my way across the park before I even realized I was moving, but now it didn't bother me. I sensed I was being prepared for something. What that might be, I had no idea, but I now found myself curious instead of concerned. I offered no complaint when I came to the tree-lined sidewalk on the far side, letting myself be directed southward again along Ninth Avenue.

As I approached the corner at Taylor Street, I spotted a teenage girl standing there, staring at the sidewalk five feet in front of her. Immediately, I knew she was the reason I had been brought here, and upon that realization, I was released from outside control. As the last of my tension fell away, I slowed my pace a bit, in order to scope out the situation.

I judged her to be maybe a year younger than me. Her faded brown dress was stained a bit and wrinkled, as if she had slept in it more than she might have liked. I could relate to that. Her unbrushed hair, which matched the dress's color, swept across her face in the breeze. She gave no indication that she was aware of this—or of anything at all. She stood with her shoulders slumped, oblivious to all the traffic, both pedestrian and vehicular, flowing around her. She was apparently engaged in some kind of internal debate that revealed itself in mumbled words and pleading hand gestures. She looked so sad and lonely that my heart ached for her.

I approached her slowly, not wanting to spook her, but that turned out to be an unnecessary concern. Even when I stopped beside her, a step or two away, she gave no indication that she was aware of my presence. She was intensely preoccupied with something other than the world around her. Something only she was aware of.

Ordinarily, I would not have intruded into her world, whatever it may be. But today was not ordinary. Having not received any instructions as to what I was supposed to do, I just said to her, gently, "Are you all right?"

She stopped mumbling. Still staring at a vague spot on the concrete, she swung her head slowly from side to side, as if she weren't even aware of doing it, as if, engulfed in suffering, she were lost to the world around her. That suffering seemed to cling to her like a shroud, and her reply cast that shroud around me too. I felt it as a physical weight.

"There's nothing," she said, sounding utterly desolate. "There's nothing."

I can't explain what I did next, because I don't know why I did it. It was something I never would have considered doing with a stranger, without their permission, without warning. It happened reflexively, and before it even consciously registered in my head, I felt my body act on its own—even without the inner prompting that had brought me here.

I reached out my hand and gently took hers.

As soon as our skin touched, she gripped my fingers so strongly it hurt me a little. We both sucked in air and held it as our eyes locked onto each other's.

I stiffened, suddenly unable to move. I stood rooted to the sidewalk as a powerful blast of energy coursed through me and passed into her. The look on her face echoed the shock and surprise I felt.

The electric jolt lasted only a few seconds, but I found I could not release her for quite a few more.

Finally, we untangled ourselves, both physically and emotionally.

I felt winded, as if I'd just sprinted for a block. For a moment, I wasn't even aware of where I was. In fact, I was surprised to find I was still on my feet. My world had been reduced to a dizzying kaleidoscope for the second time in a week—except this time, it was internal.

Slowly, my equilibrium returned, and I regained my cognizance of the world, discovering something marvelous. The girl had become very calm. She gazed at me tranquilly, her body no longer slumped, and joy now radiated from her. She had lost all traces of the weight she had been carrying, all the signs of mental or emotional or spiritual illness that she had displayed.

"Thank you," she said, her voice vibrant and steady. "Thank you so much."

To my surprise and embarrassment, she threw her arms around me and squeezed me hard.

Caught off guard, I hesitantly hugged her in return. I was not used to such displays of affection and wasn't exactly comfortable with them in public. So I just let it play itself out.

We stood like this for what seemed like forever before she pulled back half a step, leaving her hands resting on my upper arms. I dropped mine to my sides, not knowing what else to do with them.

She searched my face, awe and amazement and gratefulness filling hers.

"Who *are* you?" she asked.

I shook my head, lost in my own astonishment at what had occurred. "I really don't know."

"You must be a powerful magician. You opened the door of my prison."

I felt that was an interesting way for her to describe what had happened, as it made me feel even more as if I were in a faerie tale.

"Well," I said, shifting uncomfortably on my feet, "I'm just glad you're free."

"I wish I could repay you somehow."

"There's no need. It really wasn't my doing, anyway."

She gazed deeply into my eyes, searching me out, seeking something. This went on so long that I began to squirm.

Then she nodded.

"I understand."

She gave me one more hug—a friends' hug this time, brief and light—and then we parted.

As I headed west on Taylor, toward home, wondering what it was in me that she had understood, the Voice came to me again. But this time, the world did not disappear. Instead, it expanded.

"*You passed the test,*" the Voice said. "*Your debt is paid.*"

CHAPTER 15

I DIDN'T TALK MUCH THE REST of the day. I locked myself away in my room, and I didn't come out until dinnertime. Even then, I just spoke perfunctorily, and I said nothing at all during our Bohm session. My mind and emotions were in turmoil, and I needed time to sort things out.

After the group broke up, Sari and I said our goodnights at her bedroom door.

"You okay?" she asked, sounding concerned. "You seemed a little distant tonight."

"Oh, I'm sorry. I didn't mean to be. I just had kind of a weird day, is all."

She nodded. "I get that. If you decide you'd like to talk about it, I'm always around."

"Thanks, but I'm not sure I can even describe it to you right now."

She smiled. "That's kind of my thing."

Once in bed, I immediately fell deeply asleep and had another provocative dream.

I'm in a strange house, one I've never seen before. The interior is old, made entirely of well-worn mahogany, and feels dusty. The floor creaks under my feet. I'm in a drawing room of some sort, with parlor furniture off to my left. It's dim, but I can see fine.

The far wall holds a central doorway with a large window to either side of it, devoid of glass. Through the right-side window, I can see a grand piano; through the left one is a kitchen. In the kitchen is an old woman, small, a bit rotund, with pulled-back gray hair and wire-rimmed "granny" glasses. She's wearing a flowered dress buttoned up to her neck. She smiles at me. In the doorway between the two rooms stands an old man, tall and thin, also wearing wire-rimmed glasses. He does not smile, but glares at me out of black and unfathomable eyes. He is dressed in black, in the manner of a nineteenth-century preacher, with a white shirt and a string tie. They emit a Puritan vibe, but they're happy to see me and invite me in.

The man and I settle in on the Victorian-era furniture of the parlor, and he pours tea from an old Wedgwood teapot made of black basalt. I accept a china cup.

We sip in silence as I explore the room with my eyes. I feel there is a presence here; perhaps the place is haunted. I feel no fear, but I do feel a pressure to ask him about this. Somehow I know, however, that I should not speak.

On the coffee table, a small plate made of bone china has appeared, upon which are several corn muffins. The man gestures to them with his hand, and we both take one. We study each other, his eyes piercing mine, me trying not to flinch as I bite into the cake. It tastes like garlic and honey in my mouth. The opposing flavors, which do not mix, set up an emotional dissonance in me.

"The world," the preacher says, "is a hologram. Every part of the world contains the entire world. The bird is in the woman, and the woman is in the bird." The shadow of a huge crow with outstretched wings passes over us, briefly blocking the light of the chandelier on the ceiling. "When you recognize her, she will lead you."

I doze off in the chair, sleeping within sleep.

I dream of a huge granite boulder standing in a clearing surrounded by a dense pine forest. A gray alien stands atop it, repeatedly babbling, "We are separate, but one. We are separate, but one. We are separate, but one."

<hr>

I jerked awake to find myself lying on my back, the bed covers completely disheveled and half off the mattress. *I must have been tossing and turning like mad*, I figured. But now I remained motionless, staring unseeing at my bedroom ceiling in the early morning light that filtered through a gap in the solid blue curtains.

This light, I suddenly realized, seemed too bright. I sought out the digital clock on my nightstand; it was ten after eight. I grimaced, unhappy I had overslept like that, but I remained in bed for another couple of minutes, trying to figure out what the dream meant.

I couldn't make sense of it at all. *It was just a dream,* I finally chided myself. *They're always weird.* But this dream had left me with an uncomfortable feeling that I found hard to shake.

I decided to get up, to move around, so as not to focus on it so much anymore. But it would linger with me throughout the day.

I showered, pulling my jeans on before crossing the hall to my bedroom, where I finished dressing and made my bed. Then I headed for the stairwell.

Uncharacteristically, Sari's door was half open, and I paused in front of it. After a little inner back-and-forth, I decided I couldn't resist taking a peek inside. Flashing a guilty glance around, I took a step in.

The room was not what I expected it to look like, and I felt a tinge of disappointment. I was hoping for something more…well, *girly*, to put a fine point on it. Instead, it was laid out more like a studio. Groups of paintings leaned against the walls, and a stack of fresh canvases stood in the corner beyond her closet. I noted that two of the paintings against the far wall were tagged for delivery.

I decided to be rash and moved farther in so I could peer around the door. The other half of the room looked more like what I had expected—what I had hoped for.

But in the far southeast corner, there was another painting, set off from all the others. Only the upper right quarter of the canvas had been painted, yet I somehow intuited that this was not a new work. Rather, she had abandoned the project. I don't know why I thought this, but that's how it felt to me.

I didn't spend a lot of time nosing around in her private space; I'm sure it wasn't more than thirty seconds total, but that was long enough to burn the image of that painting deep into my brain. Because, unlike all her other works, this one was not abstract.

The figure depicted was a soaring crow.

CHAPTER 16

EMILY, THE PUNK FEMINIST, WAS the most withdrawn member of the household, tending to keep to herself. She was a serious woman for someone so young. She was twenty, one year behind Sari, who, in contrast, was vibrant and sometimes downright excitable.

Emily was rarely the first one to speak at any of our Friday night discussions. Her contributions were insightful, though, and I soon came to realize that she had a real depth to her.

I admired her for that but still found her kind of hard to talk to, so I was a bit surprised when she told me she was a practitioner of what she called "the dark arts." She wouldn't elaborate on this except to say she wasn't a Satanist. Instead, she simply followed what she called "an ancient tradition." I politely left it at that. But as I began to find my place in the household, my demonstrated knack for their practices cracked open the door between us.

The first Friday in May, about two months after I'd arrived in Portland, she stopped me in the third-floor hallway as we were gathering for our Bohm session.

"You really fit in here," she said. "It's like you were born into our family."

This, coming from the only house member who I suspected didn't even like me, made my day. But I managed to not gush over the compliment. Well, not too much, anyway.

"Oh wow, thank you. I like it here. I've never even heard about anything like this place before."

"We keep to ourselves." She flashed me a quick smile, there and gone. "I've got something you might be interested in. Would you like to learn how to scry?"

"What's that?"

"A way of seeing things that may not otherwise be apparent to you. It can move you forward in understanding yourself and your place in life. The reason you're here. On Earth, I mean. It's another way of opening a channel from your subconscious to your conscious mind." She considered for a few moments. "Think of it as like trying to remember a dream you haven't had yet."

Woah. "Holy crap. Mind officially blown now."

Emily grinned. "So I take it you're in?"

On Wednesday night at eleven thirty, we got together in the unconverted attic of the house. Emily chose this time because the full moon would be directly overhead at midnight.

It was a dimly lit space, in the central gable, whose A-frame roof girders remained exposed. The floor, which was merely a thin facade serving as a ceiling for the room below, was lined with insulation and overlaid with unfinished three-quarter-inch-thick plywood boards laid haphazardly across the supporting timbers, with eighteen- to twenty-four-inch gaps between them. The main area contained the makeshift furniture Emily needed for her spells and other activities. The space went largely unvisited by everyone else, except when they wanted to search through the boxes of their personal possessions, stored around the perimeter.

"Careful of the gaps," she cautioned quietly. "It's easy to catch your toe in here."

The room was permanently set up for scrying. Three old wooden crates had been placed so as to form the points of an equilateral triangle around a low square table, enclosing a space large enough to accommodate four people. On each of these stood a well-used three-by-four-inch wax candle, each a distinct color. As she lit them, Emily said the orange one was for clearing the mind, the purple one for deepening intuition, and the indigo, for psychic ability. I nodded, recognizing how these qualities would be useful for our purposes.

Once the candles were lit, she pulled the chain that switched off the low-wattage, bare-bulb light hanging over the table. The candle flicker was soft and calming in the surrounding darkness.

Four thick square throw cushions surrounded the table as well, one on each side, also of assorted colors. She directed me to the black one on the north side, while she took the yellow one across from it. On the east side sat a white one, and on the west, a blue one.

"There's a reason why I put you there," she said as she undid the drawstring of a navy-blue cloth tote that she had brought with her. "Or rather, reasons. North is the cardinal direction of introspection, so the scryer always uses that cushion. It's also the natural direction that a compass points, so it helps the scryer to keep aligned with their purpose. And black is the color of power. You'll make use of all these spiritual attributes tonight."

As she spoke, she pulled a highly polished, utterly unblemished black walnut bowl out of the tote and, using both hands, set it gently on the table, carefully aligning it so it was perfectly centered in the square. Its mouth was a foot wide, and its outer wall bulged out for perhaps a quarter of an inch beyond the rim's circumference, so that it looked rather squat. It was three inches deep. Carved around the outside were numerous strange symbols, which Emily said were runes. It looked solid, heavy, and steady, and it was obviously of great value to her.

She next retrieved a bottle of distilled water from the bag and filled the bowl to just below the rim, leaving a quarter of an inch of clearance. She set the bottle on the floor behind her, then took out her final item, a pyramid-shaped violet amethyst. Setting the bag next to the bottle, she then carefully placed the crystal in the center of the bowl, making minute adjustments until it was perfectly aligned. Exactly half of its height was above the water's surface.

Having completed her setup, Emily wriggled herself into a comfortable position on her cushion. We were now ready to begin.

"Scrying literally means to 'make out vaguely,' " she said. "And that's just what happens—at least, in my experience it does. I've never immediately understood the meaning of the images I've seen. I've always had to spend time meditating on them. That doesn't mean it can't happen," she added quickly. "I just don't want you to think you've failed on your first try, just because it's not clear."

I smiled. "It sounds like you think I'm actually going to see something."

She held my gaze. "I'm sure of it."

I raised my eyebrows but didn't mention that I highly doubted it, myself. I took and released a deep breath.

"Anyway," she went on, "the key to this practice is to become fuzzy."

I chuckled. "Okay."

"What I mean is, we have to let things become indistinct before they can be resolved, so you want the surface of the water to appear just slightly out of focus. That's where the crystal comes in. By focusing your attention on its point, the water around it will become background to you. And the background is where the visions are going to appear."

"Sweet."

"Oh—one last thing." She smiled. "Try not to bump the table."

I laughed.

"All right, then," she said, placing her hands on her knees. "Let's go spelunking."

We settled ourselves in and did a five-minute meditation. By the time we were fully set for our work, twenty minutes had passed and full-moon midnight loomed nigh. That was the thought I had as I opened my eyes. The entire situation sent a kind of occult thrill through me.

"Good," Emily said. "So let's start. Moisten the tip of your index finger with saliva, and mix it into the water. Try to get a full drop of it."

I followed her instructions. I have to admit, sucking on my finger felt childish. Not to mention a little gross.

"All right," she said. "Take deep breaths, and let your mind remain in its meditative state. The process is similar, except that you're staring into water instead of into your mind. Don't try to force anything; just let whatever comes, come. And don't worry about how long it might take. Just sit peacefully, eyes locked on the tip of the pyramid, but watch sidelong for anything that might appear in the surrounding water. If there's something specific you'd like to know, keep that thing in your mind. Otherwise, just let the water speak to you."

She fell silent for the rest of our time in my endeavor.

I was surprised to find that it wasn't as difficult as I had feared it might be. It really wasn't that long, relatively speaking, before a murky blue image started to form, a blob beneath the water's surface on my side of the amethyst. It was vague and largely undefined, with shifting boundaries, as if a viscous liquid had spilled into the water. It rotated clockwise and, after a bit, organized itself into a toddler's representation of a circle. As I continued to watch, the interior became compartmentalized, each section taking on a different shade of blue. At the same time, a thin outer lining formed, appearing as a kind of dull yellow-gray fog. I was able to hold on to this final vision for maybe five seconds or so before it dissolved, and the water became clear again. At that point, I raised my eyes to Emily and lifted my eyebrows.

"You saw something?" she asked, sounding more excited than I'd ever known her to get before. Of course, she still wasn't bubbling over. Everything is relative.

"Yeah. Sorta. I have no idea what it was, though. It was indistinct—confusing, even. There didn't seem to be anything meaningful to it; it didn't even seem to *be* anything. Just this rotating blue circle."

"*Everything* is meaningful. Circles are significant. The color blue is significant. Rotation is significant. Think about those things."

I offered her a chagrined smile. "Could I get a hint to start me off?"

Emily grimaced. "Well, I'd really rather not. Only you can figure out what the vision means to you."

"Just toss out an idea. Please. I feel lost in this stuff."

She sighed. "Okay. Just to get you thinking. One of the meanings of the color blue is protection."

"The protector will always be protected," the Voice intervened, startling me. I hadn't heard it for the two weeks since healing the girl at Teachers Fountain. But this time, it didn't override everything else in my consciousness. No suspension of Emily's voice into silence, no freezing of my volition, and no compulsion to do anything. Merely a statement, as if someone else was in the room with us, just a part of the conversation.

I felt the small hairs on my neck stand up, but fortunately, my fear quickly passed.

"Thanks," I said simply, not sure if I was responding to the Voice or to Emily, as both had spoken at the same time. I was a little surprised by my ability to follow both conversations, and I wondered what that might signify. But I didn't have the opportunity to think about that just then.

"This is very cool," Emily said. "You're going to be good at this. I knew you would be." She tilted her head and studied me, her piercing gaze making my skin crawl. Finally, nodding to herself, she said, "We need to get you a bowl."

CHAPTER 17

CARL HAD AUTHORED A BOOK based on his beliefs that all events in our lives are drawn to us by our spiritual state and that changing that state can change the nature of what we experience in life. He had self-published it in 2014, but it went largely unnoticed for almost a year.

Then it received an admirable review from the leader of one of the larger groups in Portland's underground esoteric community, who then contacted Carl personally. After a two-hour chat at the upscale Barista Coffee Shop in Nob Hill, he bought many copies to distribute among his followers, and the two men agreed to affiliate their people. This alliance put Carl on the map, and the men became close friends.

"Zack will be here this Friday," Carl announced at dinner on Monday.

This sparked a pleasant buzz around the table.

"Zack is a spiritual teacher," Carl explained to me. "He goes by the ascendant name of Svapnadarzaka." He stumbled a bit over this and laughed. " 'Zack' for us plebes who still can't pronounce Sanskrit. The title means 'Dreamer.' He's a trained Bwiti shaman." I had no idea what a Bwiti was, but I didn't have a chance to ask, as Carl immediately addressed the entire table. "He'd like to talk to us about maybe participating in an ibogaine trip."

After Likemind, Bohm Dialogue, and the mushroom, I felt pretty open to trying just about anything Carl might suggest at this point. I was nodding my willingness even as I asked, "What does that do?"

"It's another hallucinogen," Carl said. "It lasts much longer than psilocybin and produces a headier trip. But what it's really good for is deeply diving into our psyches. It will make you feel like you're in a dream or a movie, interacting with various aspects of yourself."

"What do you mean by 'aspects'?" I asked.

"The many personalities that are inside you."

This took me aback. "Isn't that kinda schizo?"

Carl laughed. "No, not really. Look at it this way. You know how, when you have a major decision to make, you go back and forth in your mind, trying to figure out what to do?"

"Yeah."

"Well, each side of the argument you're having is a different part of your personality. From what I understand, ibogaine takes these and turns them into various characters, entities that you can hold a genuine conversation with."

"So you haven't taken it before?"

Carl shook his head. "No. But as I said, Zack is a professional. He works as a consultant in medical programs that use ibogaine to cure addicts of other, more dangerous drugs. So we'll be in good hands."

It didn't take me long to consider. I nodded. "Okay. I trust you."

Zack turned out to not be what I expected. Tall and well-built, with black hair that was middle ground in length and style, and a face that could easily find a place on a Hollywood movie set, he could fit in anywhere—in polite society or a hippie conclave. I guessed him to be around John's age, and in ways, he reminded me of John too.

His one clothing concession fitting his role as an esoteric teacher was his blue Nehru jacket. A single two-inch-wide silver medallion dangled from a silver chain looped around his neck. This consisted of an entwined knotwork pattern depicting a spreading leafless tree and its roots, a mirror image. When I questioned Carl about it later, he told me the symbol was called the World Tree and that it represented the joining together of the spiritual and the mundane. I thought that was pretty cool.

He was accompanied by a woman who I guessed to be in her thirties. She was dressed in a colorfully patterned sari. Zack introduced her as Shylah, leaving it for me to presume that they were a couple. They radiated a sense of peace, inner certainty, and calm. I liked them immediately.

Carl and Melanie had given up their spots in the front of the room to allow our guests to occupy the privileged place. They accepted this with grace, along with a certain air of expecting to be treated in an honored fashion. Carl relinquished the floor to Zack, who led us in a different form of meditation than the house practiced before he stood up to address his subjects.

"Ibogaine," Zack began, his deep voice resonating with confidence, "is a powerful hallucinogen that will toy with your mind. It's a mystical drug that opens the portals to your inner reality. It will teach you deep things about yourself. Some of those things you'll like. Some you won't. But I can guarantee, when the trip is over, you'll have a much greater understanding of who you are.

"Naturally, everyone responds differently to it, because everyone's brain wiring, health, and circumstances are different. I could tell you about my own trips, but yours will most likely be completely different. I *will* say that sometimes I've been ecstatic, and sometimes I've been frightened. But I've always come back changed for the better.

"I do want to warn you, though, that you might feel as if you're never going to come down from it. It lasts a very long time, and it plays with time during the high. It may even influence the way you perceive time for a while after you come out of it. So I want to assure you that, yes, it will eventually wear off. But its effects on you will last a lifetime.

"It would be tempting to say something trite like, 'you'll never be the same.' " He smiled. "But actually, what you will be is *more* of the same. You'll know yourself to a depth you've never imagined before. And that will change everything for you."

CHAPTER 18

O UR SESSION WAS SCHEDULED FOR a full month
out, on the weekend after the summer solstice. To
say I was looking forward to it would be an understatement. Zack had whetted my appetite for more self-explo-
ration, and I felt like I was up for anything. Having waded
in marijuana's shallow end of the pool and swum in the
deep end of the mushroom, I now felt eager to try the high
dive.

As time usually does for me when I'm in such a
nervous anticipatory state, it at once dragged and flew
by. But before I knew it, I was two days away from my
adventure.

The weather on that Thursday in the third full week
of June was hot and sunny. Although I was used to eating
lunch a little later in the afternoon, my freneticism had
left me hungry before my shift at Flash Burger was even
finished. So instead of taking the long climb up the southern hills on an empty stomach, I turned in the opposite
direction, walking the block back to Fourth Avenue. This
placed my route on a course for Java Man.

There I met with disappointment; it seemed like everybody had decided to eat there that day, as the coffee shop

had no available seats. So I didn't stop in, but I did stand for a bit outside the propped-open doors, basking in the good memories of meeting Sari there that seemed to waft out from the interior along with the good aromas.

At last I continued on my way, my head now full of daydreams about Sari instead of angst over my stomach. Our attraction to each other had been apparent to our housemates for a while now. Not that we had ever made any effort to hide it. We had always spent time together, often sitting next to each other during our Friday night sessions, but now it appeared we had moved on from our situationship and were officially dating, to everyone's approval.

A week ago, we had gone to see the Spike Jonze movie *Her* at Fifth Avenue Cinema. The theater was owned by Portland State University and run by the students, which I thought was pretty cool. She hadn't told me much about the film, just that it was about a man who falls in love with a computer that mimics the personality of a woman. That actually sounded kind of meh to me, to be honest. The premise wasn't believable; how could someone mistake a box of wires for a real person? But it turned out to be such a powerful exploration of the depths of human emotion and the sense of *living* that these capacities engender in us, that I came out of the theater longing to have such an experience with Sari. I wondered if that was the reason she had taken me to see it.

I hoped so.

My reverie broke when I found myself at Salmon Street, where the dense urban landscape changed drastically. Before me lay three parks, nestled one after the other between Third and Fourth Avenues. The first two, known as the Plaza Blocks, were filled with trees on well-kept lawns, which were cut diagonally by broad sidewalks lined with metal mesh benches for people watching. The third was actually a federal park that held an amphitheater. Overlooked by official buildings along Third Avenue—city hall, Hatfield Court, the police station, the county jail—these popular green havens served as a welcome respite from the concrete and asphalt, and as a smack in the face to this somber display of frowning authority.

Each of the parks filled a city block. The one on whose verge I was standing, Lownsdale Square, was one of the city's memorial sites. At its center stood a bronze statue, called the *Spanish-American War Soldier's Monument*, of a Spanish soldier atop a tall obelisk-style pedestal. When the crosswalk signal turned green, I made a snap decision to stop for a moment at the memorial.

When I reached the far curb, however, I noticed a gathering of three millennials standing about halfway up the path to the statue. I couldn't tell what was going on, but they seemed pretty agitated about something.

I hesitated, not wanting to place myself in what could quite possibly be a sticky situation.

"Go join them."

Although I was only slightly startled to hear it this time, I again felt compelled to obey this Voice.

When I arrived, I discovered they were gathered around an old man who was lying crumpled on the sidewalk. He was dressed in old, worn, dingy clothing, his hair and beard long and unkempt. A rickety, wheeled suitcase was laying at his feet, its handle extended along the concrete. He was obviously another homeless person, a man whom society had pretty much turned its back on. I felt compassion for him rise within me. The group seemed to want to help him but—like me—were at a loss as to what to do. They let me sidle up to them.

"What happened to him?" I asked.

"He was walking up the sidewalk," the man on my right said, "obviously having trouble. Then he suddenly froze up and collapsed."

"Jeez."

"He won't let us touch him," the man across from me said.

"We *shouldn't* touch him," the first one berated him.

"We called an ambulance," the lone woman told me. She looked and sounded scared. "They said he probably had a heart attack and that they could be here in about six or seven minutes."

"That's a long time if this is really a heart attack," I said.

"They said it's soon enough," the first man said, "unless he becomes unconscious."

The old man was obviously conscious, so I breathed a sigh of relief. Still, I felt kind of helpless, not knowing what to do.

Then the Voice reverberated in me and around me, *"Stretch out your hand to him."*

I didn't pause to consider what the others might think of my actions; this entity's commands always constrained me to act immediately. Reflexively, before I even realized what I was doing, I crouched down and reached out to the man.

His eyes were now open, and he stared at my hand but didn't move.

I held my hand steady, waiting for a sign from him. I didn't know what that sign might be, but I was certain I would recognize it.

His eyes then flickered up at me in helplessness, and our gazes instantly locked. His eyes were watery blue and looked like they had seen all the pain the world had to offer. They pleaded with me.

This was the sign I was looking for. Slowly, cautiously so as not to spook him, I took hold of his hand.

Instantly, he squeezed mine so hard that *I* felt pain. With great effort, he pulled himself up to his knees, making my companions gasp and take a step back. Then, after taking a deep breath, he shot to his feet in a single fluid motion. I stood up with him, not even having to assist him.

The group backed away in earnest this time, scrambling and emitting various sounds of surprise, shock, wonder, and disbelief.

Then the man gripped me tightly by the shoulders.

"Thank you," he said, his voice strong and steady. "Thank you."

As the others reacted among themselves, casting befuddled and frightened glances at me, he looked around at them, beaming with joy. "Thank you all. You're good people." He turned back to me. "I'm deeply sorry, young man. I'm afraid I have nothing to give you in return."

I was still in the throes of my own shock. "Nothing is needed," I said lamely, my voice cracking on the first syllable.

"I'll never forget you."

That was when the ambulance team joined us. I'd been so blown away that I hadn't even noticed them hurrying along the sidewalk.

I left things to them and collapsed onto the nearest bench, the world spinning around me.

CHAPTER 19

Zack's "Inner Space," as he liked to call it, was a huge room lined with twelve cots and their accompanying Observer's chairs, evenly divided between the front and back walls, and arranged so the frames extended into the room lengthwise, with their heads against the plaster. Each cot, spaced seven feet apart, consisted of a folding tubular frame holding a twin-sized mattress covered with a fitted bottom sheet, a pillow, and a thin blue blanket. The walls were painted a soft green, while the ceiling was eggshell. This color scheme was designed, he told us, to reduce anxiety and help produce a sense of calm. Because the opening phases of the drug could cause nausea, a galvanized metal bucket lined with a plastic bag stood beside the head of each cot.

The plain, unadorned building, which bore only a sign that simply read *Bwiti*, was located on the outskirts of Troutdale, a city about sixteen miles east of Portland, off Interstate 84, which runs through the Columbia River Gorge and connects Portland with Boise. The drug experience was deliberately kept separate from his group's everyday activities, which were centered in the bigger city.

It only took us about half an hour to get there. Zack had told us to plan for the entire weekend.

We arrived at the appointed time of eight thirty on Saturday morning—two days after my latest Voice healing.

The weather was clear and already sixty-eight degrees and would eventually rest just short of one hundred. I was somewhat dismayed to learn that there was no air conditioning, but the large overhead fans, one above each cot, proved to be sufficient.

As we entered, Zack greeted each of us individually and introduced us to our personal Observer. Mine was a woman in her midtwenties, whose doe eyes drew me in. Her mixed black-and-blonde hair was swept back, curling casually around her ears and just grazing her shoulders. I won't lie and tell you my heart didn't skip a beat at the sight of her.

"Arthur," Zack said, "this is Saesha. She's very experienced with young people who are taking their first trip. She'll take good care of you."

"Hello, Arthur," she said, smiling broadly and proffering her hand. "It's good to meet you. How are you this morning?"

"Hey, Saesha," I said. "I'm a little nervous, to tell the truth."

"I see that. Don't worry. I've taken ibogaine three times myself and have worked with a dozen travelers. I know how to interpret the signs of a bad trip. I can bring you through anything with relative ease."

I was pleased at her use of the term *travelers*. I found it more comforting than *trippers*, which bore negative connotations in my mind. "Cool."

"If you'd like to use the restroom, now would be the time to do it."

"I'm good, thanks. I went just before we left."

At that, Saesha led me to my cot, which was the second one in from the right-hand wall at the back of the room. No one was assigned to the one behind me, but Janis was settling onto the next one over from me. I noted that the guides were arranging us so we all faced the center of the room, so I wasn't able to see Janis's face.

I searched the space, looking for Sari. She was just settling onto her cot, two down from me against the front wall, so that she was facing me. I gazed at her until I caught her eye; she smiled and waggled her fingers. I smiled back and raised my hand.

Once we were all settled, Zack walked to the center of the room to address us. After offering a brief word of welcome and reassurance, he explained to us the procedure we were going to follow. It wasn't complex, and no one had questions for him. He then indicated to the Observers that the session should begin.

Saesha handed me three green-and-white capsules, along with a glass of water. I studied the pills in my hand for a few seconds, then, giving her a look that said, *Well, here goes*, I swallowed all of them at once. She smiled and told me the drug would take about an hour to kick in. I was free to shift my position on the cot as often as I liked until it did, but I wasn't allowed to get up at any time, for any reason.

"So," Saesha asked in a hushed voice, "what are you doing with your summer? Anything fun?"

"Just hangin' mostly," I said, matching her volume. "I'm new to the city, so I spend a lot of time just wandering around in a daze."

She laughed softly. "How long have you lived here?"

I couldn't help but notice that we were speaking as if we were still in Portland. It seemed the natural thing to do, since it was the biggest city in the region and we were both living there. "Three months."

"What do you think of it so far?"

"I really like it. It's totally different than San Diego. That's where I grew up."

"I went to SeaWorld once. I felt bad for the dolphins, so I never went back."

"Yeah, I know what you mean. I usually just went to the museums and stuff."

"Have you been to OMSI?" she asked. Upon my puzzled look, she explained, "The Oregon Museum of Science and Industry. It's about a ten-minute walk south of the Hawthorne Bridge, on the east side of the river."

"Oh, okay. I've never walked the river on that side. In fact, I don't think I've even been south of the bridge. The area looked kind of funky."

"Yeah, the western shore is kind of run down along that strip. But the museum's worth a visit."

"Cool." I wondered why Sari hadn't mentioned it to me. Then I remembered her reaction to the Maritime Museum. Maybe she wasn't into museums as a general rule.

At this point, I began to drift into myself. I didn't really feel much like talking anymore, as the reality of what I had just set in motion hit me. There was no turning back now, and I found myself becoming a little apprehensive. Saesha allowed me my space, gently setting her hand on top of mine and offering me a sympathetic look. I smiled wanly, grateful for her reassurance.

About forty minutes later, I felt dizzy. Saesha noticed this immediately.

"It hit you fast," she said. "Maybe you should go ahead and lie down."

I nodded woozily. "Yeah."

I did have a mild bout of nausea, but happily, I didn't throw up, and once I was fully relaxed on the cot, it passed very quickly. But the next sensation bothered me more. My body felt like it was being pressed into the mattress, as if massive weights had been placed on my chest, arms, and legs. It took concentrated effort for me to move at all. Even though Zack had warned us to expect this, panic began to set in as I struggled even to wiggle my fingers. Knowing something is going to happen and actually going through it are two different things.

But Saesha was right there for me, lightly stroking my arm and reminding me that opening my eyes would alleviate the syndrome. I did as she instructed, and gradually, the terrifying sense of being restrained and immobile dissipated. Now I merely felt sluggish, moving simply being more trouble than it was worth, rather than a horror show.

Once fully calmed, I closed my eyes again, and kaleidoscopic images appeared behind the lids. This didn't seem strange to me; somehow, I thought they had always been there. I couldn't remember a time when they weren't, so now I just took them for granted. Lines of vibrant, electric colors swirled about, some jagged as lightning bolts, others rounded, others changing too fast to be definable. They never stopped morphing, continuously forming and transforming along an infinite progression of geometric lines. Whenever I opened my eyes, these shapes became three-dimensional, warping the air itself. Everything and everyone was distorted and enveloped in a soft blur.

Contrary to the fascination I had held for the morphing teapot while on psilocybin, I found this behavior bizarre and disturbing. The thought came to me that, unlike the mushroom, ibogaine was not necessarily my friend. A shock of alarm at this realization made me wonder if I had made a mistake in taking the drug. I started to freak out.

But Saesha lightly stroked my arm while whispering softly in my ear, and I managed not to panic. As I calmed down, the lines disappeared, so I cautiously opened my eyes again.

I stared at the ceiling, which had taken on the character of a movie screen in a theater. My vision became as if I was looking through a camera viewfinder, limited to a rectangle about the size of my cupped hands. Everything else was pure darkness. Across the center of this blank screen, in huge black letters, was the word *Destiny*.

A man in a white suit walked out onto a stage that had suddenly appeared before the screen, and he stood front and center on it, facing me. It didn't even occur to me until later that, since I was gazing at a ceiling, he was basically hovering horizontally above me. From my drug perspective, everything appeared normal.

"Do you want to know what your destiny is?" he asked.

I was so shocked, I couldn't reply to him. I recognized his voice: it was that of my healing guide—the Voice in my head, or in space, or wherever it was. I merely gaped as he offered me a sly, knowing smile, his sapphire eyes flashing.

To his right, an easel appeared, holding a large drawing pad, like those used for making sales presentations. Taking two marking pens, one pink and one blue, he scrawled a three-loop spiral of each color near the top of the sheet of paper, pink on the left and blue on the right. The loops looked like snail shells, starting small and expanding rapidly, each one's diameter three times as wide as the previous one. The final lines extended upward next to each other until they reached the top of the final arc.

He paused for a moment, watching me, giving me a chance to take this in. Then he flipped the page over the top of the board, exposing another sheet, and drew them again, this time unrolling the spirals in a downward fashion so that the outer loops now formed longer straight lines. I honestly had no idea what he was doing, but my confusion didn't seem to matter to him. He simply proceeded, using two more sheets, to unroll the two spirals in this manner, until the fourth sheet depicted two perfectly straight verti-cal lines.

Okay, I thought, not understanding. To be honest, I felt there had to be a better way of getting across to me what he wanted me to understand. Like, say, just telling me. But I was afraid to show any kind of negative response, so I simply nodded. I had a feeling he saw through my ruse, but to my relief, he showed no sign of it.

Turning the page again, he looped the blue line across the pink one—their intersection lying far enough below the top to form two prongs—and extended the blue one downward, to the left of the pink one. As I watched, still puzzled, he went page by page, alternately crossing each line over the other, until they formed another prong at the bottom. This happened in a moment, although it played out over time. I don't know how to describe that; the drug was screwing with my internal clock. But when he was finished, the page displayed two intertwined spirals, together forming a U at the top and bottom. I recognized it as a double helix. At the top of each U, he next drew a snake's head, positioned so as to face each other.

Slapping the page with the back of his hand, he announced triumphantly, "*This* is your destiny."

I frowned, having no idea what he was getting at. I felt frustrated and ashamed, and I hoped he wasn't disappointed in me. All I could do was shake my head in apology.

"No need to be embarrassed," he said. "You will understand, eventually."

His eyes locked onto mine, seeming to burn into me for hours, days, fleeting moments. I found myself falling into these endlessly deep wells, these wormholes into other dimensions. My growing fear had no end either.

Then, just when I thought I was going to die, I found myself back on the cot, all my terror gone. And without another word or glance at me, the Man in White picked up the easel and walked off, stage left. The stage disappeared, along with the word *Destiny*.

A parade of people who looked like line drawings formed by laser light—but who I knew to be alive—walked across the screen from my left to right. Well, *walked* is probably the wrong word for it, because their movements were uncoordinated and jerky, like zombies in a horror movie. They shifted and morphed in cartoonish fashion, but they were just empty shells, with no features at all inside the outlines of their bodies. Those outlines consisted of the primary colors—red, yellow, and blue. Though they had no substance, they exuded power and energy. I found these beings extremely disturbing and nightmarish; I was desperate to escape them. But even with my eyes closed, the images persisted. I couldn't even look away. I began to panic, gasping in rapid, ragged breaths.

Then, out of nowhere, seeming to come from all around me and resonating deep in my mind, Saesha's gentle, reassuring voice comforted me. Thankfully, the beings faded away as her calming words settled my nerves. My pounding heart slowed by degrees, until I was able to breathe easily again.

When I opened my eyes once more, I was surprised to find myself standing in a large clearing in a pine forest. In a corner of my mind, I knew none of this could be. *Nothing makes any sense*, I told myself. But it was easier to just accept it. At least this scene in which I seemed to be immersed was somewhat normal looking. That was important, and I let myself relax.

Until something else made me gasp.

A larger-than-life-size statue of a reposing lion was set up on the grass about twenty feet in front of me, right in the center of the clearing, oriented toward my left. I don't know how I hadn't seen it immediately; it had simply appeared, but somehow it had always been there. Its body was made of obsidian, with a brilliant-cut, fifty-eight-facet ruby as an eye. This eye had no pupil and was situated on the side of the face so that it was looking directly at me. I felt distinctly uncomfortable under its unmoving, stoic gaze. Even though I knew it was only a stone, I had an unsettling suspicion that it could see me.

A crow stood on the lion's hindquarters. This bird was alive, and there was no question that it was staring at me. I tried to stare back in a show of defiance, but my body soon began to tremble. I averted my gaze, blocking the crow out of sight with my hand, and the trembling ceased. This made me feel a little ashamed.

Turning my attention back to the lion, I was shocked to see that it had come alive, transforming into an awe-inspiring beast. Its fur was the same honey hue as any other lion's, except that it glowed with an internal, ethereal light. But the mane is what caught my attention. I can only say that it was gloriously stylized. Instead of hair, it was made up of a row of two-dimensional trapezoids, their shortest side attached to the top of the lion's head, fanning back along an arc like a Mohawk haircut. It struck me as vaguely Pharaonic. The translucent panels were tinted in soft colors—rose, sky blue, lime green, and butter yellow—and were set within thin frameworks of gold, whose sides pressed against their neighbors. They reminded me of stained-glass windows. But the eye didn't change; it remained a stone, still fixed upon me. And now I was certain it was studying me.

Or perhaps, challenging me.

Overall, this being struck me as kind of sphinxlike and was obviously a higher entity of some sort. Maybe even a deity. This latter thought sent a shiver up my spine, and the nouns and pronouns I was thinking in automatically switched to the personal and deferential.

I realized the Lion knew I was here, but He made no indication of this. I felt deeply uncomfortable under His gaze. It had been bad enough when He was a statue, but to be the object of a living beast's attention was downright frightening. Still, though I was desperate to look away, I couldn't bring myself to do so. There was something waiting for me in that eye, as if it were a keyhole into a realm of endless mysteries that were beckoning to me and that I longed to grasp. I felt like I was staring into a gateway to eternity—and I was torn between fascination and terror.

Upon thinking of the word *gateway*, massive vertigo set in. I felt as if I were falling into that eye, as if I were being drawn into a black hole. My entire being, my sense of self, rushed toward it, my body moving without moving, falling, falling, stretching into infinity. I fell forever, time never-ending. My body spanned the universe, elongating as it approached the singularity that was the Lion's eye. But I never reached it. I never even drew physically closer. I fell, but I stayed in the same place. A thought flashed through my mind: *Perhaps the Lion is pulling out my life essence.* Strangely, this possibility didn't alarm me. On the contrary, I was in awe of the Lion's power.

I wanted to have that power. I wanted to be like a god, drawing all people to me, leaving them in despair at my unreachability.

"How do I attain what You have?" I blurted out. The sound of my own voice startled me. How dare I address this exalted Being with such impunity! Of course, I wasn't sure if I had actually spoken, or if the words were just echoing in my head; perhaps it was a question I was asking of myself. But that was just semantics. The words were out there, one way or another.

To my relief, the Lion was not angry. But His answer scared me.

"Who is asking?" He replied with no emotion. His mouth did not move, as He did not speak aloud, although the words seemed to hit my ears as if He had. He remained utterly still, without so much as a twitch.

I was disturbed by His question because I couldn't answer it. I didn't know who I was!

"I'm not sure," I said, anxiety creeping into my chest.

"Finding who you are," the Lion said, "is how you attain power."

"But it's so confusing," I said. "I've been a lot of different people."

"It is wise of you to see that," the Lion said. "You have now taken the first step."

I wasn't sure what to make of this, but I didn't have the chance to think deeply about it, because my attention was immediately pulled away by the rapid fading of daylight. Thinking the sun was setting, I looked to my left, toward the west, but there was no sun on the horizon. In fact, there was no sun in the sky at all. I then realized that it was not the day that was fading but the landscape itself. I looked to the Lion for an explanation, but none was forthcoming.

Suddenly, the crow leaped off Him, cawing raucously as it flapped furiously into the air before exploding in a great flash of feathers and intense white light. It rushed toward me, encompassed me, and passed by me, all in less than a second. Then beams of light shot out from the Lion's mane in all directions, fanning back and forth like the old Hollywood searchlights, crossing over each other but not blending, never interrupting the individuality of each hue. And to my childish delight, the Lion became engulfed by a cloud of dancing stars.

His image wavered, as though I were seeing Him through heat waves. His body became two-dimensional and began spreading throughout the air, amoeba-like, as if He were a glob of melting ice cream on a hot sidewalk, swallowing the stars. Within seconds, my entire field of vision had become a smooth plane of golden hue, impenetrable to both my eyes and my mind.

A point of blue-white light appeared directly in the center of the undifferentiated space before me, seizing my attention. I could not look away from it. It began to vibrate, its oscillations coming faster and faster and faster before suddenly exploding in a silent supernova flash that knocked me off my feet, throwing me upward and backward through the air. I flew forever in the silent blast, as thousands of galaxies spun around me in a dizzying display of endless cycling, until, suddenly, I bumped into a brick wall, and everything went black.

The darkness was more impenetrable than any I had ever experienced before, an absolute absence of light. So black and empty that I could feel it, as if the matrix of space itself had weight and substance. It was thick, viscous like oil. I knew my eyes were open, but I couldn't feel the air on them, which was disconcerting. An oppressive silence pressed against my eardrums. Now unable to see or hear, I wondered if this was what death was like. As soon as this thought entered my mind, I panicked, squeezing my eyes shut (to shut out *blackness*?), trembling with the effort to block the very concept out of my mind. I didn't want to know.

The blackness permeated my entire being, blacking out all thought and all feeling and all assurance. All was lost.

Then I heard the sound of a toddler running barefoot across a tile floor. Childish laughter followed after it, fluttering like a ribbon in the wind. I reached out and grasped this unseen ribbon, and it burst into a rainbow of colors, illuminating a small area, its glow swallowed so rapidly in the murk that its radius stretched no farther than the distance from my knuckles to my elbow. The rainbow ribbon wriggled and twisted, it tugged and pulled, it wrapped itself around me in the blackness and squeezed my chest so hard I couldn't breathe. But I maintained my grip on it, and it began slowing. Slowing, slowing, slowing until it became solid. As it slowed, the space around me grew lighter, the light expanding until, after what seemed like hours, I was in full daylight and the rainbow was completely still.

I then saw that I was not holding a rainbow or a ribbon, but rather the handle of the Radio Flyer wagon I'd had as a second grader. I smiled to see the little red toy once again. But my joy almost immediately turned to fear, as the rectangular black metal, oddly concave, morphed in my hand, not visibly, but tactilely, like dough squeezing through my fingers, twisting, turning, pulsing, and beating like a heart. This disturbed me deeply, and I tried to let go of it, but I couldn't open my fingers. I began to panic.

"So this is what you do? You run away and take drugs?"

The sound of my father's menacing voice coming from behind me shocked me so much that I forgot all about the handle and the wagon. And in that forgetting, they disappeared. A shiver ran up my spine, but summoning my strength, I turned to face him.

"What did you expect me to do?" I demanded, just as angry as he was.

"I expected you to be a man. But you refused to become one. You're such a disappointment."

"Maybe if I'd had a role model, I could have done better for you."

"You could never be like me. You're a complete failure."

"No," I said determinedly. "*You* are the failure."

Darkness enveloped me once again, and I felt my father's presence dissipate. A cool breeze caressed my face, and I closed my eyes, relishing it.

I felt a sensation of moving up and down in a slow, rolling rhythm. I reopened my eyes to find I was riding on a carousel. Sporadic silent explosions of colorful lights flashed around me, like Christmas bulbs in size and hue, some of them bursting into the shapes of flowers. I found them wonderful, dazzling, reassuring. I ran my hand up and down the cold, smooth brass pole that pierced the well-worn wood of the intricately carved lion I was riding, laughing like a child at the marvelous sparks that darted out like fireflies from the gaps between my fingers.

Fear not. Heal.

This assurance came to me from nowhere and everywhere without using actual words, with no voice resonating behind it. It was more like a realization than an annunciation.

At this point, the environment faded away again, although the words remained with me. I pondered them—or at least, I tried to. It was hard for me to think. I wanted only to drift, so I let my mind take me wherever it wanted. My thoughts became a jumble, crowding into each other, making no sense to me.

After spending another indeterminate amount of time floating in deep blackness—during which I lost all sense of my body, feeling as if I were pure consciousness—the world began forming around me again.

I found myself standing in the middle of a vast field, up to my waist in golden wheat. The land was perfectly flat, wheat extending to the horizon on all sides. Rolling waves of oscillating stems flowed around me in the wind, the glumes brushing against my forearms as I swept my splayed fingers through the grains. The smell of warm vegetation filled me with deep pleasure. I felt I would be content to remain here forever under the clear crystal-blue sky.

After another immeasurable amount of time, a figure appeared at the edge of the endless field directly ahead of me. I watched as the Man in White made his way to me, the grain parting ahead of him like a ship's bow plying through water. It took an eternity for him to reach me, yet he arrived in an instant. He stopped a few paces in front of me. The crow was perched on his left shoulder, once again staring at me. Its presence discomfited me.

"Well, your trip is over," he said. "I hope you got something out of it."

"But I was just *starting* to get it." I couldn't keep the petulant whine out of my voice. "I want to stay here. Please give me more time."

"It has been thirteen hours. How much time do you need?"

And with that, I came up out of the drug.

CHAPTER 20

"You did well," Saesha told me, smiling broadly. "I'm proud of you."

"Mm."

This grunt was all I could manage to utter for the moment. My body felt like a lead weight, pressing a deep groove into the mattress of the cot. The mattress, of course, was firm enough to support me, but in the initial moments of coming to, I wasn't particularly lucid. Still, I was awake enough to fear I might never be able to move again. I was utterly fatigued, both physically and mentally.

"You'll be high for a while," she said. "The drug can linger for up to a few days. But it won't be the same all-encompassing immersion you had during the trip itself. You may still have a few sporadic visions, though, and you'll be lethargic for a while."

"Sounds like a blast," I groaned, making her laugh. I liked it when she laughed. It was a sweet sound.

"This is a period in which your subconscious mind is working through the things it was shown during the trip. Some of these things will start to bubble up into conscious-ness, where you can think about them directly. It's a very important process. In fact, it's the whole purpose of taking the drug."

That made sense to me. I nodded, my eyes still closed, because I had used up the energy I had to speak for the moment.

I couldn't help but compare what I was going through now with how the mushroom had affected me. Whereas the latter had imbued me with a pleasant glow, this drug left me dull, lethargic, and barely able to function. My body was simply unwilling to move, and it took heroic effort for me to do so. Every movement I made was met with resistance and seemed to proceed in slow motion.

After about half an hour—a little before 11:00 p.m.—I finally felt strong enough to let Saesha assist me on my passage to the yurt behind the building. She waited outside as I made a now very welcome stop at one of the three portable toilets along the way, then she took hold of me again.

It was embarrassing to need this help, but Saesha reassured me.

"It's normal," she said. "It happens to most travelers."

"Even you?" I asked, grinning slyly.

She laughed. "I had to be carried my first time."

I chuckled in return. Still, she had made me feel better about my predicament. It still bothered me, but it no longer embarrassed me.

The thirty-person-sized guest yurt contained six bunk beds, which left lots of space for other things. Two school-cafeteria-style folding tables stood along the far wall. The shortest of these, on my left, held two coffee urns, along with a box of raw sugar, five stacks of six cups each, and a three-cylinder cafeteria spoon container. The other held an array of organic breakfast cereals, granola bars, and muffins, plus a large bowl of assorted fruit. Plates and bowls were stacked on both ends. A full-sized refrigerator stood to the right of this table, filled with sandwiches, milk, and various condiments.

The room was lit by a red LED nightlight, so we had no trouble crossing the space, taking care not to disturb Carl and Melanie, who had come out of the drug sooner than I did and were fast asleep.

Saesha guided me to a lower bunk on the western wall. After helping me get settled in, she headed for the Observer yurt next to ours.

Though my body seemed made of lead, I wasn't particularly sleepy. I lay on the bunk for several hours, staring up at the gently curved slats supporting the tier above me in the shadows, contemplating my experience. I didn't even bother to try to control my thoughts, letting my mind replay the trip as it saw fit. Unsurprisingly, it focused on the Man in White. His image, voice, and manner haunted me, lingering in the recesses of my awareness until that awareness at last faded as I became immersed in much-needed and welcome sleep, still having no idea of what he signified.

Zack woke us up at eight in the morning. Groggily, I waited in line to splash my face in one of the two water basins provided and then headed straight for the coffee, which Zack had started brewing earlier. After downing a cup of dark roast, I poured another and grabbed a turkey hoagie out of the refrigerator, taking both items back to my bunk, where I voraciously consumed the sandwich as if I'd not eaten for a week.

Zack stood watch over our various proceedings from the center of the room, looking pleased.

"Who are my drivers here?" he asked.

Carl, John, and Sari raised their hands.

"Are you alert, awake, capable?"

They all answered in the affirmative, with the one common caveat that they were tired. This seemed to satisfy him.

"Don't worry about straightening anything up," he said. "We'll take care of that. I want to say that I'm pleased—and not only a little impressed—with how all of you held up last night. The first trip can be a bear, but you all handled it like pros."

Carl smiled. "Well, Zack, you know us. We're into stuff."

Zack laughed. "Touché."

Carl and Melanie didn't eat or drink anything that morning but simply spent the next hour standing and chatting with Zack. My two benefactors never ceased to amaze me; in big and in little ways, they were unlike anyone I'd ever met before. Personally, I was famished, and if I had tried to continue fasting after the ordeal of the drug, I would've keeled over. But they behaved as if it was just any other day. They were later joined by John and Priscilla, both of whom were munching on fruit.

Finally, around 9:30 a.m., we said our farewells and piled quasi-randomly into the three cars. My journey home consisted of three stages: staring at the tall cliffs of the river gorge passing by from the back seat passenger window of Carl's 2016 Toyota Yaris; my overworked mind, lulled by the vehicle's subtle vibration, drifting into a kind of fugue state; and at last, as we exited the interstate to enter the hills of our neighborhood, jerking awake with a gasp from an exceedingly odd dream in which I was once again prodded by the reassuring words from my ibogaine hallucination: *Fear not. Heal.*

It was a comforting end to my weekend adventure, and I felt confident now in my eventual recovery from the pain of my former home life.

But I had misunderstood those words.

CHAPTER 21

ON SUNDAY MORNINGS IT WAS traditional for the household to go out for brunch. As was the case with weeknight dinners, attendance was encouraged but not required. (Nothing was actually *required* in the house, other than everyone contributing to the expenses and the upkeep of the common spaces. Carl didn't even care how messy we kept our bedrooms. Some members were, shall we say, laxer at this than others.)

The following weekend, five of us gathered at a table at Brite Spot, a hip diner located across the Willamette in the Hawthorne District. This was a rather eclectic section of town, comprising shops offering everything from retro clothing and Indian imports to Ben & Jerry's ice cream. About half a mile due west of the restaurant stood the Bagdad Theater, another McMenamins project built (unsurprisingly) in an Arabic style, where they had filmed *What the Bleep Do We Know!?*—a New Age film whose message fit in vaguely with our own views.

The decor was chic alien motif. Framed posters of Grays lined one wall, graphically manipulated to resemble sixties' psychedelic art, with vibrant neon Day-Glo and odd shadow effects. Embedded in the laminated tables were old newspaper clippings of UFO sightings, NASA re-leases, and stills from 1950s sci-fi movies. Meteor-shaped hanging lamps ringed the room. Music from KGON, a local classic rock station, was piped in.

The first time we'd had brunch here, I had been struck by this decor because I had only just recently had my dream about the alien on the rock. I still found it oddly serendipitous, even two months later. But when I mentioned it to Carl, he just smiled; he didn't think it was an actual example of synchronicity, but merely coincidental. He told me that Portland was one of the first places where modern UFO sightings had occurred over the US, back in the 1940s. His explanation made sense, and I quit ruminating on it.

Sari and I sat across from each other. I liked this arrangement because it allowed me to look at her throughout the meal.

"I'm on the email list of an art gallery in Vancouver I'd like to get my stuff into," she told me. "They're hosting a couple Portland artists next weekend. One of them is supposed to be kind of eclectic, very avant-garde. I'd really like to meet her. Wanna go?"

I nodded enthusiastically. "Oh, bet."

"Cool." She beamed at me.

So, the following Saturday, we headed north on Interstate 5 in her trusty old Neon.

"My father almost never let me drive," I said, "let alone get my own car. He didn't want me having that kind of freedom."

"That sucks."

"Tell me about it."

"Well," Sari said lightly, "freedom is what we're all about here. This is a whole city built on doing your own thing."

Sounded good to me.

In twenty minutes we reached the Interstate Bridge, with its pea-green arches and towering lifts, which was the gateway to Washington. Crossing the mile-and-a-half-wide Columbia River, it funneled us into the city of Vancouver. We drove directly north along C Street for a few blocks before arriving at Evergreen Boulevard.

The main city library, five stories tall, stood on the southeast corner; we parked across from it in the visitor lot of the Providence Academy. This was a blocky three-story brick structure that was originally built in the nineteenth century as a Catholic orphanage and was now rumored to be haunted. We stood for a minute or two, contemplating this possibility, before walking the two blocks west along Evergreen to the gallery.

This heart of the city, founded as a fur-trading colony by the Hudson's Bay Company, exuded a quiet small-town atmosphere. Its streets were lined with small specialty shops. Traffic was nominal, and pedestrians strolled along the sidewalks.

"There are a lot of little artsy spaces around here," Sari said. "This one is my favorite."

Art at the Cave was not ostentatious. It shared walls on either side with a family-owned restaurant and a women's clothing boutique. The beige stucco facade was interrupted by two large arched entryways, each comprising a central glass door with display cases to either side. The items inside these could be viewed from the street. We spent a few minutes perusing them before entering.

The interior was cool, softly lit, and totally white. Not apparent from the sidewalk, due to the crowd, but taking up a large part of the center of the room was another room with a single entryway on the west side. This housed animated computer graphics.

There were three artists whose work was being displayed that day. Sari recognized Jill Falk, the one she wanted to meet, from the photo on her website. Jill stood on the eastern side of this room-within-a-room, engaged in conversation with a number of patrons.

"She's busy," Sari said. "But that's okay. I want to look at her stuff before talking to her, anyway." She indicated three paintings on the right half of the front wall of the interior room, around the corner from where Jill was conversing. They were distinctly different from the ones on the other half, done by a different artist. "We can start with those."

"Let's do it."

But I got distracted on the way over by a sculpture made up of an odd conglomeration of materials. It apparently was meant to depict a human head. I think.

"What would you call this?" I asked her.

"Hmm," she said. "I'm not sure. Technically, I guess it's ceramic art. It reminds me of something Gertraud Möhwald might have done."

She pulled out her phone and Googled the name, finding images of the artist's work. Then she handed it to me. I scrolled through the photos.

"See what I mean?" she asked.

"Oh, yeah. There is a similarity."

"Pretty cool."

"I guess."

"You don't like it?"

"I wouldn't go that far. It's certainly eye-catching. But I don't see the meaning of it."

"The best art takes a long time to understand," she said. "My feeling is, if it's so obvious that you get it in just a glance, it's probably not saying anything radical. The art I like makes you crazy."

I laughed. "Like yours."

"I take that as a compliment."

"Of course you would."

"I told you before," she said with a sly grin, "I don't like to be bored. I don't want anyone else to be, either."

We continued on over to Jill's works. At first glance they appeared to be variations on a theme, but I think this was mainly because they utilized a common basic color scheme, one mostly made up of various shades of black, gray, white, and blue. But each depiction had a specific concept to it, imagery peculiar to itself.

Something about them seemed familiar to me, like a mental haunting, but I didn't know why.

"Dude," I said.

"I know, right?"

The works were eerie, ghostlike. Uncanny. One titled *Just After the Fall* was set against a cloudy background of swirling dark. Materializing out of this was an impression of a deep-black entity with broad shoulders, which required some effort to discern from the background. This vaguely demonic being was framed by groups of whitish blurs. The image was disturbing to contemplate.

I liked it at once, and I could tell Sari did too. She seemed absorbed by it.

"This is intense," she said.

"There's something going on in there, but I don't know what it is."

"Yeah. You can almost see parts of it move. Especially those flittering white thingies."

"Whatever this black thing is"—I pointed—"it seems to be pushing out of the background. It's very, um—"

"Menacing."

"Yes!"

It was easy to get lost in this maelstrom. Gazing into it, I felt as though I were entering a bad dream. Being sucked into it.

I don't know how long we stood before this work. I felt like I couldn't tear myself away from it. But finally I managed to, feeling a bit like something in me was being left behind.

As we stepped over to the next one, a ghost of lingering apprehension accompanied me.

"Look at this odd arrangement," Sari said as we studied *Piano*. She pointed to a cluster of blurry white balls in the smeared darkness of the oils. "These, apparently, are flowers, but they remind me of spirit orbs in the way they're depicted."

"Spirit orbs?"

"Transparent balls of light that often show up in photographs, floating in the air. Nobody knows what they are. Although, of course, there are a number of theories."

"Of course." I chuckled. "I've never seen anything like that before."

"I have, in photos my Witch House friend once showed me."

"What's Witch House?"

"It's dark stuff. Demonic music and imagery. Pagan ritual mixed with horror. I never got into it myself, although I did like the retro-Goth look she adopted. But she got into a new crowd because of it, and in my senior year, we basically split up, although we remained friends to a degree." Then her expression turned nostalgic, and her voice drifted, becoming wistful. "I haven't seen her since I left Hillsboro. I wonder how she's doing now." She fell silent for a moment or two, then sprang back to her normal energetic self. "Anyway, I went hipster instead and never looked back."

"You do have a cool style."

"Our style is to despise styles, which we display by sampling from all of them. It's also very retro and environmentalist and antiestablishment. We're opposed to crass consumerism, and we're deliberately recherché. I knew instantly that I had found myself in it. It's actually one of the things that drew me to Carl."

"Sweet. He does have kind of a sixties vibe to him. And Harold too."

Sari laughed. "Harold is very into social revolution. He still thinks he can change the world. I love him for that."

I hadn't yet decided what I thought about Harold. He seemed a bit out there for me, but I had to admit he was nice enough, underneath all his freneticism, and seemed to have good intentions. He just kind of grated on my nerves sometimes.

"You know," Sari went on, "your love of old movies and music would fit you into our outlook nicely. Except for your clothes. Way too square, dude!"

We laughed. I felt like I should feel insulted, but for some reason, I didn't. Well, not "for some reason." Sari was the reason.

"But then again," she went on, "I don't know any *bros* who are into true hipster anymore. And everybody's morphing into something else, anyway."

"So hipster is dead, then."

"That's a very hipster thing to say."

I made a wry expression. "Guess I'm totally out of it."

"Don't say that. Hipster's not about being in or out. It's just about *being*."

That struck a chord within me. I nodded. "Cool." I motioned toward the next picture. "Shall we *be* over there?" I asked. Sari laughed and playfully punched my arm, making me feel rather pleased with myself.

This one was called *Here But Not Here*. The dominant image was that of a woman in a long white dress, sitting on a blue divan, her arms crossed. As with the other paintings, her face was indecipherable, and the overall figure was almost manikin-like. It was hard to tell amid the darkness and blurring, but the setting appeared something like a Victorian parlor.

A vague memory of my preacher dream flashed into my mind, which then led to a thought about Sari's crow painting. This seemed like a possible synchronicity moment to me, but it made me uncomfortable. Sari's touch on my bare arm immediately brought me back to the present.

Pointing to the lower right corner of the painting, she said, "Now *these* are orbs."

"They look like soap bubbles."

"There ya go."

"And this is the kind of thing that shows up in photos?"

"Yep."

"Wild."

"I wonder if she did these on purpose or if they just showed up."

This statement surprised and puzzled me. "How could they just show up?"

"She might have been adding light effects or something, and they turned out this way without her intending it."

"That just sounds like a mistake."

"Not at all. It's the painting making itself what it wants to be."

Woah. Now, this was genuinely startling. Especially in light of my ibogaine trip, where everything had seemed to be driven by some inner purpose and it was impossible to really know whether something was alive or not, because even those that should have been inanimate seemed to have a measure of will.

"Dude. That sounds freaky."

"I know, but that's how I feel when it happens to me."

"Does it happen a lot?"

"All the time." She indicated the painting. "I don't get orbs, though. My stuff isn't like hers at all."

"But it's in the same class, right?"

"Abstract art is a pretty wide field, so yeah. But my work doesn't really lend itself to stuff like this, all perfect shape, shading, and light. It just is." She pointed at the orbs. "I'm for sure gonna ask her about these."

In total, we spent perhaps fifteen minutes perusing the three paintings on the wall.

Arriving at the corner, we saw an opening in the artist's conversation, so Sari quickly took advantage of it and stepped up to her.

Jill Falk was a vibrant woman. She had thick, long hair, which seemed to be a mixture of brown and black, with bangs. Splashes of multicolored glitter flashed on her nails. Adorned with rows of beads and bracelets, and many rings of various shapes and sizes, she reflected Sari's hipster fashion. Her encompassing energy sparked a term to flash through my mind: *free spirit.*

I liked her instantly. She had a good vibe. But I had already decided I would not take part in the conversation to any great extent. This was Sari's thing, and I was going to let her enjoy it.

Jill turned to us, beaming, as we stepped up.

"Your work is amazing," Sari said.

"Thank you," Jill replied. "I'm glad you like it."

"There's something very dreamlike about it."

"That's what I do." She laughed.

"So it's a deliberate thing?"

"Well, my old art professor once told me that *everything* in art is deliberate. But I don't know. It just arises."

"I get that," Sari said. "My work does that too."

"Oh, you're an artist?"

"Yeah."

"Cool. What's your name?"

"You wouldn't know me." Sari laughed. "Sari Wright."

Jill joined in her laughter. "You'll get there, I'm sure. So what are you into?"

"Abstract Expressionism. I throw a lot of paint at a canvas and see what happens."

They laughed again, and I was pleased for Sari at how quickly they had connected.

"How long have you been at it?" Jill asked.

"As long as I can remember. My style seems to be changing lately, though."

"I get that. My past work dealt with color and form in a very different way than it does currently. It's evolved over time from a more surface understanding of life, dreaming, and art to more and more subtle expressions of that lived experience. I like what I'm doing now. But who knows what's next?"

"I know that feeling. Your work is so unusual. I don't think I can place it anywhere."

"I call it Liminal Oscillation. I tend to talk about it as an oscillation between form and no form, and images that appear liminally between surface and depth."

"Cool." Sari nodded, then looked at me with a slight smile. "Arthur and I cross a few boundaries on occasion."

I chuckled. "You could call it that."

Jill looked like she wasn't quite sure what to make of this, but she made no comment. I just shrugged.

Sari returned her attention to Jill. "There's something I wanted to ask you about, though, if you don't mind. Regarding *Here But Not Here*."

"Oh, that one's a little older. I changed the name for this showing." She chuckled. "But anyway, go ahead."

"There are a number of bubble-like objects in the painting. I was wondering if you put them in there on purpose."

"Bubbles? Hmm. I don't remember them. Show me."

We walked around to the painting, and Sari pointed out the orbs.

"Mostly here, but also here," she said. "And these two on the other side. What are they?"

Jill studied them closely for a few moments before stepping back again.

"Well, first of all," she said, "I can say they aren't deliberate. But this painting is not a one-off. The image is ghosted on top of itself multiple times. I do this with a lot of my works. I believe these 'bubbles' are some of the tracer layers. That is, repeated layers stacking up and down. I hope that doesn't disappoint you."

"Oh, no, not at all," Sari said. "I just thought they looked like orbs. They're so perfectly rendered."

"I'm not attached to them looking any particular way to anyone," Jill said. "Whatever speaks to you, speaks."

Sari and I nodded.

"It's almost like your subconscious is pushing up from deeper levels in your work," Sari said, "as if the ephemeral became phenomenal."

"That's the dream world for you," Jill said, laughing. "My paintings are actually influenced by my dreams. Not that these are direct images from them. I worked them off of old photographs. But my dreams are evoked in the way I represent them."

"That's cool," I said.

"You paint from photographs?" Sari asked.

"Digitally enhanced photos, yeah."

"Sweet."

"I have some unpainted stuff from years ago, when I went through my mobile photo phase."

"So you're a photographer too," Sari said, a touch of jealousy in her voice.

"Yeah. It's an interesting project."

"Have dreams always inspired you?"

"Pretty much. I record my dreams intermittently, and it's such an amazing resource. I recently read through some archived dreams that I wrote down ten years ago, and I was kind of amazed at the connections that seem to permeate through into waking life, over time. I'm also an avid lucid dreamer."

"That's something I haven't taught Arthur yet," Sari said, giving me a sidelong glance. "But I do it deliberately."

"I've been doing that for years. I've also experienced shared dreams with other people."

"Dude." I couldn't help this interjection. I mean, come on.

"I think we are always dreaming," Jill continued. "But the more superficial levels of consciousness and brain states entrain us to an idea of 'normalcy' and 'ordinary' reality."

"If there is such a thing," Sari said.

"Right."

"How would we know?"

Jill nodded. "That's the question, isn't it? Conscious awareness is so constrained by words. The only way we think we know something is by giving it a name. But I feel like words are really rigid a lot of the time, and I like to leave room for the unknown to intercept."

"Yeah," Sari said, "it seems like our perceptions are geared to a three-dimensional reality that maybe doesn't actually exist."

"And we don't even know exactly how we see *that*," Jill said. "The other night, I was in a lucid dream, and I was trying to figure out if my dream body had two eyes, similar to the ones in my physical body, that allowed me to see everything as three-dimensional. Like, how do we see things without eyes? And if we can, which we do in our dreams, are we really seeing out of our eyeballs?"

"Maybe in our dreams we're seeing out of our pineal gland."

"Well," Jill said, "the pineal does regulate sleep. Maybe there *is* a connection of some sort."

At this point I tuned out. The conversation had turned a little too philosophical for my taste. My mind kind of wandered, and I let my eyes tag along. I glanced around at the other paintings on the walls, noting a few that I thought I'd like to take a closer look at. They looked nothing like Jill's, though. I also noted that only a few of the other attendees were studying them. Most were clustered in small groups throughout the gallery, drinking wine. I wondered what they were all talking about. Somehow, I doubted it was anything like what Sari and Jill were into at the moment.

When at last I refocused my attention on them, I found I had missed an entire discussion on a different topic. I felt a little embarrassed.

"Thanks," Jill was saying. "I feel differently about them depending on where I am in the process."

"Is that why you change the names?" Sari asked with a sly grin.

Jill laughed. "Maybe." She took a sideways step and peered around the corner. "I should probably get back to my post."

"Oh yeah. Of course," Sari said. "I'm sorry for taking so much of your time."

Jill made a dismissive gesture. "Not at all. I enjoyed talking to you." She grinned at me. "You're a quiet one."

I chuckled. "I'm just trying to absorb it all. I know nothing about art. But I do really like your stuff. I've never seen anything like it before."

"Thank you. And thanks for coming, both of you."

"We loved it," Sari said.

"It was really great talking to you," Jill said to Sari. "Good luck with your dreaming."

"You too."

With another big grin, Jill raised her hand.

"High fives!" she said.

Sari and I laughed. Sari jumped right in, enthusiastically slapping Jill's palm. After a slight hesitation, I did too, although a little more awkwardly. Then Jill returned to her waiting fans.

CHAPTER 22

T HE FOLLOWING FRIDAY, I DECIDED to stop by the Dr. Martens outlet on 10th Avenue to buy some new shoelaces, as one of mine had become rather frazzled and was close to breaking. I admit I knew of this for some time and was too lazy to do anything about it. But the store was only a ten-minute walk from Flash Burger, so it wasn't as if it was unduly out of my way.

Afterward, I decided to amble down 13th, which was the most direct route to Goose Hollow. Past Alder Street, the west side became empty of buildings, which were replaced with thick stands of trees and shrubs, due to the freeway running alongside below it.

Halfway past the intersection with Morrison, I noticed a homeless camp nestled among the vegetation. It was the biggest one I'd seen in the city so far; there must have been a dozen tents of various sizes and colors, lined up in the grass and dirt. A few looked like they were store bought, but most were ragtag conglomerations of tarps, canvas, and other materials.

My attention having been snagged by this eclectic display opposite me, I semiconsciously slowed my pace, half expecting the Man in White to send me over there. Instead, I heard from someone else.

"Hey!" a vaguely familiar voice yelled from across the street. "Hey, I know you!"

I peered closely at him. It didn't take me long to recognize him as the man I'd healed of a heart attack in the park. As soon as the traffic cleared, I jogged across the street.

Five other men were joining him as I reached the far curb. One, who was drinking from a bottle in a paper bag, was quite noticeably drunk. The others didn't look particularly friendly, and I couldn't help but feel like I was being ganged up on. I felt a momentary warning pang, but I was committed now.

I addressed the man I was familiar with.

"Sup?" In response to his puzzled look, I laughed and said, "How ya doing?"

"Oh," he replied, chuckling in return. "I feel fine, as far as the heart goes." Then his tone became introspective and quizzical. His eyes narrowed. "In fact, the ambulance guys checked me out, and everything's perfect. Better than ever, in fact."

"That's really cool."

"I still don't know how to thank you for what you did."

"You being okay is enough for me. But I wasn't the only one helping, you know. The others called the ambulance."

"Which I didn't need, because of you. You didn't just help; you *cured* me. My heart is like brand new! How the hell'd you do that, anyway?"

Now, how was I supposed to answer that? I glanced at the others, who were staring at me intently. I began to squirm. What was I supposed to do—tell them that I was following the commands of a Voice that spoke in my head and channeled power through me? But what else could I say? I frantically searched my mind for a believable answer. To my relief, I hit on one that was still true, just in a different sense.

"To be honest," I said, "I really don't know."

"Well, don't that beat all," the man with the bottle said. He squinted at me and moved closer, casting a disbelieving glance over me with a look of repulsion on his face, as if he had come upon some strange new form of human. I could smell the heavy alcohol on his breath; I tried not to react to it. "Did you really fix 'im?"

"It's not what you think," I said, taking a half step backward and raising my palms in a gesture with a double meaning of surrendering and warding off.

"What *do* I think?" He glanced around at the others and, laughing coarsely, said, "He thinks he knows what I think!" Then he turned back to me, leaning forward into my space. He was droopy eyed and unsteady on his feet, kind of rolling, which made me very uncomfortable. "What do *you* think?" he demanded.

At this point, I was at a loss. But at last, the Man in White urged me on, filling me with confidence. *"You know what to do."*

And suddenly, I realized that I actually did know. I focused on calming myself down, and once I was settled, the words just came to me.

This time, *I* leaned into him and, so quietly that only he could hear, I said, "I think you're trapped. Let me free you."

The look on his face became one of derision mixed with hope. "Free?"

I indicated I wanted to place my hand on his shoulder. He stiffened, but the man from the park said to him, "Let him do it, Ben."

Ben glared at him, then cast his gaze around at the others before finally focusing on me again. Studying my face, he slowly nodded, and I rested my hand on his shoulder.

This was the first time I'd not made contact with skin when the Voice had directed me to touch someone, and I wondered if it would work. But immediately upon touching his coat, I felt the now-familiar energy run through me. And once again, as with the other people I'd healed, I watched his expression change to one of joyful surprise. By now, however, I was getting used to this, so I simply stood with my hand firmly in place on his shoulder, holding his gaze with my own, until the energy flow dissipated. My shoulders then slumped a little, and as usual, I felt somewhat drained.

And as with all the other people, he was immediately transformed. He spun to face the others and all but shouted, "He did it!" His words were not slurred now, he stood erect without reeling, and he spoke with confidence and energy. I actually thought he was no longer drunk. He held out the paper-wrapped bottle toward them. "Here. Someone take this. I don't need it anymore." The man from the park retrieved the bottle from him, a huge smile on his face. Then Ben turned to me again, his eyes narrowed, and asked with wonder in his voice, "How did you *do* that?"

"You did it yourself." I was surprised to hear these words coming out of my mouth, but I knew they were true. "I just opened the door for you."

"You're beginning to understand," the Man in White said.

But I didn't have time to relish this praise, as I suddenly became aware of a well-dressed middle-aged couple standing a few steps along the sidewalk from us, watching the proceedings. The woman stepped up to me with a dismissive look on her face. She was using a cane, and it was obvious that it was very painful for her to walk. I could almost feel it, myself. I had to admire the fact that she was out for a stroll here.

"I don't believe in hocus-pocus," she said defiantly. "Anybody can stage something, fool people like these. So I'm challenging you."

I couldn't help myself; I chuckled. "I admire your strength," I told her.

She caught the intended double meaning and smiled sardonically. "Let's see yours."

I held my hand out in offering. She clasped it, and the energy passed through us.

"Well, what the—" she muttered, a look of astonishment coming over her face. She stared at her leg as she freely bent at her knees, repeatedly and smoothly, testing them. Then she looked at me with respect in her eye—but not thanks. I gathered she was naturally taciturn like this.

Surprising me, she handed me her cane. "A souvenir," she said. Then she turned and—motioning to the man she was with, who appeared astonished—walked quickly away.

I immediately decided she was my favorite "patient" ever.

But I didn't have time to savor this moment, as suddenly I became swamped by the rest of the group. I found myself being pressed in by them, begging me to heal them. I was more than willing to do this, but the rest of the people living in the tents had joined the original five, and it was more than I could handle. I felt trapped, pressed in upon, unable to breathe or even move. My claustrophobia kicked in, and that's when I panicked.

I clawed my way out of the mass of pleading men and women and bolted back across the street—blindly, wildly, narrowly avoiding being hit by a car. I continued running for two blocks, ignoring the stares I was receiving from other pedestrians on the sidewalk. I just wanted to put as much distance between me and the clamoring crowd as I possibly could, as fast as I could.

It wasn't until I reached Taylor Street that I finally slowed to a walk, breathing heavily and shakily.

"Running away is not the answer," the Man in White said.

My cheeks burned with shame. *"I'm sorry. I didn't mean to let you down. I just felt overwhelmed."*

"It is not possible for me to be disappointed. But you have lived in this city for four months; you should be used to crowds by now."

"Crowds are one thing. Being swallowed by one is another."

"This fear is something you need to overcome."

"Why don't you work for me, the way you work through me?"

"That is not my purpose."

"Well, I don't know how to fix myself."

I had embarrassed myself on several levels at once, and while the Man in White might not be disappointed in me, I certainly was. But my affliction was real, and I didn't know how to overcome it.

If that's not ironic, I thought wryly, *I don't know what is.*

It was only then that I realized I was still carrying the cane. Suddenly, I burst out laughing.

What a doofus, I derided myself.

It seemed to take forever, but at last I reached the house.

As I was unlocking the gate, the Man in White spoke again.

"Take a walk in the labyrinth," he said.

A flash of terror, striking like a dagger in my solar plexus, made my heart skip a beat.

"I...I can't do that."

"You keep putting off facing your fears. That is why you feel you cannot overcome them."

Since my ibogaine trip, the Man in White's directions had lost their compelling nature. I was free to obey or refuse them, to listen to him or tune him out. Up until this moment, I had not refused anything. It was tempting to do so now, to continue arguing instead. But that struck me as childish, and I chastised myself for my weakness. Filling myself with all the determination I could muster, I made what was probably the hardest decision of my life.

Swallowing hard, then gulping several breaths of air to steady my nerves, I entered the grounds and locked the gate behind me. Both paths to the backyard lay only a couple feet in front of the veranda steps, fifty feet from the gate. One led eastward, alongside the seemingly endless bedroom wing of the house. Turning at the corner, it then passed by the woods and the terraced garden. The other merged with the driveway until it reached the garage, where it once again broke off as a footpath to the patio. All of these consisted of white gravel, which I found more pleasant than the cobblestone walkway leading to the front door. I liked the way it crunched under my feet.

The western route was the shortest distance from the gate to the labyrinth. As I drew near to the terrifying living structure, I began taking slow, deep breaths. I stood outside the entrance for a full minute, contemplating the rectangular opening, whose frame also appeared to be breathing, in sync with me but opposite, in and out, narrowing and returning to its rightful size. Taking a final deep breath and holding it, I pressed into the mouth of the monster, finding that I just fit, after all. Once inside, I flipped a mental coin and decided to go to the right.

The boxwoods on either side were taller than me and also gave me the frightening impression that I'd get stuck between them. I was almost enclosed in a living tunnel, which—despite being open to the sky—was filled with odd patches of darkness due to the angle of the midafternoon sun's rays striking the curving vegetation. Thoughts of becoming hopelessly lost in this terror dungeon crowded into my head—even though I knew that was an impossibility. Irrational fears are called that for a reason.

"Place your hand on the inner wall," the Man in White said. *"It will guide you in and out."*

I nodded and obeyed.

The first step was the hardest. I took another deep breath that shook raggedly on the exhalation, closed my eyes, and put my right foot forward. Hesitantly, I took another step. I kept this up, pausing for as long as I needed between steps, focusing intently on the trail just in front of me, trying to control my breathing as my heart raced. Not thinking about the looming hedge walls pressing in on both sides of me, crowding me, suffocating me. Not thinking about the five hundred feet of serpentine path that lay before me. Breathing was difficult, especially at first, and I found myself pausing frequently in my journey to take enough breaths to calm myself. But to my surprise, I didn't freak out. I pressed on with determination, repeating to myself under my breath that the Man in White was with me, that I was not alone in this place. Yet his silence made it feel as if I were.

I treated reaching the center as a victory, and from then on, the dread I'd brought in with me reduced with each step I took. I think knowing I was now on the way out of the maw of the dragon made all the difference.

I had no sense of time while in the labyrinth, but upon exiting, I immediately noticed the sun was much lower. It was only then that I checked my phone and was astounded; I'd survived in that narrow prison for forty-seven minutes.

I was still breathing a little erratically, but overall I felt an enormous sense of relief mingled with pride at having made it out of that nightmare. And maybe—just maybe—I felt a little less trepidatious about entering any others I might encounter in the future.

"Welcome to a larger world," the Man in White said.

CHAPTER 23

I AWOKE THE NEXT MORNING JUST before my alarm was set to go off. I ended up not needing it today, because I had a mission in mind. I felt fully rested and, for the first time in my life, confident in my future.

I tossed the covers aside and jumped out of bed. After quickly showering, leaving the bed unmade and breakfast uneaten, I quietly left the house, taking care not to disturb the others. I then made my way to my usual spot on the river. There was something I wanted to try.

I particularly liked the city in the early hours of the day, especially on a Saturday, when the streets were pretty much mine. The little bit of traffic this morning, flowing casually past me as if they also were in no hurry, produced a pleasant arrhythmic beat in my ears, rather than its usual hectic cacophony of rapidly varying movement, gunning engines, and squealing brakes.

As I made my way at a moderate pace, I became draped in a deep sense of assurance and purpose.

Reaching my destination, I began my experiment by engaging in my usual perusal of the far shore, settling my mind. The overcast morning muffled the light from the sun, which was already well above the horizon, bathing the buildings in a beige-orange glow. As usual, the temperature was about ten degrees colder than what I was used to in San Diego, but other than that, the conditions were near perfect for what I sought to do here.

I turned my attention to the water below me, focusing about ten feet out from the concrete retaining wall, and letting my eyes lose focus, I scried the river.

I'd been practicing at least once a week since buying my own bowl right after Emily had taught me the art two months ago. It turned out—as she had intimated—that I had a flair for it, so I was able to pick it up quickly. I had gone way beyond those murky colors and vague outlines I'd painfully tweaked out of the water on my first try. By the fourth week, I'd been seeing simple—but clear—images.

So it didn't take all that long for one of these images to form in the river: a magnificent metal framework wheel, gleaming like polished bronze, so shiny that I wondered if it was emitting light. Certainly, light flashed around it as it spun slowly clockwise. With its crossbars and clockwork and gears, it appeared like a great steampunk machine. I had no idea what it was or what it was meant to represent. But I did know one thing for sure: this was a perfectly defined image of what I had blurrily scried in my first session with Emily. As this realization struck me, the wheel suddenly vanished.

I continued to stare for several seconds at the spot on the river where my attention had been fixed, before realizing I was seeing only water. Then I mentally shook myself, pushed off from the railing, and headed home, the golden wheel looming over all my other thoughts.

CHAPTER 24

J UST ON THE EDGE OF awakening the next morning, I had an odd dream. It wasn't a nightmare, nor was it exactly unpleasant, but it troubled me, nonetheless. Or rather, it frustrated me.

At the very end, a voice had spoken to me. It was not the Man in White's voice, but it didn't feel like something my mind had randomly made up, either. It was more as if a different entity was speaking to me. What it said was just one word, a tantalizing, compelling word, and I knew in my bones that it was of utmost significance for me. But when I awoke, it dissolved out of my consciousness, retreating into my internal darkness like the dimming of a propane camp lantern's mantel as it spends the last of its fuel.

Now, of course, like everyone else, I often forget my dreams upon waking. And also like everyone else, most of the time, I don't really care. But I could remember all the details of this dream except for that one last frustrating word. I mentally scratched and clawed after it, desperate for it to return, but to no avail.

I quit the attempt after about a minute, resigned to not knowing. *It's just a dream*, I reminded myself. *It's not important*.

But after four months of living in this house, I knew I was just kidding myself. Everything that happened to me had a significance.

I got ready and headed downstairs. To my surprise, I encountered Sari at the dining table, typing on her laptop. She looked up as I paused in the doorway.

"You're up early," I said.

"Yeah. Had a weird dream I wanted to put in my journal before I forgot it." She motioned to the large mug at her left hand. "And I needed coffee."

I thought it was kind of a cute idiosyncrasy that she always used her left hand for drinks even though she was right-handed.

"That's what I'm talkin' about."

I headed for the kitchen to pour one for myself. When I returned, she was finished with her journal and waiting for me. I sat down next to her.

"I suppose I oughta start a dream journal," I said. "I have some weird ones."

"I love the weird ones." She chuckled. "But yeah, I find the journal useful for seeing what's going on inside me over time."

I nodded. "I like that idea."

"Also, a lot of the time, writing it down brings out more details."

"I could sure use that this morning. I had a dream, and I can remember everything but the ending."

"Huh, so did I. Just before I woke up."

"Really?" My interest was instantly piqued. "That's when I had mine. Is that the one you were writing down?"

"Uh-huh."

"And did it help you remember the ending?"

She sighed in frustration and shook her head. "No. I was really hoping it would. I remember that you were in the dream and that there were orbs, but I can't remember the ending."

This startled me. "What? Mine was like that too. Except you were in it."

"Okay. Now it's getting a little freaky."

"No kidding."

She pushed her laptop toward me. "Here. I need to hear your thoughts about it."

"You don't mind?"

She laughed. "Of course not. It's not pornographic or anything."

"Damn," I said, pretending to be disappointed. I grinned as she slapped my arm.

"Just read it," she said, still laughing.

So I did.

⚬

I was walking along a dirt road in an area that was mostly sandy berms, with various types of trees scattered thinly across the area. I paused as I came to a rightward bend and noticed there was a ditch next to the road, on my left. It was only around ten feet long, and it was closed all around, with no outlet on any side. I wondered if it had been dug out—though I couldn't think of a purpose for it.

The woods were thicker on the ground above it, and I jumped over it to go stand under a giant spruce. Looking back, I saw that the ditch was now filled with dandelions, with big white seed heads. They made me feel childishly happy.

As I watched, all the seed pods detached from their stems and turned into orbs, hovering in their places. But one of them floated toward me, growing as it approached. When it reached me, it was the size of a volleyball, and I saw Arthur's face in it.

Then, from out of nowhere, a quiet voice spoke to me. It only said one word.

⚬

I was dumbfounded. I dropped back against the carved wood of the chair, staring at the computer screen but no longer seeing the words on it, my mouth agape. It took me a few seconds to gather my wits about me.

"I had the same dream," I finally stumbled out, in not much more than a mumble.

"You mean, one just like it?" Sari asked.

I shook my head, still focused in front of me. "Exactly like it. Identical in every way—except one. Mine had *your* face in the orb."

I looked at her; she was frowning. I knew exactly how she felt, because I felt the same way. We stared at each other until I could no longer stand the disturbed silence engulfing us.

"Is this even possible?" I asked.

She shrugged. "Apparently, it is."

"But what does it mean?"

"I don't know. We need that final word, I think."

"Yeah, I think you're right. It's the key to the dream."

"A lost key."

"Unfortunately."

We fell silent. When Sari spoke again, her voice kind of drifted, her words seemingly directed more to herself than to me.

"Well," she said, "we do have one resource we might try."

"What's that?"

She grinned. "We live with a witch."

CHAPTER 25

"WELL, I HAVE TO SAY, this is kind of an unusual request."

Sari and I had arranged to meet with Emily later that morning in her room, which was the second one in from the staircase, between Janis's and Sari's. It looked pretty much as I imagined it would—in a word, dark. From the carpet to the walls, black was the predominant theme. Blacklights bathed the air in an eerie, almost supernatural, purplish glow. An old black steamer trunk was pressed up against the wall to our right. An ornate chair set next to the opposite wall stood out, catching my eye. With red cushions, slender curved framing, and a crowned back, it looked regal. A carved dragon's head thrust itself out of the cross rail, its long neck curving upward to the base of the crown. The chair's wood was darker than the mahogany of the dining-room furniture downstairs; it was, no doubt, deeply stained. In front of the chair, which faced the door, stood a three-foot-square mahogany table supported by a single pedestal.

A portable DVD player had found a place on her night-stand. A Simple Minds CD was playing quietly—their

Gen X anthem, "Don't You (Forget About Me)." I felt the fine hairs on my neck stand up.

"But," Emily went on, placing a hand on Sari's forearm, "since it's you, I'll see what I can scrape up."

Sari smiled. "Thanks, sis."

"It's all Gucci. Y'know, I've never tried to recover a dream before." Emily sounded intrigued by the prospect. "I know of a spell that one group uses to retrieve faded memories. But dreams aren't memories in the same way as, like, knowing what you ate for lunch yesterday. They're not recollections of events but *symbols* of events that are being sorted through by the brain. They're doubly removed. They materialize out of the mind's ether, are remolded, and then disappear back into it. So I don't know if it would even be worth trying that spell.

"Besides," she added, her tone indicating that this next statement reflected what was really important to her, "like all magic, it's best to use what belongs to you. Trying to wield someone else's spell that may not 'like' you could be troublesome. We have to respect these things. The magic comes to us, not us to it.

"So I think I'd like to try a more subtle way of doing this. It's not magic but rather a form of divination. What I'm hoping is that it will provide enough insight that it will expand your understanding of the dream, and that, in turn, should cause you to spontaneously recall the word on your own." She shrugged. "Says here in the manual."

I chuckled. It wasn't often that Emily displayed her sense of humor, which tended to be dry and farcical. This was so unexpected, given her rather dour demeanor, that it seemed to make her jokes even funnier.

Sari and I glanced at each other, and I shrugged.

Then she nodded to Emily. "That'll work," she said.

"Sweet. I use the *I Ching*, a really, really old Chinese oracle. I mean, like, *three thousand years* old. And it's based on binary code, like a computer!" Emily almost sounded excited. "It's very intuitive, which is exactly what we're looking for. It won't give you an exact answer, but it can illuminate the dream for you. From there, it's up to you what you do with it."

I studied Sari's thought process as it was reflected in her facial expressions. Seeing what I was looking for, I said, "Let's do it."

Sari nodded.

"Cool," Emily said. "Talk to each other, and come up with a question for me to ask it. Try to make it as succinct as possible. If you can put it into less than a dozen words, that would be awesome. The more concise, the better."

She retreated across the room and sat down on the chair, giving us the meager amount of privacy the room afforded.

Sari and I spoke together in low voices.

At last I said to her, "Y'know, the orbs have our faces in them. So they're kind of like reflections."

She immediately caught on to where I was going with this. She nodded vigorously.

Having thus come to an agreement, we approached Emily.

"We'd like to know," Sari said, with a sidelong glance at me, "*what does this dream reflect?*"

"That's an excellent question! I love it. This'll take me about an hour. I'll meet you in the sitting room."

"Cool," I said.

I felt a bit antsy while waiting, and I think Sari did too, because we didn't talk much.

Fortunately, Emily showed up early, about forty minutes after we had left her.

"Well," she said, "this was interesting."

Sari and I exchanged glances. She asked Emily, "So what answer did you get?"

"What I got was Hexagram Eight, which represents unity. It said you two are connected with each other. Big duh, right? I mean, we all know that. But it's even deeper than I would have suspected. You two can't be separated. It's almost as if you were one person. Your lives are deeply entangled."

Sari and I shot excited glances at each other.

"That's it!" she exclaimed. "That's the word!"

I nodded briskly. "Yeah, it is." Relief flooded through me; I felt as if an enormous weight had been lifted off my body. This was accompanied by a sense of awe directed toward Emily. "You're amazing," I told her.

Emily flashed a grin, but it disappeared as she shrugged. "All I did was throw some sticks on a table."

CHAPTER 26

The following Wednesday, I finally got my first real ride in John's hot Z28. We were retracing the route Sari and I had taken to Art at the Cave, although we were to exit the freeway six miles south of the Interstate Bridge, well before crossing into Washington. We were on our way to the summer-long Beaches Cruise-In at Portland International Raceway.

"I always go on opening day," John had told me as we were making the final preparations for the Monday Lunch Crush at Flash Burger. "It's a huge deal around here. They donate all their proceeds to local charities. Somehow, they manage to pack a thousand cars onto the grass, all of them maintained by their owners. And then there's the drag races."

"They have drag races?" I couldn't keep the excitement out of my voice.

"Uh-huh."

That was the kicker for me.

So now, at three-thirty on Wednesday afternoon, we were headed north on I-5 in John's supercool ride, having taken the afternoon off from Flash Burger. He had had Car Toys install an after-market CD sound system—his one concession to modernizing the car—and it was currently blasting the soundtrack to *Top Gun*. Cheap Trick's "Mighty Wings" reverberated throughout the interior. The exhilarating vibration of the speeding vehicle thrummed in my body, and the driving beat of the music thrummed in my blood.

John's Camaro was a sport classic, designed specifically to compete with the Mustang. To me, it looked like it was always poised to pounce, like an alert cat. With its front and rear spoilers, its slotted headlight covers that opened by sliding behind the grill, and its cowl induction set between white racing stripes, it was a vehicle that still turned heads, and I was stoked to be seen in it.

The interior was not plush, but then, this was an old sports car, after all, not a modern luxury coupe. The dashboard was simple and compact, with large round gauges set into square receptacles. The passenger side of this was wood paneled. A T-handled Hurst shifter engaged a four-speed transmission. It was built for action, and it looked the part.

I mentioned these things to John in casual conversation. He seemed to be pleased by my interest and knowledge. I think he intended to sound nonchalant, but he couldn't keep the pride from creeping into his voice.

"Three-oh-two cubic inches," he said. "Four hundred effective horsepower. Centerforce Dual Friction clutch. Edelbrock fourteen-oh-six four-barrel."

"You didn't go with a Holley?" I asked.

He gave me a quick surprised glance.

"No," he said. "This is strictly a street vehicle."

I nodded.

"But she'll do zero to sixty in seven point four," John pressed on, sounding a little defensive. "Runs the eighth of a mile in nine-seven."

"Is that something you tested?" I teased, smiling.

He laughed. "Well, yeah, I did, actually. Couple of years ago, right here at the track."

"Awesome. Did you win?"

He pursed his lips. "Nope. Got blown away by a '67 'Vette running nine-three. I was totally outclassed. Might as well have been parked."

I chuckled, but in sympathy rather than pleasure.

"But at least you can say you did it."

"Yep. That's for sure, man. I did it." His voice drifted into silence, which seemed to hang in the air for a few seconds, despite the blasting stereo. When next he spoke again, it was with his usual self-assurance. "Y'know, for a kid who doesn't drive, you sure seem to know a lot about cars."

"It's *because* I wasn't allowed to drive that I'm so into them. The heart longs for what it can't have."

John smiled paternally. "You're too young to know stuff like that. It's a revelation kept hidden by us old fogeys. You haven't even learned the secret handshake yet."

I laughed but didn't address his comments. "I kept a stash of *HOT ROD Magazine* hidden in my room. With my father mostly ignoring me, and my tutor's promise not to say anything to him, it wasn't that hard to keep him from knowing about it. Still, it was a risk. He would've thrown them out if he'd found them."

I didn't mention the other things he would do.

"That sounds a little drastic," John said. "Why would he be upset about you having those? It's not like they're porn or something."

"It was just spite."

"Mm."

I turned my gaze to the passenger window and said a bit wistfully, "And now it's all gone, anyway."

"No," John said. I turned to him, so as to hear him better, and saw he was shaking his head. "Not all of it. You carry the best parts within you."

I studied him, not sure what to feel or say, so I said nothing.

I turned my attention forward again, now thinking about our relationship, which was unlike any I'd had with an adult before. My tutor had been cool, in her own way, but she was just a caretaker. I was coming to think of John as a kind of foster father, like one of those Big Brother dudes, so now I was trying to decide whether I was comfortable enough to approach him on an awkward topic. There was something I had wanted to know for some time, and now I felt a tugging to bring it up to him. I decided to take the chance.

"You can tell me to stay in my lane if you like," I said, "and I'll shut up. But I was wondering if I could ask you a personal question."

John glanced at me, an expectant and slightly amused smile forming on his face. "Shoot," he said.

"Well," I started hesitantly, twisting toward him as best I could under the restriction of seat belts, "I get this whole steez you've got going, and it's cool, okay? It's you, for sure. But to be honest, you seem like you should be trading stocks or something. How did someone like you get into running a food cart?"

John laughed. "You think I'm a square."

"Uh-uh. I know you're not. That's why it's bugging me."

He nodded. "You see me as a dichotomy. That's fair, I suppose. I used to be an accountant. CPA. Made a bunch of money, but I hated the job. Not only was it boring as hell, but I felt like all I was doing was helping rich people stay rich. I wanted something more, to be a part of things, instead of just drudging like a cog in a wheel. Then one day I was talking to the guy who used to own my cart, although it had a different name back then. He said he was looking to sell the thing. My ears perked up, and when he told me his asking price, I jumped and never looked back."

"So you're glad you did it?"

"Best decision of my life."

I thought about this as I readjusted myself in the seat to face forward again. "Thanks."

"You know you can come to me with anything, right? Never hesitate."

I nodded and fell silent.

A few minutes later, John steered us onto the racetrack offramp. We followed a circuitous, half-mile-long route to the temporary parking area, where we then boarded one of the shuttlebuses that took us to the showgrounds. They weren't free, but since we were going to be standing for several hours, we had decided earlier to use them. Even a short prolonging of the time spent off our feet would prove beneficial. I was happy John was willing to splurge.

When he had offered to pay my way, I demurred, feeling that I should fend for myself. My father would never have taken me to an event like this, so I was grateful to John for even inviting me.

But he gave me a paternal squeeze on my shoulder and said, "What's family for?"

He couldn't have chosen better words.

We waited in a moderately protracted line to pay the entry fees at one of the makeshift wooden gates before pushing our way into the crowd. It was hard to avoid bumping into people. The huge exhibition field was packed with cars, and lined on one side with souvenir, food, and children's game booths. There was even a bouncy house. The pungent smoke of barbecue filled the air, along with the music of the country-rock band Flexor T.

Beyond the grass, the roar of engines rose up from behind a thick line of tall trees as the qualifying drag races began. I imagined this din as an entity in and of itself, a great growling beast looming over the grounds, dominating all other sounds.

I felt euphoric in this heady atmosphere, as if lifted off my feet.

"Let's see what they have to eat," John suggested.

"That's what *I'm* talkin' about."

We followed the enticing smell of woodsmoke to a barbecue booth and waited for the two customers ahead of us to be served. There was nowhere to sit, so we ate standing, as everyone else was doing.

Then we turned to our purpose for being here. Gazing around at the ocean of vehicles expertly positioned across the grass of the exhibition field, I felt slightly overwhelmed.

"Jeez," I said. "Do we have time for all of this?"

John laughed. "No. No way. We'll look at the cars we're most interested in and ignore the others. The trick is knowing which cars we want to linger over."

"How can we do that if we don't check all of them out?"

John wagged his index finger at me. "There you go being logical again."

I grinned and flashed him the Vulcan salutation.

We spent three and a half hours wandering through the tightly packed but remarkably well-aligned rows. We inspected street-racing cars equipped with Hilborn fuel injectors, tunnel rams, turbochargers, and even one with a nitrous oxide system. Not all of them were intended for speed, though. Most were being displayed for their depth of care, their unusual styling, or pure nostalgic value. All the vehicles there were in pristine condition, although some of the oldest ones couldn't hide all of their wear-and-tear. There were also a few odder ones that looked like their owners had designed and built them from scratch. Paint jobs were often deeply multilayered, some in bright, even garish, colors. A few sported hand-drawn designs. Shining chrome bumpers on the older vehicles flashed in the sun. The collection sported flamboyantly decorated interiors and intricate wheel designs, decals, and interior statuary. And the majority, regardless of age, appeared brand new, as if they had been built right here on the grass the night before.

Around six forty-five or so, we decided it was time to head over to the track for the drag eliminations. I felt torn, reluctant to leave the show, but really wanted to watch the races. I made note of as many vehicles as I could as we made our way across the lawn and even allowed myself a final lingering backward glance as we left the field.

I was thrilled when we found places on the bleachers just a little past midway along the strip. While there were a lot of people on the uncomfortable benches, we arrived just as another group was leaving. From our vantage point, the cars passing us on the hot asphalt straightaway, shimmering beyond the concrete barriers and chain link fencing, would reach their highest speeds, and if I stood up, I could just make out the finish line.

The anticipation I had felt on the drive out there returned with the first duel we watched. The realization that these speeds were being achieved by nonprofessional drivers, most of whom had worked on their own vehicles to get them into this shape, made it all the more amazing to me. It was incredibly exciting, and right from the beginning, I felt like I belonged there.

After each of the closer competitions, I found myself glancing at John to catch his reaction. He had a seldom-seen gleam in his eyes, which was the equivalent for him to what shouting was for me. He was definitely into this, but there was something more there too. This narrow highway to nowhere was the same one down which he himself had hurtled in his orange Camaro two years ago. I sensed he was itching to be out there again. To have just one more opportunity to put everything he had into beating a sliver of time on the clock.

And I found myself wishing I could have been there for him back then, at the side of this track as we were now, cheering him on even as he lost by less than half a second, one paltry little blip on the clock, a measure of time so achingly short but which might as well have been eternity. And for a brief flash, I shared his exhilaration and disappointment, the conflicting emotions roiling within me, just as they must have done in him. As this feeling welled up inside me, we glanced at each other, and I realized that John was feeling the nostalgia too.

As we turned our attention back to the races, I sighed with deep contentment, even as I was struck by a sudden realization: I had never before felt closer to any adult in my life.

When our six-hour adventure inevitably ended and we were approaching John's car in the late gloaming, he dangled his keys in front of me.

"Take us home," he said.

CHAPTER 27

"LET'S TAKE A WALK TO the Saturday Market," Sari suggested the following weekend.

Sari drove us to the lot under the Morrison Bridge because she anticipated there being a lot of people coming downtown today and it was much larger than her usual venues. The chances of finding a space were best there. Plus, it was perfectly situated for our purpose, being across the street from the river and only half a mile south of the Burnside Bridge, which was our ultimate destination. As it turned out, she found a spot right next to where I had sacked down my first night here. As a result, emerging from the car, I stood on what was tantamount to holy ground for me.

This was my first return to the lot since my arrival in Portland. Although I had spent a good amount of time in the area, I had never actually set foot in the lot itself. I had no real reason to do so. But today I found myself contemplating this space for a few seconds, wondering how things might have turned out if I had snagged a different ride at Mount Shasta. I quickly decided I didn't really want to think about that.

When I came out of my reverie and finally closed the car door, I noticed Sari gazing at me with a look of sympathetic understanding on her face. I smiled ruefully and shrugged.

We crossed the lot diagonally to the corner of Morrison and Naito, where the pedestrian signal changed in our favor as soon as we arrived. Quickly but awkwardly scissoring our legs over the metal guardrail to get to the sidewalk, we ran across the street, hand-in-hand and laughing like children, to the park's lawn, barely beating the light. From there we walked across the grass to the broad sidewalk that would lead us north to the market.

"I was so lucky to meet you," I said.

"I told you, that wasn't luck. We were meant to be. Even the fortune-telling gods say so." She laughed.

I considered before asking my next question. "How did you know this, anyway?"

She didn't answer right away; I got the impression she was reluctant to tell me. She rocked her head slightly side to side, pursing her lips as she weighed her words. At last, she took a deep breath, as if what she was about to say took as much preparation as it would to dive into a swimming pool.

"In my junior year, my Witch House friend invited me to a party being thrown by one of the rich girls in the area. Her parents were gone for a long weekend, and it was supposed to be a really big deal. She lived on a hay farm. Lots of land, so it was very private. No way was I in her clique; she didn't even go to my school. There were going to be lots of bougies there, as well as a few outcasts—just so she could show how cool she was. My friend got in for being weird, and I basically tagged along."

She giggled.

"So there I was, immersed in all the wild goings-on. I stood out as the only hipster, and some dude noticed I wasn't drinking much and offered me some Ambien. Said it would mellow me out, help me get into the scene. I figured, why not? Turned out, I liked it." She laughed.

"Don't tell me you got hooked on Ambien."

"Not *hooked*. I just took it sometimes."

"For fun."

"Of course, for fun." She frowned at me. "Don't be a square. It wasn't that big a deal."

I raised my hands, warding off her displeasure. "No, no. Not at all. It's just…it's just that it's not you. You've got your shit so together."

She gave me a wicked smile. "You didn't know me when I was in high school. It would blow your mind."

I decided that, at least for the time being, I wouldn't ping her any more on this. But I was beginning to understand why Sari had left quiet, rural Hillsboro for Portland. The freewheeling city was a better fit for her underground personality—so underground that even I hadn't suspected it.

"I believe you," I said. "Cool."

"All right. Where was I? Oh yeah. So anyway, after that, my friend and I started seeking out pharm parties together. I'd buy a few pills and stretch them out over a month. One time, a dude talked me into buying a twelve mil, and *wham!* I was gone!" She laughed. "When I finally woke up, I discovered I'd done a painting."

"The Walrus strikes again." I grinned. "Y'know, I think I like this side of you."

Sari shook her head. "I don't do that stuff anymore. Not since I moved into Carl's. I don't need to."

"Right. But that girl is still in there."

She playfully slapped my arm. "Stop that," she said, giggling. "*Any*way, thing is, the painting was about you."

I felt the hairs on my neck rise. "About me? How could that be?"

"It wasn't *a portrait* of you, of course. Remember, I'm an abstract artist. I spontaneously paint jumbles of images and forms without thinking about them, producing whatever happens to move my hand. But this one was different. It was the only one I've ever done that had a fully recognizable object in it. But that object was also a symbol, and I intuitively recognized its meaning. I've been waiting for you ever since."

I thought about the crow painting I'd sneaked a glance at, and wondered if I should tell her I'd done that. I was very reluctant to do so, but I also knew that our relationship could not be built on hiding things from each other. So I sucked it up, hoping against hope.

"Um, I think I know what painting you're talking about."

She frowned, puzzled. "How could you know that?"

"Well, your door was open one morning, and I, um, kinda took a glance around."

Sari laughed. "So you're a Peeping Tom!"

"I'm sorry," I said, chagrined. "I shouldn't have invaded your privacy like that."

"Open doors are not private. You don't need to be embarrassed. So which painting did you see?"

"The crow."

She stopped dead, surprising me. I had gone a step farther and had to turn back. "And you knew it was about *you*?" she said.

"Yeah." Very quickly, I summarized the significant part of my Victorian preacher dream, emphasizing the crow shadow. I decided I didn't need to go into my ibogaine vision.

"For real? Hashtag insane. Emily was more right about us than I think even she realized."

"But why a crow?"

"Once again, Emily could give us a better idea. But crows have always been considered kind of exceptional creatures. They're hella smart. There's lots of spiritual and magical lore about them."

As she spoke, a flash of movement behind her caught my eye. I nodded over her shoulder to indicate it. "Speaking of which."

Sari turned to see what I was referring to. A crow had stepped off the grass and was now standing on the sidewalk, gazing at us.

"Huh," was all she said.

"C'mon." I took her hand. "Let's keep going."

Sari reluctantly turned, and we continued walking. We were almost to the Burnside Bridge, where the market was held.

She glanced back again after we'd taken a few steps.

"It's following us."

"Maybe it's out for a walk too."

"They don't do stuff like that. It's really weird."

"Meh. Crows are always weird."

"It's creepy. Besides," she added, "they're very skittish, and they usually avoid people."

"I think you're reading too much into this."

"One way to find out."

Sari suddenly tightened her grip on my hand and pulled me along the sidewalk at a half run. It took me a few steps to match her pace, tipping me slightly off-balance.

Then she stopped hard again. Using her foot as a pivot point, she let go of me and spun around. I turned more slowly.

The crow was just landing, about four steps behind us on the sidewalk, and it stared at us, alternating from looking at one to the other. Right into my eyes, making my skin crawl. I half expected the bird to explode, as the one had done during my trip.

"Okay," I said slowly. "This is officially spooky."

"Tell me about it."

I shrugged. "But what can we do? Let's just go to the market, okay?"

"Sure, we'll just pretend everything is normal. Nothing to see here."

Regardless of her attitude, she continued walking with me. Neither of us looked back again, but I didn't need to. I could feel the bird's presence behind us, making my hackles rise.

It was inevitable that we would now notice every crow we came across. They were always around whenever I was here, congregating on the lawn, where they pecked in the grass and strutted around seemingly aimlessly. But as we got closer to the bridge, a handful of them began lining up, just at the edge of the sidewalk. Standing quietly, watching us pass by.

"No." Sari shook her head vehemently. "This isn't happening. I refuse to be sucked into a Hitchcock flick."

"They're not doing anything." I had meant to be reassuring, but too late I realized this was a disingenuous thing for me to say, considering that I was being creeped out too. But that was the whole point. I was trying to alleviate my own fears as much as hers.

"They're *staring*."

Yes, they were. I couldn't deny this. And now people were too, commenting about it among each other and watching us with curiosity. I wanted to shrink into a ball and disappear.

Still, I couldn't stop myself from making a quick check for our original little friend. I swallowed hard as I saw that he was not only still keeping pace but had also been joined by two others.

At last, we arrived at the square that hosted the Saturday Market. I was glad to get there because there was a substantial crowd, and I figured we could lose our avian shadows in the milieu.

At the south end of the plaza stood a large fountain gushing volumes of arcing water. As with most of the city's fountains, children loved to splash in it. I took comfort in seeing them, engaged in a normal activity on a day that had become far from normal for me—as so many days had been since I'd arrived here.

A very tall, lanky man—his unkempt silver-white hair looking as if he took no more care of it than to sweep it back with his hand every morning—was standing in front of the fountain, shouting angrily, addressing a small group of curious bystanders. When I first heard his voice, I thought he might be one of those unfortunate deranged men, who I encountered on the streets every so often, in need of genuine mental care they were unable to obtain.

I sucked in a breath, bolstering myself, as I anticipated receiving direction from the Man in White to heal him. But it didn't take me long to realize that was not coming.

The man's powder-blue sport coat, a relic from the 1970s, looked incongruous among the summer-garbed crowd. His whole appearance was haggard, as if he had lived a hard life. To say his shoulders were slumped would be an understatement. His long neck was angled almost perpendicular to the ground so that his head appeared to hang like a lantern off it. His voice, while surprisingly strong, was hoarse from shouting. Or maybe from age. Or both. Yet he was, nonetheless, filled with frenetic energy. He gesticulated wildly, an open Bible hefted in his left hand, his voice rising whenever he grew especially agitated.

Of course, I thought, rolling my eyes. He was an itinerant street preacher.

Losing interest, I glanced around the square for our corvid friends. There were more of them than before, standing under the trees just off the concrete, apparently taking in the scene like we were. Their odd behavior once again made the small hairs on my neck stand on end.

The man's audience—most of whom, I guessed from their body language, were curiosity seekers rather than genuinely interested parties—stood in random clusters before him. I felt no desire to join them. Sari and I slowed for a few steps to rubberneck as we crossed the square, but we quickly refocused our attention on our destination.

The preacher suddenly fell silent. In fact, the entire world dropped away, just as it had the first time the Man in White had spoken to me. And out of this silence came an unusual pronouncement from him.

"Behold your Beatrice."

Then I was back in the real world filled with sound and light and movement. Sari had stopped walking as I did, and her gaze was now fixed on the preacher—whose own face was filled with rage. But she looked serene. Serene, steadfast, and resolute.

Hefting his big black Bible into the air, he pointed a shaky finger at me, shouting, "I *see* you! I *know* you!"

I had no idea what to make of this. People turned, searching for the target of his wrath. This, of course, did nothing to reduce the fear and discomfort that was growing in me. It only added to my desire to run away, but I was rooted to the spot.

"You son of the devil!" the man screamed. "I know your evil works! God knows where you come from! The gates of hell have been opened!"

And on the word *opened*, the preacher launched himself into the crowd. Taken totally by surprise, people scrambled to make way for him.

Sari's grip on my hand tightened, and the power rose within me. But I felt no prodding to do anything.

The psychotic man broke through the last row of bystanders but only made it halfway to us when, without warning, he was divebombed by half a dozen crows.

Blindsided, he ducked and waved his arms in a mad attempt to fend them off. But the birds were relentless. They screamed and bit and flapped in an orgy of avian violence, as Sari and I stood—along with dozens of other people—with mouths agape, unable to believe what we were seeing. Failing utterly to ward off this assault, the preacher finally shielded his head with his Bible and ran out of the square, the birds trailing after him as he crossed Naito Parkway. Fortunately for him, the light was in his favor.

As I watched him disappear beyond the fire station, my breathing and heartbeat slowly settled back into their normal rhythms.

The people stood gawking just like we were, muttering among themselves, until, at last, they began dispersing and going about their business.

Sari released her grip on me, and we stared at each other. Awe, wonder, and confusion wrestled within me, and I could see it in her face as well. When I finally regained my composure, I said the only thing I was capable of saying in that moment.

"What. The. Fuck."

CHAPTER 28

" We have to tell the others," Sari said robotically, her tone flat.

Her voice startled me out of an uneasy reverie. We were in her car, driving west along Clay Street, about halfway home.

We had left the market square as soon as we came to our senses, and walked quickly, not speaking during our return to the parking lot. I can only assume on Sari's part, but for me, I was too rattled by what we'd just witnessed to be able to discuss it coherently.

Now, her quiet voice breaking the silence between us jolted me out of my befuddled thoughts, my mental gears grinding as they switched to her subject.

"We can't just let this go," she went on. "Something happened here. Something out of the ordinary. Something *paranormal*. It's too much to ignore."

She was right, of course. We did need to inform our housemates—or at the very least, Carl and John.

I had resisted telling anyone about the Man in White, right from my first encounter with him as "the Voice," because, frankly, I was too scared to reveal the things that were happening to me. I told myself I was worried about what others' reactions might be. Deeper down, though, I knew I was afraid for my mental health. Now it seemed he had decided to reveal himself, obliquely, giving me no choice.

"Okay," I said quietly. "You're right. But there's a lot we need to talk about first. It's even weirder than you think, and you need to take it all in to really get it."

She flashed me an intense yet expectant look. Quickly turning her attention back to the road, she nodded. "Okay."

Cautiously answering her interjected questions, but not volunteering any more information than I had to, I recounted the events I'd experienced since coming here. I started with reminding her of my perceptual blending with her while on the mushroom, then moved on to the girl at Teachers Fountain, my recognition of the Man in White—and the presence of the crow—on my ibogaine trip, and my healing of the man in the park, and I finished with the events at the homeless camp.

But I didn't talk about the more personal events, such as my encounter with the transient at the river on April Fool's Day, my horror walk in the labyrinth, and my scrying of the Wheel. Nor did I discuss my deep feelings and concerns about the things that had happened to me, that *were* happening to me. For one thing, I was still processing it all and wasn't ready to expose myself emotionally like that yet. Plus, she didn't actually need to know that stuff. So I merely gave her the essential facts.

Even so, all of this took longer than it did for us to get home, so we sat in the car, parked in front of the house, until I was finished.

Then I slumped back in my seat, as if it had taken all my energy to get this out. She remained still and quiet for a full minute. I also waited silently, my emotions roiling, as I struggled to shove my anxiety down. I desperately needed to hear her response yet was scared of what it was going to be.

"So," she said at last. "You hear some kind of voice in your head."

"Actually, it seems to come from everywhere at once. In my head is only where I put it into actual words." That still didn't sound right to me, but it was as close as I could come to an accurate description.

"Do you hear it now?"

"No. It seems to have a specific purpose when it appears. Otherwise, it's silent."

"And it leads you to people, who you then heal by touching them."

"Yeah. Except that now, I think, something is supposed to change."

"Why do you say that?"

I shook my head. "I don't know. He spoke to me just before the crows attacked, but I don't understand what he told me. He said something about a Beatrice."

Sari whipped her head around, alarmed, and studied my face, her eyes narrowed. "We were holding hands."

"Well, yeah."

"And I felt energy flowing then."

"Yeah. Energy flows—" Suddenly, what she had said hit me. I bolted upright and gaped at her. "Energy flowed *back and forth between us!*"

We were both breathing hard now. A mixture of emotions was roiling within me: astonishment, wonder, and fear. I could see the same cauldron bubbling in her eyes.

At last, Sari spoke, and her words, intoned like an incantation, caused the small hairs on my neck to stand up.

"Behold your Beatrice."

"Holy crap! You heard that?"

She nodded. "Yeah." She turned numbly in her seat and stared blankly out through the windshield again. "Yeah, I did."

I swallowed to gain some emotional control and then asked her, "Do you know what it means?"

She nodded. "Dante's *Inferno*. Beatrice leads Dante into paradise." She shifted uncomfortably and appeared to be gathering her thoughts before continuing. "I always knew that the crow in my painting was a harbinger of you. But I made a mistake. I thought it was symbolic of your mission. But it's actually symbolic of *mine*."

I was blown away—again. Immediately, the preacher from my Victorian dream spoke in my head: *"The bird is in the woman, and the woman is in the bird."*

Wrestling with overwhelming emotions, I asked, my voice cracking slightly, "And what is your mission?"

She looked at me, and her face was now calm, her voice confident, her steady gaze holding mine with clear eyes. She smiled reassuringly.

"To take on the role of your Man in White. I will guide you now."

CHAPTER 29

Two weeks later, I felt a kind of pressure in my solar plexus, urging me to go to the parlor. By this time, I had learned to listen to promptings like this one.

I had, up to now, not experienced anything on my own like the dream I'd had with Melanie there. I was, honestly, glad to have avoided that weirdness for a while. But now I wanted to experience it again. *"Dream of the '90s,"* I reminded myself with a slight chuckle, thinking back to my first weekend here.

Pleased to find the room unoccupied this afternoon, I pulled a parlor chair around to face the fireplace and settled myself comfortably in it. Then, fixing my gaze in the depths of the wood-ash-smeared pit, I let my eyes lose focus.

Let my mind drift.

Let my defenses down.

Let myself go.

I'm standing in a large cavern. There is little light, but I'm still able to see.

An older woman, dark-skinned and a bit heavyset, dressed in a kind of tunic or robe, enters from behind me and passes by on my left. She is holding a half-inch-thick wooden dowel. She uses this to draw three six-inch-long red lines in a row on the back wall, all evenly spaced. They look like they were made with a thick crayon. There are many other groups of such lines around the cavern, each made up of different quantities. I understand her to be marking the passage of time, the way inmates in a prison cell might do. There is a feeling of deep antiquity about this work, something sacred, like prehistoric cave paintings. Her movements are ritualistic. She is silent and does not look at me.

I was startled out of this dream by the sound of laughter. As had happened with Melanie, I was immediately alert to my surroundings again. I twisted in the chair to see Sari about halfway across the room, walking toward me.

"Trying to start a fire with your Superman heat vision?" she asked.

I smiled ruefully. "I was trying to see if I could enter the Dream of the Room again."

"Ah. And did you?"

I frowned. "Yeah. But it was different than when Melanie and I did it."

"You two dreamed with the room together? Cool. When?"

"A few weeks after I got here. Although I didn't do it on purpose."

She laughed again as she walked around behind me to stand to the left side of my chair. "Melanie loves to do that. The room tailors its dreams to the individual, but if more than one person enters at the same time, it produces a complex dynamic that can be manipulated by an experienced dreamer. She probably drew you into hers."

"I kinda suspected that, actually."

"So now you have your own dream with the room."

"Seems that way."

"Very cool."

"If I can ever figure out what it means." I laughed.

"Keep at it. It'll come to you." Her tone abruptly changed, becoming more nonchalant. "Anyway," she said, dropping a folded white-paged tabloid into my lap. "You're all the buzz, dude."

Street Roots was a weekly publication put out by a homeless advocacy group, devoted to articles on social justice and environmental issues. They employed homeless people to sell copies on street corners every Friday, the day it was published. A success story about one of these salespeople appeared in every issue.

I peered at the page she had opened to. The headline all but shouted at me. "Mystery Friend," it announced.

I shook my head. "What's this about?"

"Go ahead and read it," Sari said, pulling up another chair. "I'll wait. It's short."

I turned my attention back to the article. *"Who is this strange young savior who is causing a stir throughout the city's most vulnerable?"* it began.

I almost gagged on the words, whipping my head around to scrutinize Sari's face. She merely shrugged. I quickly read the quarter-page article.

"Holy crap," I said.

"Holy crap, indeed," she said. "You're famous. Famous—but unknown." She laughed. "You're Batman!"

I shook my head and rolled my eyes. "Sure, why not?" Then, making a clownish face and mimicking a Valley Girl voice, I rocked my head side to side while singsong-ingly saying, "*I'll* be Bat-man."

Sari slapped my hand. "You're silly."

"That's what you love about me."

She beamed at me. "You've really broken free since you got here. You were a downer when you walked into Java Man. It's so awesome to see you become this."

"I guess I spent a lot of years hiding from who I am. But you opened my heart."

"Aw, you're so sweet."

She leaned into me, and I put my arm around her.

I motioned to the paper.

"I wonder how this will affect what we're doing."

"Dude, this article will be read by everyone in the city who supports the homeless. And a lot of the homeless themselves. It's going to make us huge."

I grimaced as fear shot through me. "Not so sure I want to be huge."

"It comes with the territory. Don't worry, I'll be right beside you. I'll hog the cameras."

We laughed.

She continued, "But now we have no choice left. We really do need to tell the others."

I nodded. "Yeah, I guess we should. How do you want to go about it?"

"Oh, you know me," she said, tracing my bare arm with her index finger and looking sidelong up at me. "I'll be subtle."

CHAPTER 30

T HE NEXT MORNING, I AWOKE with midsummer's dawn light pressing through the glass of my bedroom's knee-to-head-height window, imbuing a quarter-inch-thick layer of air on this side of the curtains with a tinge of the latter's Egyptian-blue fabric, which quickly faded to gray and then black the farther into the room it penetrated.

I twisted onto my right side and hit the digital clock's off button, noting idly that it was two minutes before six o'clock. This was unsurprising; I'd been waking just before my alarm was set to go off for some time now.

Then I rolled back into the covers and closed my eyes again, my mind a freefalling jumble of memories, hopes, and fears. The most pressing of these, of course, was the nervous anticipation of disclosing all the things I'd been through to John and Carl.

I lay like that for ten minutes before finally deciding to get up. With a sigh, I rolled out of bed and readied myself for the day before heading downstairs for some breakfast.

I spotted John sitting at the dining-room table, drinking coffee while reading a newspaper he had spread out before him on the flat surface. I was not surprised to see him there; he was part of the minority of us house members who regularly got up early. But I *was* surprised about the newspaper. He wasn't much of one for keeping up with current events.

I wasn't very hungry, so I just grabbed cereal and coffee and joined him, selecting the chair diagonally across from where he was sitting, allowing him space so he could continue his reading.

"Morning," he said.

"Hey, John."

As I settled in, I saw that it was not the local news he was reading, but *Street Roots*. He let me get arranged before pushing it aside and turning to me.

"Interesting article in there," he said nonchalantly.

"Yeah, I guess so. I didn't know you read that."

"I don't, normally. But it was sitting on the table when I came in, open to that page."

So that's *what she means by* "subtle," I thought. I almost laughed but managed to keep it to a snort. "So what did you think about it?"

"I was wondering the same thing about you." He smiled.

I chuckled. "I have a lot to say about it. Do you have some time?"

"As much as you need."

"Sweet. I'd rather do it in the sitting room, though. It's more private."

"Sure."

I stuffed two bites of cereal into my mouth and then dropped the spoon into the bowl.

"You can finish that first," John said. "I have plenty of time."

"Nah," I said, the word muffled in the Froot Loops. I chewed rapidly and swallowed. "That's okay, I'd rather get this over with. I've waited too long as it is."

"Whatever you like."

We got up from the table and ambled to the sitting room at the far end of the hall, closing the door behind us. John motioned for me to take the easy chair that was against the wall, then tugged the other one around to the left side of the coffee table. He sat down, crossing his legs.

"This way," he explained, "it won't feel like an interrogation."

I nodded, appreciating this gesture, but I couldn't relax. I hunched forward and clasped my hands.

"I'm really sorry," I said, "for not coming to you sooner about this. But I couldn't bring myself to do it. Things were too weird, and sometimes I wasn't even sure that they were actually happening. At times it felt like a dream; sometimes I thought I was going crazy. But now things are changing rapidly, and you really need to know what's going on."

"That's all right. Everything in its own time."

"Cool. Thank you." I paused to gather my thoughts. "Something happened to me on my mushroom trip. Whenever I touched Sari's skin, I would see things through her eyes. I mean, like, if she was looking at me, I would see myself. But I'd also still see her and everything around us. From both perspectives, all at the same time."

John's eyebrows rose. "That must have been rather dizzying."

"You don't know the half of it." I chuckled. "But after a while, I kinda got into it."

"I've never even heard of such a thing before."

"That's what I figured, because as far as I could tell, no one else was experiencing it—not even her. So I was living in a private hall of mirrors all through that night, until I came down."

John frowned. "You didn't appear to be having a bad trip," he said. "I kept an eye on you, and you seemed to be handling it all quite well."

"I didn't have a bad trip. I liked it a lot. I mean, I *loved* it. It was the freest thing I'd ever done in my life. And the next morning was even better. Calmer, with—well, I guess I would call it a more spiritual experience. I felt like I was connected to everything."

"The mushroom can do that for you."

"I guess so. But I really think there's more to it than just the mushroom. The stuff you just finished reading about, I don't know for sure if it's related, but the timing is at least suspicious, in my opinion. Anyway, I was walking home from work a week later when I heard a voice speaking to me from out of nowhere. When it did, it was like the entire world around me just disappeared. This voice was the only thing I was aware of. I automatically stopped walking. And breathing. And thinking."

I paused for a second to gauge John's reaction to this. But he remained stoic and unreadable.

"This voice," I continued, "sent me off my route to a teenage girl who was obviously in some kind of deep mental or emotional trouble. Disturbingly deep. And it had me heal her."

"How did you do that?"

"I didn't consciously do anything. All I did was take her hand, and a kind of energy just passed from me into her."

John merely nodded.

"Since then," I went on, "this voice has been putting me into contact with people with different kinds of illnesses and problems, and having me heal them. The last time, there was a whole group of them. I was even healing more than one at a time, as people touched me on their own."

I decided not to talk about my embarrassing reaction to being pressed like that.

"Huh," John said. "The paper doesn't give you enough credit."

"*I'm* not doing anything. But this isn't the end of the story."

"Okay."

"In my ibogaine trip, I met a powerful man in a white suit, who—"

John suddenly jerked to attention, throwing me off my train of thought. I studied him for a few seconds, waiting for him to speak, but he just gestured for me to continue.

"Well, he talked to me about my destiny, although he was pretty cryptic about it. In fact, I have no idea what he was talking about; I didn't get him. I still don't. Anyway, the thing is, it was his voice that I've been hearing."

"The Magician," John mumbled to himself, although loud enough for me to catch it. Then he addressed me. "He's the master of dreams, the archetype of visions. It's astounding that he would come to you so soon."

"You sound like you expected this or something."

"I did. Well, not the healing part. I find that quite interesting, actually. But meeting the Magician is an important part of your journey, although it's usually a much later one." He fell quiet, appearing to be considering something. At last, he spoke again. "I knew you'd be special. That you'd be an eager student, open and willing, and wouldn't balk at the hard stuff. But even more importantly, that you would *act* on the things you were being taught. That you would absorb them, assimilate them, become them. And that you would be exceptional."

"You decided all this at dinner?" I said this half-jokingly, with a nervous laugh. But his words scared me, and that's what I was actually trying to conceal. "How could you possibly do that?"

John offered me a namaste bow as he said with a grin, "Transpersonal psychology, at your service." But he immediately became serious again. "I want you to talk to Carl. Right now."

I nodded. "I want to do that."

"Good. I'll go up and see if he can take a moment with you. Please stay here. I'll come for you when he's ready."

"Cool." But I didn't feel cool.

After John left, I suddenly realized I had forgotten to mention Sari's new role. I became ticked at myself, but there was nothing I could do about it now.

I spent the time pacing and trying to convince myself that everything was going to be all right. I didn't totally succeed before John returned.

"Go ahead up," he said. My apprehension must have been apparent, because he smiled reassuringly. "Don't worry. He won't bite."

I laughed, again a bit nervously.

Carl's personal study was located in the eastern gable on the third floor. Like the television room in the other wing, it was spacious; unlike that one, it was elegantly appointed, with cherry paneling and muted green drapes cradling the double picture windows behind his large mahogany desk on the north wall.

He spent his morning hours in this room, preparing for the transpersonal counseling sessions he held with clients throughout the workweek. Although he was not a fully licensed psychologist, he was permitted to pursue this line of work under the state's laws regulating alternative therapies, as it incorporated the holotropic breathing practices for which he was certified. He kept an office in the Pearl District—with its high-end cafés, hot nightspots, specialty stores, and the famed Powell's Books—where he drew a clientele who, in the 1980s, would have been called "yuppies." These well-off young people believed that their coolness factor was raised by their being associated with a bona fide guru. And Carl, for his part, was pleased to be regarded in this manner.

When I entered, closing the door softly behind me, he gestured to the only other chair in the room besides his leather swivel one—a utilitarian green-upholstered visitor's seat that was positioned precisely centered to the desk. He started speaking before I was fully settled.

"I only have one request of you," he said in his calm, level voice. "I'd like us to share a Likemind together. You are to provide the target, if you're willing."

I was surprised by this; it was not what I was expecting. But after everything that had happened to me in this place, I was no longer afraid to open myself up like that.

"Sure," I said.

"I want your target to be spontaneous. Don't mull it over; just hold on to the very first thing that comes to your mind."

"Okay."

"Let's start."

I readjusted myself on the uncomfortable chair, sitting up straighter and placing my feet solidly on the carpet to help me focus and become more inwardly attentive. Relaxing my body and closing my eyes, I took a few deep, slow breaths to clear my thoughts.

As soon as I succeeded, an image formed in my mind.

At the exact same moment, Carl said, "It's a coiled snake."

My eyes flew open in shock. I had never watched Carl read someone's mind before. Normally, he merely acted as a moderator for the rest of us or as the target himself, as he had for me on my first night here. Nor had I ever seen any of my housemates even come close to succeeding this fast. Not even Harold. So I had always assumed that the process worked the same way for everyone.

But Carl's mind moved at light speed, blowing me away.

I was dazzled by this display of personal power, and my admiration for Carl skyrocketed. I have to admit, he also scared me a little. It took me a moment to find my voice.

"Yeah," I said weakly.

"Bright green, kind of glowing."

I just shook my head slowly in wonder, my mouth agape.

"Snakes," he continued, "are symbols of transformation and healing. The brightness and vibrancy of this one indicates that its skin has just been shed, meaning that a stage of your growth has been completed. Things will be different now."

I nodded, thinking of Sari taking the place of the Man in White. For a fleeting second, I wondered if he knew about this. At this point, I wouldn't be surprised.

Carl's dark eyes—those almost totally black eyes, those infinitely deep wells—bored into mine. "Think of this meeting as your anointing."

I considered his words, and suddenly, something dawned on me.

He continued to gaze at me, steadily, calmly, serenely, from out of the depths of his being. His eyes seemed to swallow me whole. But for the first time, I didn't shrink away from him, didn't cast my own gaze aside. I also remained steady and calm, as a deep assurance filled my entire being.

"You knew, didn't you?" I said. "Right from the start."

His reply was casual, a tossing-off of words that actually held a meaning far richer than what they normally would signify, coming from anyone else. "I had an inkling."

I released a breath I hadn't realized I was holding and sank back into the chair. A great weight fell off my shoulders, only to be instantly replaced with another one. But this new one was not a burden. It was a privilege.

Carl said, "That is all I have this morning."

I nodded and stood up. "Thank you, Carl. For everything."

Carl had me leave the door open as I left.

On my way back to the staircase, I pondered what had just happened. This entire morning was just blowing me away.

Reaching the meditation room door, I almost bumped into Sari as she stepped into the hallway. My surprise at seeing her mingled with the happiness that rose within me.

"Hey," I said.

She smiled sheepishly. "Guess it's my turn," she said.

I frowned. "He asked for you?"

"Yeah."

"Huh."

"What's up?"

I shook my head dismissively. "Doesn't matter. I'll tell ya later."

I stepped aside to let her pass, and I watched as she made her way down the hall, wondering how John had known to confer with her.

After I heard the door close, I headed back downstairs. John was nowhere to be seen, so I figured our meeting was officially over. I stood wondering what I should do next. Then I remembered my unfinished breakfast, so I sat down at the dining table, now alone, and ate soggy Froot Loops.

CHAPTER 31

Now that I had the house's full blessing for the work I had been given, along with recognition from the city, I felt more confident entering with Sari into this new phase of my life. I was thrilled to have her as my partner, my guide, my Beatrice.

She was not of a mind to waste time, so two days later, I found myself standing beside her on the corner of Third Avenue and Burnside Street, about five blocks north of Flash Burger. Old Town's western limits were just two blocks from the Pearl, that trendy part of the city. But the neighborhood we were in was close to a hundred-and-fifty years old and considerably less ritzy, extending along the river from the Broadway Bridge to the Hallock-McMillan Building.

We had situated ourselves in the shade of a large tree that had been planted in the sidewalk next to the Wax Building, from which we were surreptitiously observing a line of bedraggled people, some with huge piles of ragtag possessions and others with nothing at all, huddled on the sidewalk along the brick wall of the Union Gospel Mission across the street. The outreach center was a primary service point for the homeless, assisting anyone who requested their help.

"Looks like they're just waiting for lunch," I said a little doubtfully.

"There's someone here who needs something," Sari said. "Something much more than just food. I feel it."

"But you don't know who? The Man in White always had a specific person in mind." *At least until recently*, I thought, remembering the homeless camp.

"No, I'm afraid not. We'll just have to play it by ear, I guess."

I turned from the street to face Sari.

"Okay. So what's your plan?"

Sari shrugged. "Go across the street and walk past them, I guess. Try to feel the situation out."

"Hmm, I dunno," I demurred. "I'm kinda thinking that might come across as confrontational. You know, invading their space or something."

"I'm sure people walk past them all the time."

"Yeah, but no one has since we got here, and I'm betting someone in that line has seen us standing here, gawking at them."

"We're pretty inconspicuous back here. But I get you. So why don't we go around the block, then?" She shrugged. "You know. Be caszh."

"Yeah, that should work. Sneak up on 'em." I laughed.

She slapped my bare arm, but she was grinning.

"Well," I said, becoming serious again. "Shall we do this, then?"

In response, instead of speaking, Sari surprised me by giving me a quick peck on the cheek.

Now with my entire face pleasantly warm, and feeling a little lightheaded yet fully energized, I took her hand and started out on my new adventure with her.

"This whole area was renovated a couple years ago," she said as we rounded the corner onto Second Avenue. "It used to be raunchier." She nodded toward the Erikson-Fritz apartment complex, a clean, three-story red-brick structure. "This was a saloon."

"How do you know so much about the city?" I was genuinely impressed.

She shrugged. "I have kind of a photographic memory. It's not perfect, but it likes trivia." She laughed.

"Cool."

The apartments took up the central half of the block, although the red-brick decor continued with the next building, whose entrance was around the corner. It struck me that there were no traffic signs or signals on this block. Pedestrians were on their own when it came to crossing the streets.

The second building turned out to be a nightclub. Next to it was an unmarked building with accordion iron grates behind all the glass.

"Carl buys his pot in a back room here," Sari said, which explained the defenses. "He was really happy when it was legalized last year."

I chuckled. "I guess so."

We continued on to the next corner. A crow was standing on the far curb; it stared at us until we stepped into the street, then took off into the air, where it was joined by several others that remained close by us.

We crossed to the mission side and paused to have a short debate about whether I should walk at Sari's right or left hand. She argued that a gentleman always took the curb side (as I had done so far), but I countered that now I should act as a buffer between her and the group, made up mostly of men, huddled along the wall. I won, so we sauntered casually, just two lovers out for a stroll on a warm, sunny, prenoon day in a cleaned-up part of the city.

I couldn't help but notice one of the buildings across the street. A giant effigy of an electric guitar stretched across the double front windows of Black Book Guitars, a vintage shop.

Sari noticed me gazing at it, and I smiled at her in response.

"I always wanted to learn guitar," I said.

"Maybe we could stop by there after."

"Sweet!"

I was genuinely enjoying the new vibe of my mission, with Sari in charge. There was no seizing of my will, no frantic desperation, no whirling of the world around my head, making me dizzy. We were just two people out to help other people. Except that we were magicians.

As we drew near to the tail end of the lunch line, I took a deep breath, and Sari gave my hand a quick squeeze just before we walked past our first prospect.

We attracted a few glances and stares, as I had anticipated, but mostly, we were essentially ignored.

That is, until a man's voice called out from behind us. It had an odd quality to it that I couldn't quite describe. It just felt wrong, somehow.

"What are you?" the man demanded.

I let go of Sari as we stopped and turned to look for him. He was pretty easy to spot: a bedraggled man in a worn gray overcoat, who, when we passed by him, had been sitting cross-legged on the sidewalk, leaning back against the wall. Now he was bent as far forward as he could get, staring at us.

We headed back to him.

"What *are* you?" he said again. This time, it was obvious he was addressing me and not the two of us.

The man in line in front of him gestured toward him and said to me, "Don't worry none 'bout him, son. He ain't right." He tapped the side of his head. "You two might want to move along, though."

I held the speaker's eyes for a moment, then nodded and returned my attention to the first man, who did have a confused, kind of wild expression on his face.

"What are you talking about?" I asked him calmly.

"Why you all lit up?"

This was the last thing I had expected him to say. I was so startled I couldn't speak at first.

"Lit up?" I asked him. "What do you mean?"

He waved his hands through the air in front of him, making me think of a mime washing a window. "Lit up. Colors. In the air. Lights. Flashing."

I frowned at Sari, who looked as puzzled as I was. She shrugged.

"Gordon," the other man admonished him, "you are screwed up."

"*Lights!*" Gordon barked. His gaze flitted jerkily around me, as if I were surrounded by a cloud of gnats whose individual movements he was trying to follow, all of them at once.

I kept my own focus on his face, waiting patiently until our respective gazes met, and when they did, I locked on.

Immediately, I felt power rising up within me, of a different quality than what I was used to experiencing in these healings, and I knew intrinsically that it came through Sari. It mixed with my own energy to become stronger than any I had yet channeled.

It also somehow opened me up to this man's mental state. I could see he was imprisoned in his mind, trapped in a delusion he could not escape, left by society to his own ineffectual devices. I felt my compassion for him grow, and I recognized that some of this was Sari's contribution as well.

The men and women immediately around us had become background for me; I was laser focused. Sensing the crow's presence as it circled about fifteen feet above our heads, my body vibrating with the energy I was receiving from Sari, I spoke to Gordon with gentleness but also firm authority.

"Gordon," I said, "wake up."

Immediately, he jerked to alertness, the way your body reacts when you're drowsy and sense that you're about to fall over. His eyes began to clear, and he gazed back at me in a way that made me think he was seeing reality for the first time in a long while. First his countenance relaxed, then his entire body followed. He looked around at the gaping, muttering crowd with a puzzled look on his face, as if he had no idea how he had come to be in this place. Then he addressed me.

"Thank you," he said, his voice calm and even. "It's been a long time. A long, very tiring time."

Sari said to him, "You can rest now."

He nodded, then with a shrug gave an *I dunno* look around at the others, who were gawking at him in astonishment and at me with a mixture of wonder and fear.

His friend demanded of me, "How the hell 'd you do that, son?"

"Sometimes," I said slowly, feeling as if I was being fed the words, "people just get stuck." I shrugged in turn. "I helped him get unstuck, is all."

"Whatever you did," Gordon said, "I'll never forget you. I know it sounds unlikely, but if there's anything I can ever do for you, I'm here for it."

I only had time to nod, as some of those who had witnessed this encounter were now shuffling toward us, asking to be made unstuck.

CHAPTER 32

THIS WAS AN AUSPICIOUS START to Sari's and my new mission. We healed a few others over the next four weeks, but we weren't as swamped with petitioners as I had at first feared we would be.

Sari's priority was a matter of quality over quantity; she led me only to those in the most need. This was perfectly fine with me. I liked dealing with worst-case scenarios, giving hope to the most hopeless.

On the last Monday of August, I noticed on my way to work that canvas tents were being set up in Lownsdale Square. I wondered out loud about this when I arrived home that afternoon, mentioning it to Harold. This sparked him to reminisce about his adventure with Occupy Portland, a protest march six years ago that turned into something quite unexpected.

"It was groovy, man," he told me. "Ten thousand frickin' people showed up for it! Can you even imagine that? We swamped Pioneer Square and shut down the MAX!" He laughed. "It was outta sight, man. We weren't violent or anything, we were just tired of the One Percent owning us, and we wanted to make some noise about it.

"That night, we set up tents in the Plaza Blocks. We had no permit to camp, but Mayor Sam was cool and let a couple hundred of us tandem off the permit of another group. But it turned into more than just an overnighter for us. We stayed for over a month, camped out like hippies at Woodstock. People sold stuff and handed out brochures. And argued with the suits on their lunch hour!" He laughed again. "We had our own medics and even put up a free soup kitchen. TV reporters showed up. It was outta sight, man."

The nostalgia in his voice, mixed with his usual excitability, touched something in me. Harold really was a dreamer, believing the world could be a better place. And I was kind of proud to have been called to support this dream in my own small way.

"What you're doing ain't small, dude," Harold had chided me. "Don't you even think that."

On Wednesday, the heat wave that had plagued us for four days, sending temperatures into the nineties, had finally broken. So I decided to stop off at Lownsdale Square on my way home and check out the goings-on.

I entered the park from Fourth and Salmon, the same point I'd used when I healed the old man, as that was the shortest route from Flash Burger.

When I reached the center, I noticed, scattered among the trees around the southwest arc of the circle, that ten camping tents had been set up. They all had multiple signs and posters tacked to them, displaying slogans or symbols, and tables in front of them, holding pamphlets and flyers. Each of these had one or two attendants. People milled about, dressed in every form of fashion imaginable. It struck me that the scene looked a lot like what Harold had described.

Immediately to my left, on the northeast arc of the circle, stood a large squarish structure whose door was open; its walls looked like they were made of blue plastic. As I moved beyond this, into the circle itself, I saw that a folding table had been set up on the far side of it. It had a banner tacked along its front, bearing the words *Street Roots* in the periodical's distinctive blocky black lettering.

A woman, who I guessed to be around thirty, was sitting on one of two metal folding chairs behind the table; the other was empty. I sauntered over.

She smiled and greeted me as I stepped up. "Hi."

"Hey." I indicated the park setup with a sweep of my arm. "So what's up here, anyway?"

"Various advocacy groups are trying to mitigate people's fear of the homeless," she said. "The uneasiness they feel often turns into anger, especially when the camps encroach on otherwise-nice neighborhoods. The one at Powell and 57th is a good example. People are pretty miffed about that one, but they can't get rid of it. The police do periodic raids, but the camp just keeps coming back." She frowned. "I don't know what the draw is for them there. It's just a tiny parking lot in a residential district."

"Seems weird."

"It does. Everyone would like to see this stuff fixed. The problem is, no one can agree on how to fix it. Just doing routine sweeps to kick the squatters out doesn't work. They just go somewhere else for a while, produce the same problems, and then return when they're kicked out of the new place. We'd like to approach the problem in a better way."

I nodded in agreement through all of this. "I'm very interested in helping the homeless. I do what I can."

"Oh? What are you involved with?"

I blanched at my faux pas. Scrambling to find something reasonable as a cover, I said, "Well, mostly I bring them food and personal stuff. Y'know, like soap and things like that."

This wasn't a total lie; Sari and I did this one day the previous week and were considering making it a part of our outreach.

"That's good work." She lifted herself partially off the chair and stuck her hand out across the table. "I'm Julie, by the way."

"Arthur," I said, our hands clasping in the center of the table.

"Good to meet you, Arthur."

"So," I asked, scanning the brochures and pamphlets on display, "do you work for this shelter company?"

"I'm an editor for *Street Roots*. We sponsored them this week."

"Oh, of course. Big banner right here."

We both laughed.

"Anyway," she said, returning to her story, "it costs money to fix these situations properly, so we're trying to show that things could be done to make it better for the homeless without breaking the bank, which in turn would make things better for everyone else as well. We want people to feel that the money for the latest projects we have in mind will be worth it so we can persuade them to pay a small added tax."

She grinned at this last part, and I laughed.

"I get that. So what kind of fixes *do* you folks have?"

"Besides cleanup crews and providing outhouses and garbage pickup, there's those." She indicated the structure next to the table. "They're two-person sleeping pods made out of polyurethane. This makes them light and strong, so they're easily transportable and can be put up and taken down quickly. They come with built-in cots, overhead lighting, heaters, and storage cubbies. The company has a similar unit for washrooms so people can keep clean."

"That's awesome." My enthusiasm was real. "I love this idea."

"It's taken a consortium to put the whole project together. We're now trying to get the new mayor to give his okay."

"Will that be a problem?"

"Our initial contacts with him have been positive. That's why we're allowed to do this this week."

"Sweet."

I wanted to go peer inside the pod, but there were several people lined up to do the same, so I decided to wait. I took another glance around the area. Something struck me.

"Is it my imagination," I asked Julie, "or are there a lot of cops around?"

"I think they're afraid of another Occupy. They've been out in force all week."

"Are you afraid of being thrown out or something?"

"Oh, no." She laughed. "Not at all. This isn't that situation. I think they're more concerned about how events like this can draw people who might make trouble, is all."

"Oh, for sure." I kicked myself for my stupidity. I was really on a roll today. "Of course."

I motioned to the stack of *Street Roots* on her table. "Mind if I take one?"

"Oh, please do. It's last week's, of course, but we do mention this event in it."

"Sweet."

But before I could pick up one of the tabloids, a commotion at the pod door caused me to turn my attention toward it again. A man in shabby clothing was arguing with the company representative, who was standing in the open doorway with his feet spread apart in a stabilizing stance, his arms crossed. It immediately became apparent to me that the shabby dude, who seemed to be growing angrier as he continued his complaint, was being blocked from entering the structure.

"Speak of the devil," Julie said, briefly drawing my attention back to her. "Some people think we're offering free beds." She shrugged. "Been happening off and on all week. It gets worse at nightfall."

I nodded as I turned back to the confrontation. "I bet."

"They're confused and desperate. The ones we really want to help."

I felt a sudden urge to walk over and touch the homeless man, to see if that might rectify the situation. But I had no prodding from the Man in White and no energy buildup from Sari, so I decided against it. I'd never before imposed myself like that on someone without these directions, and I didn't think it would be a good idea to start now.

I was impressed with the representative's ability to remain calm under the barrage of the homeless man. And also with his ability to fend him off without the argument becoming physical. Still, the homeless dude kept pressing, and it was only a matter of time before this would happen. His complaints were growing louder as he became more agitated, so I could now hear his words clearly.

"I need to get changed!" he insisted. He pointed into the doorway. "It's changing in there!"

That's a weird thing to say, I thought. He wasn't carrying a change of clothing or a bag or anything else. I had no idea what he was talking about, as his words made no sense to me.

"I wonder if he has mental issues," I remarked, half to myself and half to Julie.

"It wouldn't surprise me," she said.

At this point, a police officer walked over to the pod and tried to talk the man down, but the man only pushed the cop away.

Julie remarked, "He won't get away with that for long."

"For sure."

The man became even more agitated, now waving his right fist in the air. The cop grabbed his wrist.

"Now it's going down," I said, my breathing fast and shallow, my attention riveted on the action. The scuffle was no more than five steps away from me. That was a little too close for comfort, and the thought flashed through my mind that maybe we should move away. But I hesitated.

The officer couldn't restrain him. The man spun quickly in a rather impressive—if clumsy—martial arts move and threw the cop off him, just as another officer stepped in. Together, the two officers tried to wrestle him to the ground, but he proved to be slippery as well as strong.

I'd never seen such a thing before in my life. I stood rooted to the spot, as events now happened so fast that I no longer had time to get out of there.

"I think he's on drugs," was the last thing I said to Julie.

The remaining events seemed to take place in slow motion. One of the officers was shoved backward out of the melee. I could see that he was going to land on me, but I didn't have time to get out of the way. So I just reflexively raised my arms to ward off the impact. My hands pressed into his shoulder blades as he struck me, his momentum driving me backward. He was almost twice my weight. Unable to prevent his fall and trying not to have him land on top of me on the hard sidewalk, I shoved myself to the side and staggered to a standstill, watching him topple over, horror now freezing my movements.

But before he even landed, a third cop grabbed me from behind and wrestled me to the ground. Sharp pain stabbed my knees and then my hands as they hit the concrete. The cop shoved his knee into the small of my back and, twisting my arms behind me, handcuffed me. I was so shocked by how rapidly everything was happening that I didn't react at all.

He then pulled me roughly to my feet and began forcefully marching me down the sidewalk toward 3rd Avenue and Main, the corner on the opposite side of the park.

As I was double-timed through the crowd—which parted for us like the Red Sea—the officer gave me my Miranda rights. I paid little attention. I had seen enough cop shows to know what my rights were. So when he asked if I understood, I robotically mumbled, "Yes," not really caring one way or the other. But I was keenly aware of the eyes boring into me as I was unceremoniously pushed through the crowd.

My head spun with a whirlwind of images and faces. The looks and startled reactions I received scared me more than the judicial prospects I was facing.

Has the Man in White abandoned me? I shoved the thought out of my mind, refusing to even consider it.

The cop behaved as if he was deliberately trying to humiliate me. If so, it was working. I couldn't bring myself to look into the pedestrians' faces as we passed by them. My unseeing gaze remained fixed on the slabs of concrete immediately before my feet, my attention preoccupied with the policeman's harsh grip on my left arm and the cold sharp bite of metal pinning my wrists. I tried not to think about what was happening, focusing instead on not stumbling as I was pressed along.

Because I knew I was in for a world of hurt.

CHAPTER 33

WE HAD TO CROSS BOTH Third and Main to get to our destination. Our first stop was the intake room, where I surrendered my personal possessions at the window of a partitioned office before being directed to a table where I sat and filled out a seemingly interminable amount of paperwork. Then I was taken back to the intake window.

"Do you have anyone you can call?" the intake officer asked. "A parent or guardian?"

I knew Carl wouldn't legally qualify as that, but I really had no one else.

"Yes, sir. His number is programmed into my phone." Emphasizing that I needed the phone, I added, "I don't remember it."

"Why not?"

I answered very carefully, not wanting to sound impertinent. "Because it's in my phone. I don't memorize people's numbers."

The clerk scowled at me but turned and retrieved my phone from the translucent plastic bag in which he had placed it. He annotated this on a form, then slid the phone to me through the oblong opening at the bottom of the window. Finally, he stood staring at me, his arms crossed.

I turned aside and tried to ignore him and the other officers in the room as I opened the contacts app.

Carl answered on the third ring.

"Hey Carl," I said, trying to keep my voice from quavering. Didn't quite succeed. "Um, I'm kind of in trouble."

"What's up?"

"I got arrested."

"Inciting a riot?" I could hear the smile in his voice.

"No," I said, marveling at his intuition, even though I knew he was mostly joking. There were always levels to him. "But it's probably just as bad. They haven't told me what the actual charge is yet."

"What have they told you?"

"My rights. That's about it."

"So what happened?"

"I was at the homeless event in Lownsdale, talking with one of the sponsors, and things got hairy around us. They say I pushed a police officer. But I didn't. I really didn't, Carl."

"Okay. Are you all right?"

"Well, I'm not really hurt." *Surprisingly enough*, I thought.

"Good. It's important to try to stay calm. Don't argue or resist in any way. Do whatever they tell you to do; don't put up any kind of a fight at all. But you don't have to answer any questions that might make you look bad, or anything you're uncomfortable with. Okay?"

"Okay."

"You at the juvie center?"

"I don't think so. Just a minute." I addressed the officer at the window. "Where am I, sir?"

"The Multnomah Justice Center."

"Thank you." I turned away again. "The Justice Center."

There was a pause before he responded, his voice flat. "Really."

"Apparently, they thought I was older."

"But by now, they must know you're not."

"I'm sorry, Carl. I really don't know what's happening. They're not telling me anything."

Carl's tone became a mixture of sympathetic and directive. "Okay. Listen. Don't worry. They can't hold you indefinitely, because you're not an adult. We'll come get you."

"Thanks, Carl."

I hung up and turned to the window again.

"So?" he asked as I pushed the phone to him.

"Someone's coming."

"Okay. Let's move on, then."

They took me farther inside for fingerprinting and mug shots. Afterward, I was led into the interrogation room, where I was directed to a hard chair behind a large metal desk.

They left me alone. There was nothing to look at in the barren space but empty gray walls and a heavy locked door in the corner. No distractions. So I sat with my thoughts and my rising anxiety, and I tried not to freak out.

I must have sat there for at least ten minutes before the interrogator entered. I wondered whether this delay was deliberate.

He sat across from me and placed a folder on the desk in front of him. He didn't greet me as he opened it, but merely introduced himself as Detective Robbins. He perused the paperwork as he began questioning me.

"So," he said, his voice flat and authoritative. "Your name is Arthur Cedric Johannsen, correct?"

"Yes, sir."

"May I call you Arthur?"

I hadn't expected him to ask permission. I couldn't keep the surprise out of my voice. "Of course."

He nodded. "So, Arthur. You are seventeen years old."

So they do know, I thought. "Yes."

"Your license shows a California address. But the one you put on the induction paperwork is for Portland. Why the discrepancy?"

"I moved here last March."

"Yet you haven't changed your license."

I grimaced. "I'm sorry, sir. I forgot to. I don't have a car, so I didn't think about it."

"Okay. You'll want to do that."

"Yes, sir."

"I'm surprised your parents didn't remind you."

"They didn't come here with me."

I could see he didn't like my answer. I felt a pang of fear.

"So who are you staying with?" he demanded.

"Some friends."

"Family friends?"

"Not really."

"How long have you known them?"

"About six months."

"Six months. So basically, you're living with some strangers you met when you got here."

I felt agitated and scared. "It's not like—"

Robbins held a hand up. "We'll come back to this."

I shut up.

"So," Robbins said, "tell me what happened today."

"I do some work with the homeless," I said, hoping I wouldn't have to go into details. "I was talking with a woman who was part of the event in the park, when a fight broke out around her table. I was trying to get out of the way, but before I could move, I was run into by a police officer, who, I guess, got pushed or something. Everything I did after that became automatic, a reflex reaction. I tried to counter his weight, to keep him from knocking me over. I managed to do that, but he ended up on the ground. But," I added firmly, looking at Robbins directly for just this final statement, "he was already falling." I couldn't maintain my gaze, so I dropped it. "I just didn't want to hit the sidewalk with him on top of me."

Robbins made no comment but merely pursed his lips as he flipped through the pages before him. Finally, he addressed me again.

"Y'know," he said, his casual tone belying the menace in his words, "your 'friends' could be in trouble for harboring a runaway."

This sent a shock of genuine panic through me, but I somehow found the courage to remonstrate.

"I'm not a runaway."

He glared at me. "Do your parents know you're here?"

I turned to the wall, anger mixing with the fear. "No, but—"

"Then, technically, you're a runaway."

I faced him, keeping my voice as steady as I could. "My father kicked me out of the house. It wasn't my choice to leave. As for my friends here, I have to stay *somewhere*. And I didn't want to be in California anymore. I just couldn't handle those memories."

Suddenly and unexpectedly, I wanted to cry. It must have been the strain. I looked away again, angry at my incipient tears, determined to not let them embarrass me.

I knew Robbins was studying me, but I couldn't look at him while I was in this condition. I wanted to just shrivel up and disappear.

When he next spoke, his voice was gentler. But not by much. "What memories, son?"

I tried to focus my thoughts and control my emotions. This took more effort than I would have liked, the seconds seeming to drag on, but Robbins waited patiently.

Finally, I said, "My mother abandoned me when I was a baby. My father blamed me for her leaving. He wanted nothing to do with me, and he made that very clear."

Telling him this was difficult for me. I was afraid that getting into the subject would cause him to scrutinize the small scars on my arms and the big one on my neck. They weren't that obvious, but people like him were trained to spot such things. I don't know why I didn't want him to know. Maybe I was afraid he'd blame me for them, like my father had.

"A broken home is a hard place to live in," Robbins said.

I shrugged. It wasn't that I was blowing off his sympathy, but rather that I didn't want to address these things. I didn't like thinking about them at all, and I had managed to put them out of my mind for several months now. I didn't want to talk about it anymore, so I remained silent. But this made him study me even more closely—exactly what I'd been trying to avoid.

Robbins asked quietly, "Did he ever hit you, son?"

I continued in my stubbornness as shame and anger flooded through me. I took a deep, ragged breath, struggling to hold in my emotions, trying to find a way to answer his question without answering it.

As I finally released the breath, my chest trembled, causing the air to flow erratically. I choked back an impending sob, hating myself for showing so much weakness. And that act, of trying so hard to hide these things, had the odd effect of doing the opposite.

"Yes," I whispered.

Out of the corner of my eye, I saw Robbins lean back in his chair. "Okay," he said gently. "It's okay."

We sat in silence for a while. As surreptitiously as possible, with my index finger, I wiped away a tear that was forming in the corner of my left eye.

After a bit, he asked, "Would you like some water?"

I hesitated a second, then nodded.

He gathered his papers and left the room.

He was gone a lot longer than I expected him to be, but eventually, he returned, along with a woman in uniform.

She handed me a paper cup, and I gulped the water down.

"Okay," Robbins said as he sat down. "Because of your age, the judge has agreed to move up your arraignment. I suspect he'll release you to your guardian. So you should be out of here within a couple of hours. However, there's a hiccup."

This caused me renewed alarm. I searched Robbins's face for a clue to what was happening, but he held up his hand and smiled. It was a brief smile, more like a flicker, but it was at least enough for me to know it had happened.

"Don't worry," he said. "It's just coordination. I can't keep you here at this facility because it's for adults only, and there's no sense in transferring you to the juvenile center at this point. So I've arranged to let you wait in the anteroom outside the main office. Officer Hamlin"—he indicated the woman standing next to him—"will stay with you, but I'm afraid you're going to have to be handcuffed while you're in there."

I grimaced.

"Yeah, I know," Robbins said. "But I have no choice. I'll cuff you in front this time, which should be more comfortable. On the plus side, you'll have a private restroom."

Well, that's something, anyway, I thought. I nodded.

He stood and motioned for me to do the same as he walked around the table. Holding my wrists out, I allowed him to handcuff me.

Then Hamlin ushered me into the anteroom. It was a bit cramped but relatively quiet and not too unpleasant, as was promised.

I sat in silence for the next hour, working over in my mind everything that had happened to me today. It didn't make me feel better, but it was hard to keep from thinking about it. In fact, I felt a little peeved.

"What happened to 'the protector will be protected?'" I asked the Man in White.

"Are you injured?"

I grudgingly replied, *"No."*

"Are you imprisoned?"

"No."

"Being protected does not mean being sheltered from life."

I had no argument to offer against this.

At 4:05 p.m., another officer arrived to take me to see the judge.

He was lenient with me, and to my indescribable relief, I was released into John's custody. I found it hard to look him in the eye. As I walked with him out the glass doors of the facility and down the broad concrete steps, I couldn't lift my gaze off the ground.

Driving home, we talked sporadically and, even then, only about mundanities, neither of us mentioning my predicament. At last, I fell into silence, and thankfully, John honored it.

My heart felt like it was sinking into a swamp, and my throat was so constricted, I could hardly swallow. But it wasn't until we pulled up at the house that, deliberately fixing my attention on the passenger window so John couldn't see my face, I allowed a single tear to fall.

CHAPTER 34

A S WE WERE WAITING FOR what I expected would be an awkward and uncomfortable dinner, for which I wasn't even hungry, John asked me to join him in the sitting room.

The last time we'd met there, he displayed the stoic manner of a spiritual adviser. This evening, he was much more supportive. I can't even begin to describe the emotions that were roiling within me.

"Well," John began, "the police didn't impress me much. They spent more time questioning me about our relationship than talking about the charges against you. In fact, they warned me about charges they could bring against Carl. While—"

Guilt and fear shot through me, causing me to interrupt him by blurting out, "Are they going to do that? Will you get in trouble because of me?"

To my relief, John shook his head.

"No," he said reassuringly. "Don't worry about that. I was about to say that *technically*—because of your age— we're harboring a runaway. But unless your father files a complaint in California, the police won't do anything here.

It was mostly an attempt to get me to confess to things that aren't going on."

"I'm so sorry, John." My voice broke, which annoyed me. "I never meant to hurt you."

"You haven't hurt anyone," he said. "Don't even think that. They were just on a witch hunt, trying to dig up dirt. They can't take you away from us or send you back to California. However"—and here his tone became more serious—"they *are* accusing you of assault on a police officer. That's not a light charge."

I blanched, even though I had been fairly sure all along that was what they were going after me for. Hearing it out loud made it real for the first time. "But I really didn't do anything. They have to know that already."

John shrugged. "The police have to look into crimes, even where none exists. It's kind of their job to do that, I suppose. But people often end up on the short end of it."

With this comment, he was sounding a little bit like Harold. Except without the obvious disdain in his voice that characterized the retro hippie's attitude toward authority.

"That's all they would tell me," John went on. "Would you like to talk about it?"

I nodded and related everything to him as best as I could remember, starting with my desire to see the homeless event and ending with the officer crashing into me.

"Pretty stupid of me to put my hands on him, I guess," I said ruefully. "But it was reflexive." John made no response. "Anyway, as soon as that happened, another cop came up from behind me and tackled me." I shrugged. "That's it."

"Hmm," John said. "Sounds like the police have it backward."

"I think the detective who interrogated me thought so too. He didn't say that, though. He just took me to what I think was, like, a visitors' waiting room or something, and let me stay there with a babysitter. He's the reason I wasn't locked up in juvie."

"He might be a good one to have the lawyer talk to."

"Yeah. Too bad I don't have one." I couldn't help sounding a bit sarcastic, even though that's not how I meant it. My emotions were all over the place, not under my control.

"Maybe you do."

It's amazing how fast hope can displace despair. We grasp at any lifeline offered us.

"Really?"

John nodded. "Possibly. I'll take you downtown in the morning so you can get set up with your probation officer. While you're going through that process, I'll call a friend of mine. He's a pretty good lawyer. He won a case for me when a client sued me, back when I was a CPA. I can't say we're particularly close, but we still have an occasional beer together. While I can't guarantee he'll represent us, I do have kind of an in with him."

His use of the plural pronoun at once surprised and pleased me. Represent *us*.

"Thank you very much," I said, addressing both his offer and the sentiment.

"I'll do what I can to help you. But no one can predict the future. We just have to take it one step at a time."

I nodded. "Yeah, I guess so."

This ended our conversation. John stood and said, "I'm hungry. How about you?"

CHAPTER 35

DINNER WAS POLITELY SUBDUED. No one really wanted to talk about my predicament, especially me. The perfunctory sympathy and well-wishes were sufficient, and I expressed my gratitude in a comparable manner.

Afterward, Sari took me up to her room.

After closing the door, she turned and threw her arms tightly around me, pressing her cheek into my chest. We held each other as if we'd never let go again.

"This is such a bummer," she said into my shirt, her voice distorted by fabric and tears.

"I'm sorry," I said. "I'm really sorry."

She pushed away far enough so she could look me in the face. Her cheeks were damp, but her eyes flashed.

"Sorry because the cops in this city are bastards?" she countered.

"I'm sorry for letting you down."

"You didn't let me down. You could never let me down." She laid her head against my chest again, gently this time. "It isn't fair."

"No, it isn't. But now I have to deal with it. I have no choice."

Sari gazed determinedly into my eyes. Hers were on fire. "*We'll* deal with it! I'll unleash crows everywhere!"

The childish threat, seemingly surprising her as much as it did me, startled both of us into laughter.

"My Hitchcock Mistress," I said teasingly.

"We must have this power for *something*."

"We know what we have the power for."

She relented, sighing. "I know. But still."

I nodded. "Yeah. But still."

And as we stood there with our bodies pressed together, comforting one another, I wondered if she might not just have a point.

CHAPTER 36

THE LAW OFFICES OF DAVIS, Berner & Young were located on the fourth floor of a mixed commercial building on Salmon Street. The Tuesday following the incident, we arrived there at 9:15 a.m., fifteen minutes before our appointment.

Evan Davis was about the same age as John, with professionally groomed graying hair and deep blue eyes. He didn't give me the impression of being in any way a playful person. This was fine with me. I wasn't looking to toss a football with him.

He was only vaguely friendly toward John as well.

John's being there made me feel more assured. I needed someone at my back in this legal world of ultimate grownup-ness, even more so now that I was facing someone so gruff. I wondered what the basis of their friendship actually was. They didn't seem to be all that compatible, which made me even more uncomfortable.

"Thanks for seeing us, Evan," John said as we were shown in.

"Not a problem," Evan said. He held his hand out to me across the desk. "Good to meet you, Arthur."

"You too, sir."

He motioned to the two client chairs in front of his desk as he settled into his huge leather one behind it. Ours were stiff and uncomfortable; I guarantee that his was not.

"So," Evan said, getting right down to business. "The charges against you are quite serious." He picked up a page off his desk and perused it. I assumed that he already knew what it said and that this was just for show. "Assault and obstruction of a police officer." He laid the paper back on the short stack again. "Are they true?"

I was startled. I hadn't expected such a direct question, such a curt question. It took me a moment to regain my footing, and even then, I didn't quite succeed. "I don't think so."

"Why not?"

I glanced at John, who indicated that I should tell the whole story. So I did.

When I was done, Evan shot a barrage of rapid-fire questions at me, pounding in notes on his computer as he did so.

"So," he said, "you weren't actually involved in the altercation."

"No, sir."

"You didn't throw any punches. At the other fighters, the pedestrians, the officers?"

"No. I did not."

"And you did not strike the officer who you say ran into you."

"That's right."

"You did not push him when he backed into you?"

This gave me pause; the phrase "backed into" imbued the situation with a different connotation. It made me stop and question my memory. And now, I honestly couldn't remember my reaction. Everything had happened so fast, it was all basically a blur in my mind. This scared me.

"I don't know," I said at last. "Maybe. I mean, I was trying not to fall on the sidewalk. So I raised my hands and may have pressed against him, just to keep my balance. But I didn't deliberately try to hurt him or anything."

I felt like I'd just blown our case. But Evan didn't linger on my response.

"And it was a different officer who tackled you and arrested you?"

"Yes, sir."

"Okay. Now, this woman you were talking to at the table. Do you happen to know her name?"

"Yes, Julie. She works for *Street Roots*. An editor, I think she said."

"Do you think she would remember you?"

"She should. We talked for quite a while before it happened."

"So she can corroborate the events as you've described them."

"I would think so. It happened right in front of her."

"Good. I'll track her down."

This sounded as if he had come to a decision. I glanced hopefully at John, who apparently was thinking the same thing.

"So," he asked Evan, "does that mean you're taking us on?"

"Yeah, I'll do it. I believe we may have something here. I'll have to look at the police report to be sure, and that may not be available for a while. But the fact that they released you without a legal guardian makes me think they know they don't really have a case. They're going through the motions, probably wishing this would just go away." He pointed a finger at me. "No guarantees, there," he added sternly.

I got the message. But I also remembered how I had been treated toward the end, being placed in a comfortable room. Now that event made more sense. I tried to keep my hopes in balance with my fears. I nodded to let Evan know I understood.

"However," he said, "we do have a bit of luck. I've worked with Alice Brokell, the Deputy District Attorney who has taken your case, for years. She isn't a hardliner. I think the case might be a good candidate for a decline of charges, which means, if they agree to it, it won't even go to court. All records of the arrest will be sealed. Unless," he added quickly, "you want to countersue the police officers involved."

Hell no. "I'm not looking to go after anybody," I said quickly.

Evan nodded. "It would probably go nowhere, anyway. The police are pretty solid in this city."

I knew what he was implying by that statement. I was thinking about Occupy again. "It's okay. I just want it all to be over."

But Evan was already turning to address John. "Do you have anything you want to add?"

"He's a good kid, Evan. He works for me. He also does a lot of work with the homeless. I've been helping him out while he gets established here. So I'll be covering the fees for him."

Before I could feel too guilty about John's footing the bill, Evan turned back to me.

"What kind of work do you do with the homeless, son? Food bank or something?"

I glanced uncertainly at John.

"Go ahead and tell him."

"I, um," I said. I swallowed hard. Then, speaking quickly and flatly, I blurted, "I heal them."

Silence pressed against the walls of the room like the breath the sky seems to hold in that moment before a thunderhead breaks loose.

"You're *that* guy?" Evan asked.

Now my face was so hot, I imagined it was brick red. "Yeah," I said weakly.

Evan leaned back in his leather desk chair, which tilted under his weight. "Well, I'll be damned."

His steely gaze held me for longer than I liked. I felt myself crawling inward, trying to hide inside my own skin.

Then, to my great relief, he dropped his stare and addressed John again.

"I'll do it pro bono," he said.

"Wow, Evan. Thanks. That's generous of you."

Evan held his hand up, palm outward. "It's not all selflessness. This case can help my reputation."

"I have no concerns about your motives. We're both very grateful."

"Yes," I said. "Thank you very much, sir."

Evan almost, but not quite, smiled. Then he waggled his fingers at us.

"Now get out of here before I change my mind."

CHAPTER 37

I'M HIKING ALONG A FOOT trail in a mountainous region on a clear summer day.

I come around a corner and see an ancient castle before me, situated on a hill across a shallow ravine. It's made of worn dark gray stone. It has a single turret, part of its upper wall broken, set in the corner nearest to me. This tower seems deeply menacing, bearing a single square window near the top, whose unadorned opening is tinged with the light of sunset, as if the glow is coming from inside.

I get a creeping sensation along my spine, a feeling like I'm being watched. Not by someone, but by the window itself. My stomach tightens, and my every instinct tells me to flee.

But even as the intention to move is forming in my mind, I hear a voice calling to me from inside the castle, and immediately, I know I must go to it.

As soon as I realize this, I find myself standing at the entrance. Before me is a gate made of crisscrossed thick steel bars backed by heavy sheets of battered wood. I push on it, and it swings open easily. I pass through it cautiously, the hackles on my neck rising.

The space inside is large and rectangular, bound by stone walls four stories high. Although I recognize this as the courtyard, I'm surprised to find that it's covered by a roof; normally, these spaces are open to the sky. I don't know how I know this.

The interior is gloomy, lit only by the sunlight seeping in from the open gate. The interior wall to my left stops one floor short of the roof, forming a mezzanine with the outer wall at its back, to which a broad set of stone stairs runs along the wall behind me. The platform's inner ledge is unprotected.

A wizened old woman in a rough black dress and cloak stands on the very edge of this, gazing down at me. I feel a touch of vertigo at the sight of her.

I climb the stairs and stand before her. She peers intently into my eyes, searching within me, discovering me. Devouring me. Her own eyes are empty, colorless, lightless. I cannot see an end to the depths of her. Fear grips me, and I tremble, but I cannot force myself to turn away. An eternity passes in a single second.

At last, she speaks. "The subconscious becomes conscious," she intones.

I feel as if my body has fallen over the ledge, shed and discarded like dirty clothes, leaving my soul bare and at her mercy.

She gestures toward the courtyard, and I turn to see what she's indicating. Below us, I see an army of demons, all in black armor, marching across the floor. Stunned, I cannot look away. But after a time has passed, I sense movement behind me and turn back to her.

The woman takes my right hand, pulls it toward her, and places something in it. Before I can see what it is, she closes my fingers over it, and immediately, I find myself again back on the trail, across the valley from the castle. The sun still burns brightly in its blue sky, and everything feels right.

I open my hand to see what the old woman has given me. It is a three-inch-tall, solid-gold replica of the staircase.

I awoke with the final strains of "Stairway to Heaven" fading from my awareness. Those last slow words, drawn out, despairing, and plaintive, as if Robert Plant were reluctant to lend them voice, sent a chill up my spine.

It had been two weeks since my meeting with Evan. As had been true for every morning since my arrest, I remained still for a while in the predawn darkness, which was lasting longer every day, now that September had crested the hill of summer and begun its quiet slip toward autumn. I would lie on my back, my eyes not opened yet, trying to force myself not to focus on my situation. Which, of course, made it the only thing on my mind.

I had no way of knowing how my case was faring. That *not knowing* was the worst part of my whole situation right now. Since my mind had no anchor of assurance to hold it in place, it would toss on the dark sea of every conceivable dreadful thing that could happen to me, and I would become convinced that every one of them *would* happen.

"We make our own future," the Man in White said, echoing the words I'd said to Sari six months ago. It kind of annoyed me to have them thrown in my face.

"What did I do to make this one?"

"You will know once it plays out."

There was no doubt in my mind about one thing: this voice belonged to the Man in White from my ibogaine trip. They both spoke in the same spirals. He immediately picked up on this thought.

"You make the mistake," he said, *"of thinking things are linear."*

"One thing follows another, doesn't it?"

"One thing produces an infinity of following things. The only one of those that matters is the one you decide is real."

"I decide is real?"

"It is always your decision to make. Right now, you have two choices laying immediately before you. You can sit in your tent, sulking like Achilles at the unfairness of the universe, or you can use what you have already created to help you climb out of it."

"What I already created?"

Suddenly, the dream image of the golden staircase burst into my mind, cutting off my question. The Man in White did not make further comment, and after my usual amount of time waiting on him had passed, I decided he wasn't going to.

I glanced at my clock: 5:53.

On impulse, I tossed the bedcovers aside and swung my legs off the edge of the mattress. I moved to the window, where I pushed aside the curtains and stood peering out into the darkness that would begin to dissolve within mere minutes.

My room looked out over the front lawn. Much smaller than the backyard, yet bearing ample trees and flower beds, it provided a bulwark of privacy from the neighborhood. Under certain conditions, I could catch glimpses of the houses across the street through breaks in those trees; I imagined this would be especially pronounced once bare winter moved in. But the blank air shrouding the morning was not even broken by a streetlight, as none had ever been erected on our block.

There lay, out in that darkness, a comfort in the silence and stillness that was not present during the day, when the human part of the world was frenetically dashing about. I knew there was also color hiding within that blackness, as the leaves of the dogwoods were starting to blush with red, and those of the maples, yellow orange. All it would take was a mere hint of sunrise to cause that soft beauty to break forth.

And now, finding myself touching the stillness that lay within my own personal darkness, I stood there at the window, breathing softly, feeling my heart's infinite rhythm, waiting for the dawn to break within me.

CHAPTER 38

O N ALL THE OTHER WEEKDAYS, we ate dinner an hour later than we did on Fridays. We sat down together earlier on that day to allow ample time for our Bohm session. So starting in late spring, as the weather was warming up, I had made it a practice to set aside the period of five to six in the evenings to contemplate in the garden.

This Wednesday evening, my dream of the castle having lingered in my mind all day, I was sitting in my usual spot on the patio, counting crows.

Emily had once talked to me about the Middle Ages practice, born from witchcraft, of divining the future by the number of crows one encountered unexpectedly. Because crows were so ubiquitous in Portland, and especially because of my newfound ties with them, their presence here really didn't mean anything to me. However, I couldn't help but note that, as I remembered from the ancient rhyme she had recited for me, the three crows currently pecking underneath the oak tree signified an upcoming wedding—thus proving that their presence here was mere happenstance.

As was their wont, these crows were spending more time strutting around as if they owned the place than actually looking for food in the grass. I chuckled at how they managed to seem at once cautious and bold in their behavior. The truth was, though, that I mostly thought they looked arrogant.

"Confidence is often mistaken for arrogance," the Man in White said.

I snorted. *"What do crows have to be confident about?"*

"They have deep knowledge."

I frowned. *"Really? What is it they know?"*

"The dark things of the earth."

"Well, that's pretty nondescript."

"It is impossible to describe spiritual realities. We can only experience them."

"I think I'm kinda experiencing dark things right now."

"You should take advantage of this privilege."

Now I actually chortled. I couldn't help myself; it was the only response I could make.

"You dismiss things out of hand," the Man in White said. *"This is foolish. Do you not yet realize that you cannot truly become Light until you walk through the Dark?"*

"Become light?" I was so taken aback by his statement that I said these words out loud. Startled by the sound of my own voice, I focused and redirected my attention inward and outward, as I always did when talking to him. *"What does that even mean?"*

"It is impossible to explain, which is why I am giving you a living example instead."

"Are you saying you're responsible for what's happening to me?"

"I am responsible for you. *You are in training."*

"Well, I don't think I care for the way you train." I meant this to be tongue-in-cheek, but there was more than a little truth in my complaint.

"Do not be childish. Did you learn how to stand by having someone tell you how to do it or by falling down until you were able to find your balance? You are on the verge of something much greater than merely standing. You are becoming One. To truly enter into this state, it is imperative that you grow in every way—emotionally, physically, spiritually."

I felt chagrined. I somehow received the impression that his words had deeper meanings than what I normally understood them to mean, and I felt bad for being so dense.

"I'm sorry. It's just that I've never had anyone help me grow up before."

"I know. But now you have someone."

As these words penetrated my mind, I suddenly realized that I felt the same way toward the Man in White as I did toward John. And also that, in the space of a mere seven months, I had gone from having no father at all, to having two.

CHAPTER 39

T HREE WEEKS LATER, IN THE second week of
October, autumn had arrived in its full glory. In San
Diego, we used to drive an hour every year to reach Mount
Laguna, where my father said the colors were the best. But
here, all I had to do was look out my bedroom window.

But when I woke up at my normal six o'clock on
Sunday morning, I was unable to view those glorious
colors, as sunrise was still an hour away. Finding myself
wide awake but reluctant to get up just yet, I grabbed my
phone to play another game of *Planescape: Torment*. I
was finding the app useful for distracting myself from the
weight of my situation.

Evan Davis had called me on Friday. It had been a full
month since John and I had met with him, and in that time,
a cloak of dread had wrapped itself around me, becoming
a normal part of my emotional wardrobe. But if his news
was not one of salvation, at least it was positive.

"I've talked with the *Street Roots* editor you mentioned, Julie Elsher, and she's agreed to serve as a witness
for you. She's believable, which is good for us. By the
way, your court date has been scheduled for Tuesday,
November twenty-first."

Happy Thanksgiving to me, I thought. But what I said was, "That all sounds good, Mr. Davis."

"I'm meeting with the DDA on Wednesday. Let's see if we can nip this thing in the bud."

John had agreed that this was a good sign but cautioned me about becoming overly optimistic. The proof that I was heeding his warning was the state of my disheveled bed-clothes, which—in the semidark, lit only by my phone's screen and my alarm clock—I noted were bunched up around me. The nightmare I'd been aroused from by my own frenetic movements hadn't been particularly pleas-ant, although I couldn't remember it now. It had dissolved upon waking.

"*It is good,*" the Man in White said, "*to not take things for granted.*"

I nodded distractedly, still focused on my phone. It didn't occur to me at that moment that I was becoming nonchalant about hearing this voice in my head. "*I try not to,*" I replied.

"*Yet you assume you are awake right now.*"

Now, this startled me so much that my phone slipped from my hands and dropped with a thump into my lap.

"Wha—" The sound of my voice breaking the early morning stillness made me cut the word short. Switching to inner thought, I asked, "*What are you talking about?*"

I received no answer.

There was something wrong about the darkness I was now enveloped in. It was thick, almost viscous in its impenetrability.

I reached for my phone to switch its flashlight on, but I couldn't find it. Consternated, I frantically swept my hands across the bed, searching for it to no avail.

"Huh," I mumbled to myself.

I leaned back against the pillow I had earlier propped up on the headboard, glancing at my alarm clock as I did so. But this only added to my puzzlement; I couldn't read the numerals. The line segments constituting them were all randomly lit so that the only thing produced was a jumble of red-orange sticks. And I don't know quite how to describe this, but they also didn't cast any light beyond the clock's face. The familiar soft glow, which I had always used as an orienting marker in the night, was somehow being absorbed back into the display—even though I could see the lit-up LED strips clearly. The room was intensely dark, a kind of darkness I had never experienced before, a darkness so thick that I could feel it pressing against my skin.

Suddenly, I sensed movement in the room. There was no sound whatsoever, just air being displaced.

My heart pounding as it was squeezed by a growing fear, I strained to see who or what was there, but couldn't make anything out at all. There was absolutely no light in the room to see by.

And then, suddenly, there was.

An abrupt, silent explosion of blinding white made me reflexively throw my arms across my face and avert my gaze, squeezing my eyes shut. But within a few seconds, the white became tinged with turquoise, softening it.

Tentatively, I opened my eyes, and finding I was now able to tolerate it, I dropped my defenses. The silent supernova, in the form of a three-foot-diameter ball hovering midway between the foot of my bed and the door, was subtly vibrating, the trembling becoming stronger and stronger until the energy field suddenly collapsed as if being sucked into a black hole, leaving the room filled with normal noontide light.

Normal. That is, except that it was nowhere near noon.

At the foot of my bed stood a gorgeous woman, who appeared to be in her midthirties but who I knew had no age at all. Her tightly curled blonde hair, which reached below her shoulders, was partially covered by a cap that looked vaguely like a beret, and she carried a staff that was topped with a figure-eight symbol. She wore a full-length semisheer white dress that was wrapped in a rainbow. An actual rainbow, which glowed around her. But the most striking things about her were the golden eagle wings that were folded back behind her shoulder blades. Her gold-flecked green eyes blazed, flames dancing within them.

I was so entranced by this vision that the sound of my own voice startled me. Indeed, I couldn't believe I was even daring to speak.

"Are you an angel?" I asked incredulously, even though I don't believe in angels.

"I am the goddess of resolutions," she said. "I am here to tell you that the storm is dissipating."

Upon this, everything went black and silent again, and I actually felt the emptiness she left behind, like a hollow place in the air. Once more, the darkness was palpable and oppressive, and an abject fear that I had been cast into nothingness ran like an electric shock through me.

Then the air began to tremble, as if every atom in the room was vibrating in unison. This built up, becoming faster and faster and faster until, suddenly, the darkness itself imploded into a baseball-sized dot of black, which hung for two seconds in the once again normally lit room before dropping onto the carpet in front of the door.

In that spot, peering up at me, stood a crow.

This is all an ibogaine flashback, I told myself. *It has to be.*

"*It is not,*" the Man in White said. "*You are in the superconscious.*"

I frowned. "*Without the holotropic breathing?*"

"*The talisman of passage is in your hand.*"

My hands had been resting on my thighs throughout these events. Now, with a shock, I realized that the fingers of my left hand were curled around a heavy, solid object that felt like worked metal, with precise, sharp corners and polished flat surfaces. I turned my hand over as I opened my fist to find I was holding the golden staircase from my castle dream.

"*How did* that *get there?*"

"*You dreamed that you were holding it.*"

"*I don't remember that dream.*"

He ignored my comment.

"*The talisman belongs to the superconscious,*" he said, "*so it took you there. It used your Gateways to do this. Now that those are open, you must learn to control them so they do not rule you.*"

I stared at the statue, feeling apprehensive. "*This thing is dangerous.*"

"Life is dangerous. Spiritual life is doubly so. But you will learn your way."

"You're always so confident. You make it sound like I can do anything."

"You can *do anything. The sun is up. Exit the superconscious whenever you wish."*

And just by thinking that I wanted to leave this realm, the normal world instantly reappeared around me, leaving me feeling as if I had never left it.

I looked down at my hand again, to find that it was empty.

But now I knew how to fill it.

CHAPTER 40

Evan Davis's personal assistant called me just before dinnertime on Wednesday afternoon to set up another appointment.

It took me a few minutes to find John, who turned out to be sitting on the patio with Priscilla.

"Sorry to interrupt," I said, "but I have Mr. Davis's office on the phone. He wants to meet with us as soon as we can. She said to set aside two hours."

John frowned. "That doesn't sound good."

"That's what I'm thinking too," I said, trying to keep the fear out of my voice. I held out my phone to him. "Maybe you should talk to her."

John nodded and took over the conversation. He set up a meeting for early Friday afternoon, then handed the phone back.

"We'll just close down the cart after lunch," he said.

"I'm sorry, John. I keep pulling you away from work."

"This is more important. Friday afternoons are slow, anyway. Nobody wants to be downtown after three."

"That's Friday the thirteenth," Priscilla noted. Then, grinning, she bumped shoulders with John and added, more ominously, "In *October*."

This puzzled me. "Why is the month significant?"

"That's the date," John said, "when the Knights Templar were betrayed. That's the origin of the superstition, so this one is supposed to be especially unlucky. But don't worry. We're going to break it."

"I sure hope so."

I shivered as the wind suddenly gusted, prompting me to survey the blocked-in sky. The air felt like it should be raining. Noting my friends were in short sleeves, I asked, "How can you sit out here like that in this cold weather?"

"I just checked it a bit ago," Priscilla said. "It's in the upper forties. That's not cold."

"It is to normal people."

"Well, there ya go."

We all laughed.

"Let's go eat," Priscilla said.

"I guess it is that time, isn't it?" John said.

So two days later, at one thirty in the afternoon on the unluckiest one of the year, I once again found myself with John in Evan Davis's office. As was his wont, he launched right in as soon as we were seated.

"The DDA has agreed to drop the charges," he said.

A waterfall of relief gushed through me, making me physically slump a little in the chair, as if my anxiety had been the only thing holding me upright. I reflexively looked to John, who smiled and nodded. That was about as much enthusiasm as he ever displayed.

"However," Evan went on, "there's a slight glitch. In the meeting, I thought it would be in our favor to mention your work with the homeless." He addressed John. "Make him look civic minded, good kid caught in a bad situation kind of thing, right?" Back to me. "Well, it both worked and backfired on me. She now wants to meet with you to discuss exactly what kind of work you're doing. I promise you," he added quickly, with a flash of raised palms toward me, "I didn't say you were the street healer everyone's talking about. But she jumped to that conclusion on her own, and when she suggested it, I had to tell her the truth."

I blanched as fear crept into my heart, but I managed to keep that out of my voice as I said, "I understand, Mr. Davis. It's not your fault. I would have thought it would make a difference too. A good one, I mean."

"I'm afraid I share responsibility in that as well," John said with a sidelong glance at me. "I was the one who made Arthur tell you about it in the first place. He wasn't going to."

"You didn't make me, John," I said. "I did it willingly. We were all thinking the same way."

"So we'll all plead mea culpa, then," Evan said. "I'm sorry, Mr. Johannsen, but I'm afraid the burden has been placed on you now, because you'll have to answer the bulk of the questions. The reason I asked you to come here today is so we can hash out the testimony among us. A rehearsal, if you like. We don't want to go in dry."

Addressing John, he continued, "She'll also want to know about the situation and the living conditions in your home. We should talk about that today too."

"That'll be no problem."

"Good. Shall we begin, then?"

"Let's do it," I said.

CHAPTER 41

B Y THREE-FIFTEEN THAT AFTERNOON, EVAN was satisfied that we had a good handle on how we should engage in our discussion with the DDA the following Wednesday. He had coached us on our responses to the most likely questions Ms. Brokell would ask us, and while my nervousness had not been vanquished, I at least felt I might be able to avoid making a complete mess of things.

It had been raining lightly when we arrived at the office, and it was still mostly cloudy now, but the midafternoon peekaboo sun had warmed the air up a bit by the time John and I reached the street.

I felt a desire to mull things over privately, so we said our farewells and went our separate ways, him heading home, and me, the river. I loved Carl's house for its otherworldly feel, and the backyard was a magical mystery always beckoning, but the riverside was where I did my practical thinking.

I traced a winding course, along several different streets, that finally let me out at my usual contemplation spot, about fifteen minutes' walk from Evan's office. I settled myself at the railing and stared out at the suburban skyline across the dark green expanse of water, noting how the fleeting sunlight stabbing through momentary gaps in the clouds sparkled on the waves and flashed off a few windows in the distance.

I let my thoughts drift with the current as I languidly swept my gaze up and down the river, pausing every so often as something caught my eye. My breathing settled into the long and slow rhythm it always adopted when I was contemplating—a result, I believe, of my now-daily personal meditation sessions.

The water flowed below; the gulls swooped above. I noted that there were more of these beautiful—but noisy and mean—gray-and-white birds than usual, circling over the river. I supposed the past three days of storms had driven them inland. The ocean was eighty miles away, so I was rather impressed by how far they were willing to travel. I watched awhile as they swooped and screamed, admiring their gracefulness and chuckling at their haughtiness.

After a while, I let my gaze drop to a point close enough to shore that I could actually see the current. I stood idly watching the passing water, my mind calming with the stream, as if it were washing away all my doubts and fears, carrying them to the ocean, cleansing my spirit of its shadows.

And as I contemplated the possible meanings underlying this strong course of water, the words of the transient who had accosted me in this spot seven months ago came back to me: *"But if you stay in the flow, it all flows with you and around you, and you make it. You* make *it, man. You make it all happen."*

And in that instant, my eyes were opened, and I found myself in the flow. The world seemed to expand and contract around me, simultaneously, in a flash. But it wasn't just around me; it was also *inside* me. I was it, and it was me. I understood *everything*. I saw the world for what it truly was; I saw myself for who I truly was. I knew my place in it all, and I knew its place in me.

And then, just as suddenly, I didn't see, and I didn't know, and I didn't flow. I felt myself drop back into my normal, bland, everyday way of being and understanding. It was the emotional equivalent of hitting a wall. Disappointment welled up in me, along with a longing to regain that wonder, that awareness, that awe of it all—at what the universe was and what it was doing. But I may as well have been attempting to pick up fistfuls of the water flowing below me, as the elusive insights of truth slipped through my fingers.

I sighed deeply, reconciling myself to my loss yet glad for that momentary transformation.

"You just had the Taste," the Man in White said.

"I want the whole meal." I laughed.

"It is the first step toward Enlightenment," the Man in White said, ignoring my joke and speaking over my laughter. *"You will have a number of them before you achieve that permanent state."*

"What, exactly, is Enlightenment?"

"It is the moment-by-moment awareness that all things are the same thing, that all events are the same events, that all feelings are the same feelings."

My dream of the preacher came back to me. *"The world is a hologram."*

"Yes," the Man in White said. *"Nothing moves, but everything happens."*

His statement blew me away; it was incomprehensible to me. I shook my head.

"You have to experience it," the Man in White said, *"in order to understand. And even then, you probably will not understand. But it is not necessary to do so. The experience is all that matters, and it only matters when it occurs all the time. Everything else in life is merely rehearsal."*

"Do you *experience it all the time?"*

"Yes. I am always One."

"And do you understand?"

"No."

I laughed again, but I think I knew what he was getting at. And suddenly, I felt a yearning, an almost desperate longing, to re-enter that mindboggling state of serenity and never leave it.

"How can I get what you have?"

"Wash your bowls."

This statement confounded me. My mind seemed to go blank; I was at a total loss as to how to respond to his words.

"It is a Zen teaching," he explained. *"It means to live your life as if you have already achieved the goal. Even mundane things are to be experienced as a higher order."*

This was the first time the Man in White had explicitly explained something esoteric to me. I wondered, briefly, what this implied.

"Oh. Well, that's what I want to do. It's what I'm trying to do."

"I know."

And for the very first time, in those two simple words, I thought I detected a slight tinge of emotion in his voice. He almost sounded proud.

CHAPTER 42

T HE FRIDAY AFTER OUR LEGAL coaching session, I put on my best clothes—basically what I wore on my city tour with Sari, except that I'd bought a dress shirt for this occasion—and rode with John to the Mark O. Hatfield Building, a blocky multistory structure with rectangular pillars along its front, located across Third street from Lownsdale Square. There, we met with Alice Brokell in her sixth-floor office. Evan Davis was already there.

I was nervous, to say the least. John's being with me relieved some of that; I was glad I didn't have to face this alone. But it also meant that Flash Burger was once again closed for the morning. Despite his repeated insistence that it was not an issue with him, it was for me.

"It may not be official," he told me, "but I consider myself your guardian. This is not a nuisance for me; it's an obligation to a son. An obligation I will gladly discharge to the best of my ability. We'll see this through, together, whatever it takes."

I wished my real father had felt that way.

We didn't have to wait long in the anteroom before being escorted into Alice's office. I guessed her to be around Evan's age—that is, somewhere in her midforties.

After the introductions were made, she had us take our seats. She rested her elbows on the desk and steepled her hands, slowly rubbing them together as she spoke. Since she did this frequently during our interview, I assumed it was an unconscious habit.

"Normally," she said, "this would be a deposition, where we would have a court recorder present and you would be under oath. And we may yet get to that. But I would like to have a more informal talk with you before we do, because, as I'm sure you realize, your case is a little unusual."

"Yes, ma'am," I said.

"But let me begin by saying that, as I've already indicated to your attorney, Mr. Davis"—she nodded toward him—"I have declined your case. The evidence shows that you were not an intentional participant in the melee but, rather, a victim of it. So as far as that incident goes, you can put it behind you. Your record will be sealed."

"Thank you, ma'am," I said. "I appreciate that so much. You have no idea."

She shrugged and replied in a sympathetic tone. But her words didn't match her voice, so while she may have intended to reassure me, she ended up making me squirm inside instead. "It's not a favor. It's my job to follow the facts. But those facts brought up another aspect of your tenure here, and I wish to address that this morning. Because it's also part of my job to make sure you're safe. Today will be an informal session, but what happens next depends on what I hear."

"I understand."

"Good. So let's begin at the beginning. I understand you left your home in California to come here?"

"Um, not quite. It wasn't my intention to come to Portland."

"What *was* your intention?"

"I don't know, to tell the truth. My trip was kind of haphazard. When I could find work, I'd stay awhile in a city to build up some money and then leave when the bug hit me. It was mostly random, except I always headed north. And I only did that because that was the direction I started out in, and I saw no reason to veer off it." I almost said *felt* instead of *saw*, but I caught myself in time. The appropriate word might have just brought up more questions.

"I see. So you have no ties here? No friends, relatives?"

"No relatives, ma'am." I tossed a glance at John. "But I'm making friends."

She made an expression that was half smile and half grimace. I swallowed hard. *Don't say stupid things!* I chided myself.

"Okay," Alice said. "But you left home of your own accord."

I narrowed my eyes. "Mm, that's sort of true. My father kicked me out. But I was happy to leave, to be honest."

"So you and your father didn't get along."

I snorted. "You could say that."

"The interrogating officer seems to believe you were abused at home."

I had not yet gotten over this term being applied to me. It made me uncomfortable, made me feel like a victim. And I hated feeling that way. I swallowed before answering, just to give myself a couple more seconds.

"He kind of figured that out on his own, ma'am. But yes. I was."

I tried not to squirm in the seat.

"So how did you end up here?"

I shrugged. "I just started walking."

"Just started walking," Alice repeated, smiling for the first time. "A lot of us wish we could do that sometimes."

I smiled back. Despite my fears and nervousness, I thought I might be able to like Alice Brokell.

"So you didn't even have bus fare?" she asked.

"My father was rich, ma'am. But I was kept poor, so I hitchhiked."

"You were *kept* poor?" Alice frowned.

"My father provided everything for me, and I wasn't lacking for stuff. But I wasn't allowed to do a lot of things on my own, and he withheld money from me to prevent me from 'sneaking around,' as he called it." I couldn't help but add, with a sly grin at the memories, "But I snuck around anyway."

She ignored this.

"That sounds like a difficult situation to be in."

I just nodded, hoping we could get past this line of questioning quickly. To my relief, she was finished with it.

"I'm very sorry for what you've been through," she said, and her tone sounded sincere. "But let's talk about where you are now. How did you come to meet John?"

"I was getting something to eat at Java Man when I met a girl there. We sat and talked, and she asked me to go home with her and meet the people she was living with."

"And how many people live there?"

"There are nine of us all together. But we fit in the house easily. It's very big."

John interjected here, "It's a mansion, actually. In Goose Hollow."

Alice looked as if she recognized it. "You mean that huge place with all the land around it?"

"That's it."

"I've been by there. It looks amazing."

"It suits our needs."

She turned back to me. "So what are your accommodations like in this huge house?"

"I have a private bedroom and a separate private bathroom right across the hall. I don't really know how big they are, but—"

Here, John interrupted me by raising his hand. "His bedroom is twelve by twelve. He has full run of the house and the yards. Nothing is off-limits to him, and he can raid the refrigerator whenever he likes."

Alice appeared to simultaneously approve of the arrangements and to be annoyed at John's interruption of her questioning. But she simply nodded and said professionally, "More than sufficient." She studied me for a few moments before continuing, "Well, you seem to be well fed and healthy. What do you do during the day?"

"I work part-time for John at his hamburger cart."

Alice addressed John. "And you have registered him, I presume?"

"His BOLI certificate is on the cart wall."

She turned to me again. Her next question took me by surprise, and I spoke more out of emotion and impulse than I would have liked.

"Are you happy in this house, with these people?"

"Oh, for sure. I love my housemates, and I love Portland." I blushed and dropped my gaze to my lap, fidgeting with my hands and chastising myself for sounding like a bubbly girl.

But Alice surprised me again, this time by laughing.

"Glad to hear we're pleasing *somebody*," she said. She turned to Evan. "All right, then. I'd like to move on to these healing activities you told me about. Is there anything you'd like to add here before we do that?"

"Just that," Evan said, "in my dealings with him, I find Mr. Johannsen to be a fine young man, who has never been in trouble before, even though he comes from a broken and sometimes violent home. He is resilient enough to have made his way here without incident. And his benefactors are treating him with the utmost care. I actually know John from other situations, and I feel confident in vouching for his integrity."

"Thank you. I will accept your testimony," Alice said. "So Arthur, when you say you heal people, what exactly do you mean by that?"

I shifted in my chair, marshaling my thoughts. This was the tricky part, the part I had been dreading. I told my story carefully, making sure to mention only those things Evan had approved, in the way we had rehearsed it. And while I couldn't avoid all the weird stuff, I didn't get too deep into it. I most certainly didn't mention to either of them the Man in White or the drugs—I wasn't *that* stupid.

"We do something called holotropic breathing," I concluded, after speaking for what seemed like hours but couldn't have been more than ten minutes. "It's a psychological therapy that helps us to kind of open up our minds to inner strengths we normally aren't aware of. Carl, the owner of the house—who lives with us, by the way—is licensed with the state to practice it. He has a clinic in the Pearl. He oversees all of our sessions."

Alice addressed John again. "I may wish to talk to him."

"That should be easy to arrange," John replied.

"Good." She turned back to me. "Go on, please."

"Well, apparently, I had an unusual reaction to the therapy. Somehow, it made me able to kind of suck up negative energy from people, which causes them to become healed." I gave a little half shrug. "I dunno. It's just something that happens to me."

Here, John indicated he wished to speak by raising an index finger. "If I may add something?"

Alice nodded.

"Carl and I think Arthur is 'healing' psychosomatic illnesses."

I stiffened slightly at this statement. I had argued against using this explanation when we were rehearsing, because I knew it wasn't true. But John and Evan had countered that it would be better than allowing the conversation to become paranormal. I'd eventually given in, seeing the wisdom of their position, but I still wanted to cringe at actually hearing it being offered in testimony. *At least he isn't under oath*, I thought.

"I see," Alice said. "So the people are being healed of things they only imagine they have?"

"Well," John said a bit hesitantly, "technically, it's more than just their imagination. Psychosomatic illnesses can sometimes be the result of overworked emotions, often caused by traumatic experiences. Arthur seems to be able to soothe those emotions."

She looked at me, and I detected a hint of wry humor on her face. "So you're a faith healer."

Why didn't we *think to say that?* Though ticked at myself, I managed to grin. "It seems that way, ma'am."

"And you didn't know you could do this before you came here?"

I shook my head. "No. But to be honest, I had no opportunity to find out, when I was growing up. I may have had it all along and just not known about it." I didn't believe this for a second, either, but again, it was another reasonable explanation that didn't require me to get into the wild things.

"Well, I'm not aware of any complaints in this matter. How about you, Evan?"

He shook his head. "No. No incidents at all."

"All right, then. I think I've heard enough." She leaned back in her chair. "Young man, you have quite a story to tell. And as unbelievable as some of it is, I do believe you. You are intelligent, articulate, and you're not impulsive. I'm sorry for the things you've had to go through, including since you came here. But in my judgment, you're handling it all well.

"As far as I can see, you haven't done anything wrong. If anything, you're trying to help. And frankly, we could use a little more of that around here."

"Thank you, ma'am," I said, a rush of relief running through me.

"I'm glad things are working out for you, Mr. Johannsen. Not everyone can come away unscathed from the kind of life you've had. I'm sorry our city had to give you another scare, but I think you're resilient enough to bounce back from it.

"You're free to go. My assistant will prepare some paperwork for you on your way out. Take it to your probation officer. Then you'll be finished, and you can put this incident behind you.

"But please," she added quickly as I stood up, "be careful on the streets."

I grinned. She had no idea.

CHAPTER 43

WHEN I ARRIVED HOME, I found Sari in the library. She looked up from the book she was reading as I paused in the doorway, an anxious-yet-hopeful look on her face. I intuited that she had been waiting there for me; I wondered how long.

"Hey," I said quietly.

"Hey, you."

"Everything's all right. Nothing's going to happen."

"Oh my gods!" She jumped up out of the chair and wrapped her arms tightly around me. "I am so glad!"

"I guess I am too," I said teasingly. "Especially now."

She pulled back a half step, keeping her hands on my upper arms, and gave me a faux stern look accompanied by a grin. "You are such a silly boy!"

"It's what you love about me."

"I love everything about you, Arthur Johannsen."

"And I love you, Sari Wright. With everything I have in me, everything I am."

We embraced tightly again.

As we finally released each other, I gazed intently into her eyes and said, "I have something I'd like to show you.

I'm not sure if it'll work, but I feel like this is the right time. Can we try it?"

She studied my face. "I suppose," she said, puzzled.

"Cool." Then I warned her, "This will be a bit jarring."

"I think I'm pretty much jar-proof at this point."

I chuckled. "We'll see."

I took Sari's left hand with my right one and guided her around to stand at my right side so that we were facing the same direction.

While it wasn't necessary for either of us to close our eyes for this to work, I found the practice to be both easier and more comfortable on a psychological level, so I suggested we do so.

Then, making a fist with my left hand, I imagined gripping the golden staircase tightly in it, focusing my attention inward and outward, the way I had become accustomed to doing when dealing with the Man in White. Although the talisman was imaginary, it felt real, with genuine heft and a recognizable physical shape. Then I conjured up an image in my mind of us entering a portal together.

Almost immediately, my eyes flew open of their own accord as, suddenly, the world exploded into a jumbled pattern of colors and vague images. Each of the sections shared defined black borders with their immediate neighbors, looking a lot like a jigsaw puzzle. Like a morass of amoebas, these globules kind of oozed around each other.

Then, abruptly, all the colors, acting like a reverse prism, were sucked in together to form a single large white sphere that filled the center of the room, enclosing us. This sphere, in turn, was surrounded by impenetrable blackness, in which I could see nothing at all. It seemed to spread out into infinity.

Just as I was coming to terms with the dismaying loneliness this unsettling vision produced in me, the blackness was drawn into the white sphere, where it became a small black dot. I remembered seeing this happen before and anticipated what was to come next.

I was only partially correct: instead of forming into a crow, the dot exploded into an uncountable number of crows, which flew out in all directions, filling the air so completely that they became another mass of darkness in which Sari and I were fully immersed. I was unable to see anything at all.

Sari's hand jerked in mine at each of these explosive junctures, and when all the lights went out—so to speak—she was left tightly squeezing my fingers. I gently rubbed my thumb along her hand to reassure her, and I felt her relax a little.

Taking an amount of time I couldn't determine, the darkness slowly dissipated until we stood immersed in a kind of milky-blue light. The library seemed to gently ripple around us, almost like a reflection in deep water, but more lazily. That was the word that came to my mind, anyway. All in all, I found it rather soothing.

However, a tiny portion of the blackness had coalesced as clothing around a very old woman in a shabby dress and cloak. I was shocked to recognize her from my dream of the castle. This brought up many questions in my mind, but I didn't have the chance to try to analyze the situation just now, as all my attention was focused on what was happening.

Gazing intensely at Sari, the woman reached out a closed hand to her.

Sari, who was returning her gaze calmly, responded by immediately extending her right hand, palm up, allowing the woman to place something into it. She quickly closed Sari's fingers around it before I could see what it was. Then she vanished.

Sari and I stared incredulously at each other; she looked like she wanted to say something but couldn't find the words.

"Are you all right?" I asked softly.

She drew and released a deep breath.

"Where are we?" she asked, her voice filled with wonder and her eyes wide.

"In the superconscious."

"I've never had anything like this happen during holo-tropic breathing before."

"I don't think that practice produces precisely the same thing as this. What we're in is more like a dream world, I think. Or something in between. I dunno. But the Man in White assured me that this *is* part of the superconscious."

"Maybe there are different aspects to it," Sari pondered, "with different ways of accessing it." Then, suddenly, she brightened. "Anyway, I can now get here on my own."

And at this, I knew with certainty what I had suspected: the woman had given her a talisman with the same powers as mine. I was burning to know what the artifact was, what it might represent to her. But I knew not to ask, of course. I was not permitted to know these things, just like no one else was supposed to know anything about mine.

Sari said, "This constitutes a new level of things between us."

I nodded. "It does."

She appeared to be happy at this prospect. Then, suddenly, she gave a start and looked into my eyes, smiling coyly. "Did you just ask me to kiss you?"

Now it was my turn to be startled. "What? Um, no." I had thought it, though.

"How bizarre. I distinctly heard you say that."

Tentatively, hopefully, achingly, I asked, "Do you want me to?" My heart was pounding.

She didn't say anything and didn't need to.

Slowly, shyly, we turned, wrapping our arms around each other.

I closed my eyes, but somehow I knew how Sari was moving and reacting.

We hesitated a second or two, our lips a bare fraction of an inch apart, as I breathed in the smell of her skin and hair. The pounding of my heart made my entire body vibrate.

Our kiss was soft, better than anything in the real world, better than the dream world—the fulfillment of all worlds, containing no doubt, reservation, or demand. My next thought drifted up, unbidden, out of the labyrinth of my mind.

I think I'm going to like this.

CHAPTER 44

I'M BEING HANGED FOR A *crime I didn't commit. I can feel the rough rope of the noose scraping the skin on my neck and pressing into my throat, making it difficult for me to swallow.*

I feel no fear, though; just sorrow, regret, and self-recrimination. I hadn't done what they accused me of doing, but I know I am guilty, anyway.

The hangman tightens the noose even more so that I am choking before the trapdoor is even opened. I struggle to breathe, struggle to untangle myself from the rope, but there is nothing I can do. The rope seems to be alive, writhing like a snake, tugging tighter and tighter on my throat as blood floods my vision. Everything around me shakes violently. I panic.

"Slow your breathing." Melanie's calm, softly accented voice surrounded me as if it were emanating from an ethereal plane. "You're hyperventilating. I'm going to bring you back now. Just relax, and follow my voice."

I did as I was told. As I gradually reached a state of deep calm, a sudden revelation gripped me, and I understood the meaning of my vision. At the same moment, I realized I was lying on the carpet in the meditation room, and then I fully awoke. At 9:06 p.m. on Friday night, my second holotropic session thus ended.

I looked up into Melanie's sympathetic eyes. She smiled at me in reassurance.

"My mother didn't reject me," I said, my own eyes damp and my words catching in my throat. "The umbilical cord was wrapped around my neck. They tried to do an emergency C-section, but there were complications. She died giving birth to me. My father lied about her wanting an abortion and treated me like shit because he blamed me for my mother's death."

And I broke down crying.

CHAPTER 45

S UNRISE FOUND ME STANDING ONCE more on the Vista Bridge, looking out toward Mount Hood looming above the tall buildings that, in turn, appeared to rise out of the thin fog filling the shallow valley. I was here because I needed to be alone, but this time, it wasn't because I was unhappy.

At a little after eight o'clock in the morning, the air was cold, and the light rain offered cover for my tears. This time, they were tears of gratefulness. For having escaped from an unjust situation. For having survived my father's brutal, misplaced hatefulness. For having found a home and a family at last. And for having found someone who I loved deeply and who felt the same toward me—and with whom I shared unbelievable abilities.

But most of all, I was grateful for having learned the truth about my mother. Her bravery, her strength, and her determination to bring me into the world no matter the cost to herself. She died giving me life, and she did so willingly, out of the depths of her love. And the love I now felt toward her made me realize the truth.

No earthquake could ever destroy such a home.

CHAPTER 46

THERE IS A DARK PLACE I am afraid to enter. It is not dark in the sense of being absent of light, but rather, like being absent of existence. It's not even physical but, instead, is kind of a knowing that it exists, a hole in the fabric of my mind. As I stand before it and gaze into it, I realize I'm missing a significant amount of time. This hole is the psychic manifestation of that.

Feeling deeply uneasy, I turn away and walk, through a dimly lit room, over to a desk upon which lies a slightly crumpled piece of paper with a paragraph on it, handwritten in black ink. I pick it up and recognize it as part of a story I had started writing a long time ago—before I was even born. It is about this dark hole.

Dispassionately, I tear it into shreds.

I awoke with a deep sense of peace radiating throughout my whole being.

I wasn't totally certain that what I'd just experienced was merely a dream. That's how it was in the Dream of the Room; realities mixed and mingled, much like in the superconscious, but not exactly like it. I was coming to realize that reality is thoroughly layered, and there are Gateways between those layers.

In the reality I was now in, I was sitting in the parlor, in front of the gold-threaded white stone fireplace, my gaze languidly focused on the flames dancing in its firebox.

I took a deep breath and let the air drift slowly out of my lungs, drawing myself even deeper into my meditative state. The house was still and quiet; I didn't hear so much as the creak of an upstairs floorboard. The crackling of the fire and the heat it radiated brought me a deep assurance that I was home.

I hadn't known what was in store for me when I set out on my indeterminate journey last February. I had made no plans beyond simply walking, hitching, and working. But with every step and every random ride along the way, with every hard workday and every harder night, I had never doubted that I was on the right path. A dream had carried me here, a dream had changed me here, and now a dream was about to open a door to my next destination, my next way of being.

And so it was that, on this darkling evening, for the first time in my life, I awoke from slumber, believing in myself.

I half stood and repositioned the chair so I could look out on the backyard through the sliding glass doors. The sun was well set on this Sunday evening following my visit to the Vista Bridge, and twilight, losing a competition with a moon three nights past full, illuminated the backyard in an otherworldly light. I found a kind of melancholy comfort in this early dimness. Autumn had reached its peak, and the deciduous trees along the back fence were in their full glory, the glowing colors punctuated by dark evergreens.

"It is time for you to enter your future," the Man in White said.

"I think I'm ready."

"I am certain of it. Take a step into it now, and become certain of it yourself."

I closed my eyes to conjure my talisman, but it didn't appear. Puzzled, I opened them again.

"You no longer need it."

"So what do I do?"

"Just walk out the door."

Although I knew he meant it metaphorically, I took it literally. The two concepts were now forever etched in my mind as being the same. So I stood and moved to the door, slid it to the side, and stepped out, barefoot, into what I expected to be a cold evening. But the crazy swirling, mindboggling abstract images that normally encompassed me when I entered the superconscious did not occur.

Instead, the world around me simply became midday in summer. The air was brighter and clearer than I had ever experienced before, but there was no sign of the sun in the cloudless blue sky. All the trees were in their full greenery, except for the oak in the corner. That one was bare, the grass around it thick with mottled leaves—discarded colors, a splattering from a dropped palette.

What season am I in, anyway? I wondered, frowning.

Beyond the trees at the yard's northern perimeter stood a huge structure, towering one hundred feet into the air. Its lower portion was obscured, as if it were standing in a holler (a word I learned from Melanie) between the house and the city. It looked like a great clockwork Ferris wheel with compasses and stopwatches affixed between two gleaming brass rails defining the outer of several internal spaces. Between these instruments lay intricate scrollwork, reminding me of paisley and fleur-de-lis patterns. Five spokes radiated from the center to the outermost rim. In the right quadrangle of the wheel, encompassing the lower third of the structure, another spoke curved around to form a Golden Mean spiral. All these components rested in the empty interior space enclosed within the wheel, affixed to nothing yet remaining solidly in place. The entire thing blazed like fire, flashing in the sunless sunlight as it slowly and silently rotated clockwise.

This was, of course, the Wheel that I had scried in the river. I found myself mesmerized by this marvelous object, this materialized imagination, and for a long time, I could not take my eyes off it. The image burned its way into my mind, filling me with childlike wonder.

"The Wheel of Being," the Man in White said. *"It is always cycling."*

"Cycling? Do you mean, like, reincarnation?"

"That, and more."

I was surprised by the deep sense of peace this Wheel filled me with, far deeper than any of my meditation sessions had produced. Its presence was reassuring, comforting, protective. And suddenly, I realized that this structure was the reality behind the statue of the Dancing Shiva displayed in the study, expressed in that deity's raised hand—a universal gesture meaning *be still.*

An odd mixture of feelings washed through me, a sense of being firmly planted and yet without weight at all—physically, emotionally, mentally. It was not like floating but, rather, more of a being-yet-not-being. I was at once here but not here, material but immaterial, grounded but flying. And at this core of being and nothingness lay a deep residing peace such as I had never known before, but which felt like it had always been in me. It was not like my meditation sessions, during which I had wrapped myself in calmness through observing my mind as a vast, dark cavern receding into infinity. Instead, it was a profound, infused tranquility arising from the innate realization that I had become everything, at all levels and in all forms, and that everything encompassing me was also *me*. I was the trees and the shrubs and the grass and the fallen leaves and the sky, I was the Wheel and the house and the obelisk on the terrace. And I was the labyrinth, that personal nightmare that I had vanquished by simply allowing it to swallow me.

All of these things were me. There was no differentiation between us. I even felt the atoms vibrating in my body, in the plants and in the structures, and in the air between us all; infinitesimal dots of energy manifesting as physical objects out of the primordial ether.

I closed my eyes and expanded into infinity.

I don't know how long I stood like this, enraptured and yet unmoved, but when I opened my eyes again, I found myself standing just a few steps away from the oak tree. I was getting used to doing this, moving without moving. And as I looked upon this magnificent being, its graceful branches reaching up into the crystal sky as if it were stretching upon awaking from a deep slumber, I began to perceive it differently than I ever had before. More clearly, seeing it for what it actually was.

The tree was a woman.

I couldn't determine her age. She was, simultaneously, all ages, although an impression of youth filled my mind. Her body formed the tree's trunk, while her bare arms were raised upward as the two lowest branches, forming a living Y. She had wild, windblown, multicolored hair that reflected the cycle of the seasons and that cascaded down to her waist, tendrils waving gently across her body in an unfelt breeze. These colors were reflected in her flashing eyes, whose hues were constantly changing.

She was wearing a dress the color of summer leaves, and it clung to her body from just below her shoulders down to her knees. A bronze-and-black-mottled python was loosely entwined around her, coiled upward from her ankles to her elbows. The serpent peered back at me from above her right shoulder, its amber eyes hooded.

It was impossible for me to differentiate between the woman and the tree. My awareness flashed as rapidly as a strobe light between seeing her as the oak and seeing them as separate beings.

We are separate, but one.

These words startled me as they flashed through my mind. I knew them, of course, but I still didn't know what to make of them. Should I consider them just the memory of a dream, or were they a dream of the present? And who *did* they apply to?

I stood transfixed, unable to even think about moving, as if my legs had pushed like roots deep into the earth. For a moment, I wondered if I had become a tree as well.

"She is an Ultraterrestrial," the Man in White said, startling me out of my trance. *"A dryad. She embodies the oak tree on the spiritual plane. Or if you prefer, she is the tree in the fourth dimension. She is more ancient than you can imagine. She is a representative of the earth, a manifestation of Gaia. Listen to her."*

"Why is she wrapped in a snake?"

"The serpent is a symbol of personal transformation. She bears it, even as it envelops her. Even as it will you."

Great depth of knowledge, compassion, and a hint of amusement now shone steadily in the dryad's eyes, replacing the earlier flashing, as she weighed me, searching deep within me, unearthing all my failures and the successes in me, too. I was torn between fear that she might reject me and fear that she might accept me. But somehow, my own gaze remained steady, my demeanor surprisingly calm.

"You are no stranger to goddesses," she said. Her voice was like the susurration of leaves in a summer breeze.

"I've encountered some before," I said. I was surprised, not just by the steadiness of my voice, but that I was speaking at all.

"One such as me?" she asked.

"No. Not exactly."

"Prettier?" She smiled coyly.

"Oh—no." I shook my head vigorously. "No way."

Her smile broadened. "Such a sweet young man."

The python slithered around her, its black mottling rippling along its thick, tarnished-bronze skin, as it drew its head forward, reaching toward me, its yellow eyes piercing me, its countenance gargoyle-like. Beneath its inscrutable reptilian stoicism, it appeared to be anticipating something.

"You have been traveling long, for one so young," the dryad said. "Yet you are not really so young, are you?"

I knew she wasn't referring to my trip from San Diego. And yet, at the same time, she was.

"In this place," I said, "I'm not sure what time even means."

Suddenly, a shadow descended upon the backyard. Reflexively, I looked up at the sky, but it remained clear and blue yet filled with a light unlike daylight or dawn or dusk, whose origin and true nature were lost to me.

"Time," she said, drawing my attention back to her, "means whatever we want it to mean."

At this, the shadow passed.

"I'm beginning to feel that *everything* is relative here."

"It is not just here. It is true throughout the universe. Everything is connected to everything else. Everything *is* everything else."

"Is there any real meaning, then?"

I was startled by the sound of another voice, a man's voice, entering the conversation. I recognized it immediately, and I flushed with pleasure as the Man in White walked up and stopped directly in front of me, exactly half the distance between the dryad and me.

I had no idea where he had come from, but the relief that passed through me upon seeing him, my familiar guide, pushed all trepidation out of my mind. I now knew everything was going to be all right.

"You make your own future," he said. "That is the only real meaning. You have always known this."

"And now," the dryad announced, "it is time to enter the future you have made."

The python then unwrapped itself from the dryad's body. It slithered to the ground and coiled beside her, its head raised like a cobra's. The goddess's eyes flashed like emeralds, and her flowing autumn-colored hair was swept as if by a sudden gale—although no wind stirred. It settled around her body as she stepped lightly over the exposed, gnarled tree roots to wade through the ankle-deep pile of fallen leaves, kicking them lightly with her bare feet.

Now I wondered if my impression that she was the tree itself had only been an illusion. I supposed she could have been it and not it at the same time. Things tended to work that way in the superconscious.

She stopped at the Man in White's left hand. She was now only, like, five steps away from me; being this close to a goddess made me tremble. But her eyes softened, and when she smiled, I relaxed.

Suddenly, a white easel board appeared on the grass to the Man in White's right. On its top sheet, written horizontally in red, were the numerals zero through nine.

"The cardinal numbers, right?" the Man in White said. "One of the first subjects taught to children. But let us have some fun with them, shall we?" He picked up a black marking pen from the easel tray. "What if we create a new sequence of numbers from this one? Let us start with the zero and the one." He wrote these numerals beneath the corresponding ones in the original sequence. "But instead of continuing in the normal manner, let us add the one to the zero." He wrote another 1 next to the first 1, under the 2. "Then, add these ones together." He wrote a 2. "Now the two to the one." He wrote a 3. "And three plus two equals five."

He continued to draw out the sequence on the bottom row until the numerals reached the end of the upper sequence: 8, 13, 21, 34. Then he placed the marking pen back on the tray and studied what he had written.

"This sequence is called the Fibonacci series, after its discoverer. Not a particularly impressive discovery, though, is it? It looks like a children's game. And maybe he *was* just doodling."

He chuckled and turned to face me. It fleetingly occurred to me that I had never heard him laugh before. I didn't have time to consider what this might mean, though.

"But sometimes," he went on, "astounding truths can arise from seeming child's play. Newton watching apples, for instance. Einstein discovered relativity by imagining he was riding on a light wave. Those revelations revolutionized our thinking about the universe. But what Fibonacci discovered revolutionized what we think about *existence itself.* Because this sequence of numbers is the basis of the Golden Mean spiral, which I have already shown you."

I nodded.

"That figure is found in many parts of our universe," he went on. "It is the shape of galaxies, and the way the leaves of some plants are arranged on their stems. Snail shells, hurricanes—even the swirls of cream when it is stirred into your coffee. From the mundane to the sublime, the universe manifests the Golden Mean spiral.

"Ancient peoples worshipped it. We find it all throughout their cultures, in jewelry, art, and religious statues. It is as prolific as the snake symbol, that winding, climbing serpent that both kills and heals."

At the word *serpent*, the python raised its head a couple feet higher, its dry skin rasping, its body fluid as water.

The Man in White flipped the page over the top of the chart. On the next one was a drawing depicting two snakes wound around a rod topped with a ball, looking like they were preparing to strike it. I gasped when I saw this, and he smiled.

"So you *did* learn something on the drug." He tapped the page with the back of his hand. "The caduceus," he went on, "has been used for eons throughout the world's cultures as a symbol of healing. Today, the python will make you whole. Because the Fibonacci series is also"— and finally, with a dramatic flair, he flipped to the last page, on which was depicted a scientific diagram of a DNA molecule—"the basis of life."

Before I could consider this pronouncement, the Man in White turned his attention toward the labyrinth, prompting me to look that way as well. My heart leaped as I saw Sari walking across the lawn toward us, and I turned to face her.

She was wearing an ivory lace tank top above a white calf-length skirt with a green-and-red floral pattern, a crown of petunias on her head. Like me, she was barefoot. John, his left arm hooked around her right one, escorted her. Carl followed three steps behind them.

I acknowledged my two mentors and benefactors, the guru led by his high priest, with a nod. But my focus was totally on Sari, and our gazes became locked as she drew near.

John delivered her to me, and we savored a minute of happy gazing at each other before turning to face the Man in White. John continued around us and took a position behind me and to my right. Meanwhile, the dryad assumed a mirror stance behind Sari, while Carl took her spot next to the Man in White. Thus this elegant dance provided us with a maiden of honor, a best man, and a witness.

Orbs clearer than crystal arose from the grass around the two of us, drifting in the air from the ground to our knees, sometimes bumping into us like wayward soap bubbles.

The wedding ceremony was, to say the least, like no other in history.

The snake uncoiled, rising straight up until it was fully extended, except for a loop acting as a base upon which it balanced. It then split down its center, the halves pulling apart like the images in a kaleidoscope, to form two whole serpents side by side. This action made me think of cells dividing, the second snake materializing from out of the original, with no indication of how it had come to be. Just the phenomenon that, where there was once one python, now there were two.

This action was mesmerizing, but I didn't dwell on its being impossible. Nothing was impossible in this place. So I simply acquiesced to the reality of it, not questioning it in my mind.

"Please face each other," the Man in White said.

I was happy to oblige. I gazed into Sari's eyes once more, mere inches away from mine, and breathed in the smell of her sweet skin and hair.

Although my focus was riveted on her, I was still aware of what was happening around me. I seemed to have acquired 360-degree vision, but now, such a thing didn't faze me. I took everything that happened for granted.

I noted the pythons as they dropped to the ground and slithered toward us. Once reaching us, they coiled up and around both our bodies in opposite directions, binding us together within a double helix, squeezing us gently. Unspeakable joy arose within me like water in a well, in synchrony with the serpents' slow, twining climb. I experienced something else also, something I absolutely cannot describe. There are no words to use for it because it was not possible for it to be happening.

I distinctly felt my DNA changing.

I could tell by the expressions on her face—of wonder, joy, and astonishment—and the flashing light in her eyes that Sari was experiencing the same thing. Genes that had laid dormant in humanity for forty thousand years were being activated, transforming us into higher spiritual beings and connecting us in a way no one in history had ever been before.

I don't know how long this process went on. It seemed like it lasted forever, but perhaps it was only an instant. Time had no real meaning here.

But at last, the serpents uncoiled and slithered back to the oak tree. There they formed a ring on the ground around its trunk by swallowing each other, starting at the tails and ending at the midpoints of their thick mottled bodies. I intuited that they had formed a portal to the dryad's realm, the Land of Symbols, and that Sari and I would be able to access it any time we wished. The pythons had become our mutual talisman.

The Man in White interrupted my thoughts, but I was glad he did, because he said the one thing I most wanted to hear at that moment.

"You may kiss the bride."

I had thought that our first superconscious kiss in the library could never be exceeded. I was wrong.

Sari and I continued to face each other after that bliss, relishing the events of the day. Our union was now official, recognized by the powers that represented the world.

Sari ticked her head in a sideways nod toward our officiator.

"Is that your Man in White?" she asked me.

"Yeah."

"He doesn't look how I thought he would."

"What did you think he'd look like?"

She shrugged. "I dunno. The Wizard of Oz, I guess."

I laughed, and after a moment, she joined in.

I had never been happier in my life. The only thing that mattered to me right now, in all the world, was Sari. The connection I shared with her, which we had both felt from our first meeting, had now become something more, and so had we. I could *feel* her experience of life, and I knew that she could feel mine. We had entered a recursive reality, a joyous inner hall of mirrors, and we never wanted to leave the funhouse. We were separate but one. Right down to our molecules.

My heart pounded in my chest as we fell forever into each other's eyes. I felt more than close to her, and I knew she felt more than close to me. This experience, at once physical and spiritual, real and imaginary, went far beyond simple perception, far beyond what I had experienced with her on psilocybin.

Our lives had now become a perpetual dream, a world where anything could happen and where we could do anything we wished.

That was a huge responsibility, I thought. For a moment, I wondered if I could shoulder it.

But only for a moment. There would be time enough to figure all that out once we returned to our other world. For this moment lingering in eternity, we simply stood together, enwrapped in each other as no lovers had ever been before.

ACKNOWLEDGMENTS

I would like to thank artist Jill Falk. When I saw her work at Art at the Cave, I knew I wanted to include it in my story. I contacted her to get her permission, and I ended up interviewing her. We had a wonderful two-hour talk over breakfast. Her thoughts about dreaming and art fit in perfectly, so on a whim, I asked her if she would like to become one of the characters. To my great joy, she was eager to do so. I am pleased to offer you a small taste of her captivating world through her own words, which I have presented, unaltered, as dialogue in the book.

You can find Jill's work at www.jillfalk.com

ABOUT THE AUTHOR

Corbyn Travers began his quest for utopia in 1967. Turning twelve during the Summer of Love, he avidly embraced the best of the hippie counterculture ideals and has been seeking the perfect community ever since. Along the way, he discovered that the world is not exactly what we think it is. His greatest hope is that everyone will one day find these things out for themselves and we will all be able to live together in peace and harmony.

Connect with him at corbyntravers.blog and @corbyntravers on Instagram.

www.ingramcontent.com/pod-product-compliance
Lightning Source LLC
Chambersburg PA
CBHW061422150726
47987CB00001B/65